PRAISE FOR CATHER...

WIFE BY WEDNESDAY

"A fun and sizzling romance, great characters that trade verbal spars like fist punches, and the dream of your own royal wedding!"
—Sizzling Hot Book Reviews, 5 Stars

"A good holiday, fireside or bedtime story."
—Manic Reviews, 4½ Stars

"A great story that I hope is the start of a new series."
—The Romance Studio, 4½ Hearts

MARRIED BY MONDAY

"If I hadn't already added Ms. Catherine Bybee to my list of favorite authors, after reading this book I would have been compelled to. This is a book *nobody* should miss, because the magic it contains is awesome."
—Booked Up Reviews, 5 Stars

"Ms. Bybee writes authentic situations and expresses the good and the bad in such an equal way . . . Keeps the reader on the edge of her seat."
—Reading Between the Wines, 5 Stars

"*Married by Monday* was a refreshing read and one I couldn't possibly put down."
—The Romance Studio, 4½ Hearts

Fiancé by Friday

"Bybee knows exactly how to keep readers happy . . . A thrilling pursuit and enough passion to stuff in your back pocket to last for the next few lifetimes . . . The hero and heroine come to life with each flip of the page and will linger long after readers cross the finish line."

—*RT Book Reviews,* 4½ Stars, Top Pick (Hot)

"A tale full of danger and sexual tension . . . the intriguing characters add emotional depth, ensuring readers will race to the perfectly fitting finish."

—*Publishers Weekly*

"Suspense, survival, and chemistry mix in this scintillating read."

—*Booklist*

"Hot romance, a mystery assassin, British royalty, and an alpha Marine . . . this story has it all!"

—Harlequin Junkie

Single by Saturday

"Captures readers' hearts and keeps them glued to the pages until the fascinating finish . . . romance lovers will feel the sparks fly . . . almost instantaneously."

—*RT Book Reviews,* 4½ Stars, Top Pick

"[A] wonderfully exciting plot, lots of desire, and some sassy attitude thrown in for good measure!"

—Harlequin Junkie

Taken by Tuesday

"[Bybee] knows exactly how to get bookworms sucked into the perfect storyline; then she casts her spell upon them so they don't escape until they reach the 'Holy Cow!' ending."

—*RT Book Reviews*, 4½ Stars, Top Pick

Seduced by Sunday

"You simply can't miss [this novel]. It contains everything a romance reader loves—clever dialogue, three-dimensional characters, and just the right amount of steam to go with that heartwarming love story."

—Brenda Novak, *New York Times* bestselling author

"Bybee hits the mark . . . providing readers with a smart, sophisticated romance between a spirited heroine and a prim hero . . . Passionate and intelligent characters [are] at the heart of this entertaining read."

—*Publishers Weekly*

Treasured by Thursday

"The Weekday Brides never disappoint and this final installment is by far Bybee's best work to date."

—*RT Book Reviews*, 4½ Stars, Top Pick

"An exquisitely written and complex story brimming with pride, passion, and pulse-pounding danger . . . Readers will gladly make time to savor this winning finale to a wonderful series."

—*Publishers Weekly*, Starred Review

"Bybee concludes her popular Weekday Brides series in a gratifying way with a passionate, troubled couple who may find a happy future if they can just survive and then learn to trust each other. A compelling and entertaining mix of sexy, complicated romance and menacing suspense."

—*Kirkus Reviews*

NOT QUITE DATING

"It's refreshing to read about a man who isn't afraid to fall in love . . . [Jack and Jessie] fit together as a couple and as a family."

—*RT Book Reviews*, 3 Stars (Hot)

"*Not Quite Dating* offers a sweet and satisfying Cinderella fantasy that will keep you smiling long after you've finished reading."

—Kathy Altman, *USA Today*, "Happy Ever After"

"The perfect rags to riches romance . . . The dialogue is inventive and witty, the characters are well drawn out. The storyline is superb and really shines . . . I highly recommend this stand out romance! Catherine Bybee is an automatic buy for me."

—Harlequin Junkie, 4½ Hearts

NOT QUITE ENOUGH

"Bybee's gift for creating unforgettable romances cannot be ignored. The third book in the Not Quite series will sweep readers away to a paradise, and they will be intrigued by the thrilling story that accompanies their literary vacation."

—*RT Book Reviews*, 4½ Stars, Top Pick

NOT QUITE FOREVER

"Full of classic Bybee humor, steamy romance, and enough plot twists and turns to keep readers entertained all the way to the very last page."
—Tracy Brogan, bestselling author of the Bell Harbor series

"Magnetic . . . The love scenes are sizzling and the multi-dimensional characters make this a page-turner. Readers will look for earlier installments and eagerly anticipate new ones."
—*Publishers Weekly*

NOT QUITE PERFECT

"This novel flows extremely well and readers will find themselves consuming the witty dialogue and strong imagery in one sitting."
—*RT Book Reviews*

"Don't let the title fool you. *Not Quite Perfect* was actually the perfect story to sweep you away and take you on a pleasant adventure. So sit back, relax, maybe pour a glass of wine, and let Catherine Bybee entertain you with Glen and Mary's playful East Coast–West Coast romance. You won't regret it for a moment."
—Harlequin Junkie, 4½ Stars

NOT QUITE CRAZY

"This fast-paced story features credible characters whose appealing relationship is built upon friendship, mutual respect, and sizzling chemistry."
—*Publishers Weekly*

"The plot is filled with twists and turns, but instead of feeling like a never-ending roller coaster, the story maintains a quiet flow. The slow buildup of a romance allows readers to get to know the main characters as individuals and makes the romantic element more organic."

—*RT Book Reviews*

DOING IT OVER

"The romance between fiercely independent Melanie and charming Wyatt heats up even as outsiders threaten to derail their newfound happiness. This novel will hook readers with its warm, inviting characters and the promise for similar future installments."

—*Publishers Weekly*

"This brand-new trilogy, Most Likely To, based on yearbook superlatives, kicks off with a novel that will encourage you to root for the incredibly likable Melanie. Her friends are hilarious and readers will swoon over Wyatt, who is charming and strong. Even Melanie's daughter, Hope, is a hoot! This romance is jam-packed with animated characters, and Bybee displays her creative writing talent wonderfully."

—*RT Book Reviews*, 4 Stars

"With a dialogue full of energy and depth, and a twisting storyline that captured my attention, I would say that *Doing It Over* was a great way to start off a new series. (And look at that gorgeous book cover!) I can't wait to visit River Bend again and see who else gets to find their HEA."

—Harlequin Junkie, 4½ Stars

STAYING FOR GOOD

"Bybee's skillfully crafted second Most Likely To contemporary (after *Doing It Over*) brings together former sweethearts who have not forgotten each other in the eleven years since high school. A cast of multidimensional characters brings the story to life and promises enticing future installments."

—*Publishers Weekly*

"Romance fans will be sure to cheer on former high school sweethearts Zoe and Luke right away in *Staying For Good*. Just wait until you see what passion, laughter, reconciliations, and mischief (can you say Vegas?) awaits readers this time around. Highly recommended."

—Harlequin Junkie, 4½ Stars

MAKING IT RIGHT

"Intense suspense heightens the scorching romance at the heart of Bybee's outstanding third Most Likely To contemporary (after *Staying For Good*). Sizzling sensual scenes are coupled with scary suspense in this winning novel."

—*Publishers Weekly*, Starred Review

FOOL ME ONCE

"A marvelous portrait of friendship among women who have been bonded by fire."

—*Library Journal*, Best of the Year 2017

"Bybee still delivers a story that her die-hard readers will enjoy."

—*Publishers Weekly*

HALF EMPTY

"Wade and Trina here in *Half Empty* just might be one of my favorite couples Catherine Bybee has gifted us fans with so far. Captivating, engaging, lively and dreamy, I simply could not get enough of this book."

—Harlequin Junkie, 5 stars

"Part rock star romance, part romantic thriller, I really enjoyed this book."

—Romance Reader

FAKING FOREVER

"A charming contemporary with surprising depth . . . Bybee perfectly portrays a woman trying to hold out for Mr. Right despite the pressures of time. A pitch-perfect plot and a cast of sympathetic and lovable supporting characters make this book one to add to the keeper shelf."

—*Publishers Weekly*

"Catherine Bybee can do no wrong as far as I'm concerned . . . Passionate, sultry, and filled with genuine emotions that ran the gamut, *Faking Forever* was a journey of self-discovery and of a love that was truly meant to be. Highly recommended."

—Harlequin Junkie

SAY IT AGAIN

"Steamy, fast-paced, and consistently surprising, with a large cast of feisty supporting characters, this suspenseful roller-coaster ride will keep both series fans and new readers on the edge of their seats."

—*Publishers Weekly*

Changing the *Rules*

ALSO BY CATHERINE BYBEE

Contemporary Romance

Weekday Brides Series

Wife by Wednesday
Married by Monday
Fiancé by Friday
Single by Saturday
Taken by Tuesday
Seduced by Sunday
Treasured by Thursday

Not Quite Series

Not Quite Dating
Not Quite Mine
Not Quite Enough
Not Quite Forever
Not Quite Perfect
Not Quite Crazy

Most Likely To Series

Doing It Over
Staying For Good
Making It Right

First Wives Series

Fool Me Once
Half Empty

Chasing Shadows
Faking Forever
Say It Again

Creek Canyon Series

My Way to You
Home to Me
Everything Changes

Paranormal Romance

MacCoinnich Time Travels

Binding Vows
Silent Vows
Redeeming Vows
Highland Shifter
Highland Protector

The Ritter Werewolves Series

Before the Moon Rises
Embracing the Wolf

Novellas

Soul Mate
Possessive

Erotica

Kilt Worthy
Kilt-A-Licious

Changing the Rules

Book One
of the
Richter Series

CATHERINE BYBEE

Published by Montlake, Seattle

www.apub.com

Amazon, the Amazon logo, and Montlake are trademarks of Amazon.com, Inc., or its affiliates.

ISBN-13: 9781542009911
ISBN-10: 154200991X

Cover design by Caroline Teagle Johnson

Cover photography by Regina Wamba of MaeIDesign.com

Printed in the United States of America

To the graduating class of 2020:
may your future life celebrations be filled with all the
pomp and circumstance you've been denied this year.

CHAPTER ONE

Claire Kelly maneuvered around the auction table, her eyes in constant motion as she watched for anyone who might think to take one of the many pricey trinkets on display. A form-fitting black dress hugged her frame and stopped before her knees. She wore her strawberry blonde hair straight, and only a minimal amount of makeup dusted her features. Claire silently swore at the pain of her feet pinched into shoes that brought her to a height three inches taller than what her driver's license said she was.

The guests at the charity auction were dressed to impress. The women wore cocktail dresses, and the men wore suits. Because the event was invitation only, the philanthropic, star-filled guest list mandated serious security. That was where Claire came in. Well, she and her colleagues at MacBain Security and Solutions.

She preferred the *solutions* part of the job as opposed to a *security* detail, unless the security detail gave her the opportunity to kick someone's ass for breaching it. When the guest list was drawn from Hollywood's famous, Billboard's top artists, and people who frequent the Forbes list of richest Americans, ass kicking would have to wait for another day.

"Ready for a break, Loki?"

Claire smiled at the use of the nickname she acquired in her boarding school. A name she had needed to keep her identity ambiguous should the headmistress stumble upon the covert communications between her and her best friend, Jax. "Yes, please," Claire said into the small microphone none of the guests could see she was wearing.

After rounding the table, Jax smiled at her briefly and took Claire's position so she could step away.

Everywhere Claire looked she saw bling. The women wore dangling earrings encrusted in diamonds, and necklaces sporting every possible gemstone out there. "There's some serious money here," Claire said into her microphone to everyone on the team who cared to listen.

"I'm not sure why this surprises you," Sasha replied.

"If they didn't have money, we wouldn't have jobs," Lars added.

Twilight settled into night, and strings of lights illuminated the outside venue in a magical way. The massive Victorian had coastal views and a large piece of property. The charity event was raising money for a home for orphaned children and teens. It had grown through the years, according to Neil, and with it the celebrity guest list that made the event a who's who of the rich and famous.

In the six and a half years she'd been employed with Neil MacBain, Claire had met several of the people milling about the lawn. No longer did she feel starstruck when she saw a familiar artist or celebrity. She was numb to it, in all reality. Between the famous people that Neil and his wife knew, and all of their close, personal friends, it appeared that he knew just about everyone.

Claire walked around the back of the house to where the small mobile office was parked. She pressed in the code on the keypad and smiled at the camera focused on the door before making her way inside.

Lars was one of the oldest members on the team. He was not quite five ten with a bit more of fluff around his middle and a sprinkling of gray hair, but that didn't fool her. The man could move if he needed to. She'd seen him do it. He sat at a desk filled with monitors that displayed livestreams from all the cameras around the venue.

"It's perfectly boring out there," Claire announced.

Lars pushed the microphone in front of his lips out of the way. "Just the way we like it."

She motioned toward the door. "You need a break?"

He shook his head. "I'm good."

She glanced at the monitors again. "We could use someone trying to smash and grab right about now," she said almost to herself.

Lars chuckled.

"Be careful what you wish for." The voice in her ear belonged to Neil.

"I thought you weren't working this event," Claire said.

Lars pointed to the monitor. Neil stood beside his regal blonde bombshell of a wife. He wore a suit, but his clothing was the only thing that blended with the crowd.

Neil was a brick house of a man. The perfect bodyguard. Which was what he leaned on after he left the Marines. He hid behind the title of bodyguard until he married. Then he branched into a team environment. Years later he had the crew here in California, and another one in the United Kingdom.

"Look who cleans up well," Claire teased Neil through the microphone.

"What have I said about chatter on the line?"

Claire rolled her eyes and shook her head, but kept her mouth shut.

The announcement for the silent auction tables closing was broadcast over the PA, which gave her a job to do.

Pushing off the wall, she patted Lars on the back. "That's my cue."

Back outside the trailer, she pulled down on the hem of the cocktail dress she still hadn't completely gotten used to wearing. *Blend in,* she'd been told. The place had security everywhere. The men wore three-piece suits and looked like they were personal bodyguards. And in reality, there were a few of those there as well. But Jax, Sasha, and Claire wore dresses. Granted, there was an awful lot of spandex in the dresses they wore, on the off chance they needed to interact with anyone up to no good. But they were still dresses.

3

When the auction table came into view, those at the event who were bent on winning something hovered over the items and waited for the countdown so they could write their names in the final and winning spot. Which meant the table was packed with people.

Claire noticed the back of Jax's head at the far end.

"Everything good down there?" she said into her mic.

Jax didn't respond.

Claire tapped on the microphone that looked like one of the many beads on her dress. "Yoda?" She used Jax's nickname.

When she didn't respond a second time, Claire tapped on the microphone again. "Lars, is there an issue with the mics?"

Her earpiece crackled, almost like it was underwater.

"Great." The state-of-the-art, high-end toys were shockingly reliable in difficult situations like jumping between rooftops and surviving hand-to-hand combat, but apparently walking around a lawn party was when they failed. "If anyone can hear me, my audio took a hike. I can't hear any of you."

Silence met her.

Instead of returning to the trailer, Claire waded through the crowd and did her job.

She was in charge of the east end of the table, and Jax was on the west.

The announcer started the final countdown, and a buzz went up among the hovering guests.

Claire smiled at people as they stepped in front of her, but then looked around them to lay eyes on one of three extremely pricey items up for auction. Items that were small enough for someone to walk away with.

A man stood in front of the pair of diamond earrings. The woman with him smiled as he wrote his name slowly.

Next was a sapphire-and-diamond tennis bracelet where a lone woman was also writing her name.

Then there was a Victorian brooch that was previously owned by some famous woman Claire didn't know. The starting bid was twenty thousand dollars. But at last look, the bid was nearly double that. It, too, was where it needed to be.

"Three, two, one. Thank you, ladies and gentlemen, it's time to step away from the auction to enjoy the rest of the evening." With the final direction from the announcer, she heard the first chords of a guitar strummed from the stage. The band hired for the evening welcomed everyone.

The coordinators for the event started to push in as the guests dispersed.

Her gaze ignored those acting as they should and instead found a man who switched places with the woman gunning for the bracelet. His back to her, Claire started to move forward.

His hand reached out to touch the jewelry. Something many of the guests had done all night. But when Claire peered closer, she saw something dangle in his fingers for less than a second. With a flick of his hand, he switched the bracelet on the table with whatever he had in his palm. If she'd blinked, she would have missed it.

Her heartbeat sounded in her ears as her adrenaline started to pump.

"We have a situation," Claire said into her mic as she moved to intercept the man.

The silence that followed had her cussing dysfunctional equipment.

She didn't run, didn't call out. These events called for diplomacy, so unless someone was flashing a weapon, the team was meant to apprehend and deal with any situation with as few witnesses as possible.

The thief kept his back to her as he slowly walked away. Unlike the other guests, he wasn't headed to a table or the bar line that never seemed to end. He headed toward the back of the house to where the catering vans were clustered.

Claire looked away for less than a second to signal to Jax. Only Jax's view was blocked by the exiting guests. When Claire looked back, the man was slipping around the house and out of view.

She reached down and took off one spikey heel and then the next before she picked up her pace.

"Someone lifted the sapphires and is headed to the back of the house. If anyone can hear me. Male, approximately six one, wearing a black suit." Just like every other man there. "I didn't see his face. He is on the heavier side and needs a haircut."

As soon as the voices behind her drifted away, Claire started to run, her shoes dangling in her hand.

The side of the house was deserted, only the fleeing thief swiftly walking away.

"Hey!" Claire yelled.

He didn't look back.

Instead, he started to run.

Claire had the advantage. If there was something she took pride in, it was her ability to beat anyone on the team in a one-hundred-meter dash. So she dashed. Her skirt hiked higher and her legs took off.

She was on him before he reached the pavement.

Her arms tackled his waist from behind and brought him to the ground.

He rolled with her.

Claire attempted to grab on to his skin through his clothing and found her hands filled with padding. Almost like he was wearing something under his suit.

He used her hesitation to twist out of her grasp and scramble to his feet.

Only she was faster. She kicked his legs out from under him before he managed to run a second time.

She jumped onto his back and had his right hand twisted behind him and her knee to the back of his shoulder blades, pinning him to the ground face first. "You're not getting away, buddy," she said between pants.

He heaved his body and Claire put more pressure on his arm. "Okay," she heard him say. And then, for whatever reason, the man's body started to shake.

With laughter.

She pulled on his arm again.

"Okay, uncle."

Something about his voice.

"Who are . . ." Her hold softened, she moved her knee from his spine, and the man twisted out from under her. Without warning, she was on her back and he was straddling her.

Clear, calculated, and well-practiced moves started to unfold inside of her. Her arms and legs moved at the same time. Her knee came up and met something entirely too hard to be mistaken for flesh, especially male genitalia, which was what she was aiming for. Even without that jarring surprise, she twisted her legs up with his and heaved her weight until he was on the ground under her.

And he was still laughing.

Claire brushed the hair out of the man's face and finally saw him.

Her mouth opened and her eyes narrowed.

"Cooper?"

Their eyes connected. "Hello, Yearling."

~

Cooper Lockman hadn't seen her in nearly six years.

Six long, education-filled years.

Six years in absence because it was the right thing to do.

Six years where not one day escaped that he didn't think of her.

Claire's surprised expression was followed by flailing hands that slapped at his chest in a much more playful way than when she was tackling him. "What. The. Actual. Fuck!"

And he laughed.

"You're the one that asked for drama." Neil's voice sounded in both of their ears.

Cooper could see Neil's words register in Claire's head at the same time they did his.

Claire settled on top of him. Her legs spread over his hips, her body upright . . .

Slowly, she started to smile.

When she did, her body relaxed on top of his, and it was then that Cooper realized that six years had changed absolutely nothing.

He placed his hands on her hips to move her off of him.

Once she was on his side, he felt he could actually say something intelligent. Something other than . . . *God, you're beautiful and just as amazing as the last time I saw you.*

"I thought we lost you to Europe," she said.

"And become an expat? Never gonna happen."

Her smile moved from happy to radiant seconds before she threw her arms around him in a hug of unadulterated happiness.

Cooper allowed his arms to encircle her in response.

He closed his eyes and found himself lost in the moment.

Not that it lasted.

"I trust no one is hurt."

Cooper looked over Claire's shoulder to find Sasha standing several yards away.

"Never better," Cooper told her.

Claire stopped smiling in a millisecond, and without warning she placed her hand on the cup that protected his sexual future. "I knew it."

He brushed her hands away before her touch made him turn red.

They pushed off the ground at the same time. Cooper shrugged out of his jacket and lifted his shirt to tug on the Velcro that kept the fake pounds around his waist.

"When did you get back?" Claire asked.

"Last week."

"Are you back to stay, or does Neil have you slated for the London team forever?"

He opened his mouth to offer an ambiguous reply only to be cut off.

"The reunion can wait. We still have work to do." Sasha walked up to the two of them and handed Claire the shoes she'd tossed to the ground before she did a full body tackle to take him down. Not that he resisted all that much.

Claire pulled at the hem of her skirt and smoothed a hand over her stomach. "Is my dress okay?"

Cooper wasn't sure the question was directed at him since she turned a full circle in front of both him and Sasha.

"You look like you've been rolling around in the grass," Sasha said, her Russian accent always apparent.

He reached out and pulled a leaf out of Claire's blonde hair.

Claire was all smiles. "Or maybe people will think I snuck away to get lucky."

He laughed.

"Run a brush through your hair. It's getting dark, no one will notice the grass stains on a black dress." Sasha turned to Cooper. "Relieve Lars. We'll recap at the end of the evening."

Claire turned toward the back door of the Victorian home. "Glad you're home," she called out over her shoulder.

"Me too."

Then she was gone.

He brushed at his pants. "That was fun."

CHAPTER TWO

"I forgot how hot he was." Jax stood in the doorway of Claire's room in the Tarzana house they shared.

It was after one in the morning, but they were still buzzing from the late night. Claire was slipping out of the formal clothes and into a pair of boy shorts and a T-shirt to sleep in. And Jax was talking about Cooper.

"Don't let him hear you say that. He will remind you every chance he gets about that 'one time' you said he was hot." Claire motioned toward the disguised camera in the hall that she knew was equipped with audio as well. The home had undergone some extensive security adaptation back when Neil's wife had lived there. The man took protecting his family to serious extremes. When Jax made the move, she and Claire both decided that the internal cameras and audio needed a kill switch. The last thing either of them wanted was for their coworkers to see what they were doing in their personal time. Like talking about the hotness that was Cooper.

Jax flopped on the end of Claire's bed and curled her pajama-covered legs under her. "Any idea what this special meeting we have tomorrow is about?"

Claire shook her head.

Neil had told the team to sleep in but be at the office at ten in the morning.

"Neil's cryptic. You never know what the man is thinking until he actually tells us."

"I hope it's fieldwork."

Claire walked into her bathroom and turned on the hot water in the sink to scrub off her makeup. "You and me both. Running after Cooper and taking him down was the highlight of my week."

Jax spoke from where she sat on the edge of the bed. "Neil knows you get bored. I think that's why he arranged a decoy."

"He's right. Things need to pick up or I'm going to be signing up for those weekend murder mystery things for a little excitement." Claire used a washcloth to work the mascara off her eyelashes.

"Those look lame."

"Better than sitting at a computer all the time."

Back in her bedroom, she climbed onto her bed and faced her best friend.

"It's crazy how much stuff Richter taught us that we never use," Jax said with a sigh. The more tired her best friend got, the more her German accent showed up.

Richter was a military-style boarding school in Germany where they both went to high school. Emphasis on *military*, right down to arms training and hand-to-hand combat. The school housed many secrets inside of its halls. From murderous faculty to recruiting for special agents and covert assassins. All that changed thanks to Neil's team. Not that the team had any real recognition for their efforts. No, they moved in, exposed the wrongs, and moved out. "That was an exciting night," Claire said, reminiscing about the evening Richter changed its ways forever.

"Feels like yesterday."

It had been six years. Jax had had a semester to go before she could graduate from Richter, and Claire had moved with her new chosen family to Southern California.

Neil set her up in the Tarzana home, and Sasha paid for her to go to college. Sasha had attended Richter years before Claire landed there. When Sasha had returned, searching for direction, Claire had taken their mutual understanding of each other as a sign. A sign to liberate herself from the walls of Richter and venture out on her own. Only she hadn't been on her own. Sasha had been there, along with AJ, her now husband. Claire had always viewed Sasha as an older sister. Sasha made sure that Claire had what she needed, but didn't helicopter and assume the role of parent.

Claire looked up to the woman. Respected her.

Claire worked for the security business nights and weekends when she was in college. The summer after Jax graduated, she moved in and joined the crazy. The difference was, Jax returned to Europe a couple of times a year, since that's where her family lived. Claire spent her holidays with Neil and his family, or Sasha and her chosen family.

Neil, the big, stoic dude, busted her ass all the time. He was half father, half boss. And Claire did whatever she needed to to earn the man's respect.

Jax unfolded from the bed. "I'm exhausted."

"Me too. Good night."

"'Night, Loki."

~

There was nothing formal about her work when Claire wasn't on a personal detail. She arrived at nine thirty and was dressed to go for a late-morning run once the meeting was over. Which meant she wore running shorts that hugged her legs, a pair of Adidas, and her hair pulled up in a ponytail. She would have loved to say she wore some kind of special running bra, but since nature teased her in that area, the garden-variety sport top did the job.

She walked into their main headquarters and straight to the surveillance room. Up on the wall of monitors were views from cameras on many of their clients. Most were angles from front doors, or backyards. But all of them could be expanded with the flip of a switch. Security was a serious business for the rich and famous.

"Good morning," she said as she walked into the room.

Rick turned around in his chair and offered his signature smile. "Hey, Yearling."

She rolled her eyes at the nickname she couldn't shake, regardless of the fact she'd been on the team for over six years. "I'm surprised to see you behind the desk." Rick was Neil's right-hand man on many occasions. He was almost the size of the other man, but with an easier smile. The two of them went back to their days in the Marines. They'd been to hell more than once, from the stories Claire had heard.

"Favor to Neil," he said.

"Is this about today's meeting?"

"Yup" was all he offered before changing the subject. "Judy told me everything went like clockwork last night."

"Did your wife tell you about the false heist?"

Rick laughed. "I heard about *that* from Lars."

Claire moved to the coffeepot that never seemed to empty. "It's probably wrong for me to crave that kind of excitement."

Rick glanced back at the monitors. "It's normal for people like us."

"I'm not sure that applies to me or Jax. We never saw combat."

"No, but you both trained for it."

She supposed that was true.

The door to the room opened and Neil popped his head in. "Good, you're right on time," he said to her.

"I'm a half an hour early."

He looked her dead in the eye, blinked. "Like I said, right on time."

She shook her head. In the early years, she had to arrive fifteen minutes early, and then somehow, after she graduated with a degree in criminal justice, Neil pushed that fifteen minutes to thirty.

She could lie and say she hated his expectations.

The truth was Claire liked the boundaries and structure.

"You gonna tell me what today is all about?" she asked.

He looked at his watch. "In about twenty-five minutes."

Claire returned her attention to the coffee, smelled it, and decided to put her effort into a fresh pot. "I don't know how you guys drink this stuff," she said as she walked out of the room to find water.

"Grows hair on your chest," Rick called out behind her.

"Not my goal," she called back.

By the time she had a cup of drinkable coffee in her hand, half the team had arrived. By quarter to, everyone was there, including Cooper.

She motioned a hello and stood back while several others quizzed him on his time in Europe.

Jax sat beside her, similarly dressed since they planned on doing their workout together. "He's even cuter in jeans and a T-shirt," Jax whispered in Claire's ear.

"Are you thinking of kicking Lewis to the curb?" Jax had been dating Lewis for a good six months. The man was finishing up his law degree and prepping to take the bar exam.

"I'm not married."

Claire looked up to find Cooper smiling at her. It was nice to see him back. She'd been surprised when he left, but that was when Jax moved in, taking Claire's mind off his departure.

Neil walked in the room with another man and cleared his throat. "Have a seat, guys."

Chairs scraped against the floor as the team turned to give Neil their attention.

"I see everyone had a chance to welcome Cooper back," Neil started. "With him here, I'm likely going to be replacing him overseas.

After today's meeting I'll be looking for volunteers, if any of you are interested."

"It's a cush job," Cooper announced.

"Stupid cold in London this time of year," Jax said.

"Neil had me all over the place. Not just London."

Neil cleared his throat a second time and they stopped talking among each other. "Details on that later." He turned to the man standing beside him. "This is Detective Thomas Warren."

Detective Warren looked around the group with a slight smile.

"He is the lead on a local task force that is targeting human trafficking. I'd like you to give him your undivided attention." With the introduction made, Neil stepped back and leaned a hip on one of the many desks in the room.

"Thanks, Neil. I appreciate you all coming in. Like Neil said, I'm part of a larger group of detectives that has been working on identifying and apprehending the organizations that are responsible for human trafficking in our area. Specifically, child sex trafficking."

Claire glanced at Jax, who sat silently beside her.

"Our team uses outside help on a continual basis. That's where you come in, if you choose to take on the task. There has been an increase in child sex traffickers finding their victims in several local high schools. While many believe that this only happens in the inner city where the income and poverty level among the community is a factor, that wouldn't be entirely true. More and more private schools and Title One schools are reporting kids dropping out and seemingly disappearing as well. There appears to be a much more organized effort to target younger and younger teens across the board." Warren indicated Neil. "Neil and I became acquainted through a mutual friend. I know each and every one of you in this room has a special set of skills that would soar your rank if you ever decided to join the force."

"Most of us are retired military. We're not interested in being cops." Lars spoke for many of them.

Warren shook his head. "And I don't blame you. The rules we have to abide by tie our hands more often than not. But you guys don't have that. What you do have are skills to infiltrate the local schools, help us identify at-risk teens, and point us to those who prey on them. More importantly, you're able to keep yourselves and the victims safe should they ask for your help."

"This sounds like something your department can do undercover," Claire said.

"And we have. In the past we've managed to identify several victims and those that pulled them into the sex trade."

"Then why do you need us?" Claire asked.

Warren took a second to look at all of them. "We need fresh eyes, young eyes." He looked directly at Claire and Jax. "My department has successfully gone undercover acting as teachers, office staff, and the occasional student. All of which turned up the gangs involved. Only now our resources are coming up dry. And no one believes these self-proclaimed 'entrepreneurs' have stopped manipulating teens into prostitution."

"Entrepreneurs. Really?" Isaac asked.

"That's a stretch," Cooper added.

Warren kept talking. "The pimps we've managed to take down claim no gang affiliation. Of course, many of them lied to keep face with their people. And by gang, we aren't talking anything as big as those we see in downtown LA, or any of the bigger cities. Some of these guys have a small culture, some as small as a half dozen, or as large as several dozen. Not very organized, but even then, they recruited and pimped their victims independently."

"You mean the money didn't go into the gang," Lars said.

"Exactly. But, as our sting started outing these dirtbags, some formed bigger organizations and changed the way they operate. And that's the issue we're having now. Our crisis in over twenty schools has seemingly gone underground almost overnight."

"The unorganized became organized," Cooper stated.

Warren pointed at him. "Right. And I've been asked to go out, hire a team, and flush out the problem. We still have dropouts, runaways, kids that fit the profile, and some that are just flat-out disappearing."

"Flush out the problem," Jax repeated. "That sounds as if you're questioning your team."

Warren lost any amusement in his face. "I've had solid men and women on my task force."

"That wasn't a denial," Claire said.

The room grew silent, answering the question.

"My superiors want to rule out a team issue within before an internal investigation led by the feds occurs," Warren admitted.

"So you'll be telling us who your men are if we take on this task?" Cooper asked.

Warren shook his head. "No. I don't want you following my team around and waiting for them to fuck up. I want you to go in and find the scum that are behind these kids disappearing or being sold. If in that investigation you uncover any of my men"—Warren's words broke off, his fist clenched at his side—"any of my men with dirty hands, it won't be because you're profiling them. My team is sharp. They'll know if they're being followed. As any of you would, too. If they're dirty, they'll hide. Nobody wants that."

It took a minute for Warren's words to register.

Neil cleared his throat. "What Detective Warren is asking of us is to put together a team to have eyes and ears at two schools. Jax and Claire would be on the inside, different campuses. You're both young enough to pass as high school seniors. We put Cooper at the higher risk school as an assistant coach and substitute teacher. I'm actively searching out a new member for the team to go with Jax. The details will be hammered out later."

"This sounds extensive," Claire said. And not at all like the Hollywood party detail they normally handled.

"We'll be putting those new PI licenses to work." Neil directed his comment to both Claire and Jax. They'd wrapped up their degrees in college and licensed themselves in six states so far. Along with a concealed carry permit, it gave them license to protect themselves, and others if needed. Legally.

"Will the school administration know we're there?"

"Limited. Only the principal and vice principal will be aware of who you are. And we want to keep it that way. There is speculation that there might be someone on staff directing the perps to the kids most likely to fall for their lies."

"That's fucked up," Lars voiced.

"No more than a dirty cop," Cooper pointed out.

"Dirty cop is worse."

"I'd rather it be staff than the other. Even better, I'd like the connection to have nothing to do with the people that say they're there to help." Warren looped his thumbs inside the pockets of his slacks and rocked back on his heels. "If you choose to work with us, you'll report to Neil, and he will report to me. We'll have a deeper briefing if you take this on."

Claire rubbed her thumb against the palm of her other hand. Nothing ticked her off more than someone preying upon kids. A look around the room told her the rest of the team thought so, too. That aside, the job sounded a hell of a lot better than babysitting celebrities.

"Okay. Thanks for your time." Warren moved to shake Neil's hand. "I'll be in touch."

There was a chorus of goodbyes as the man exited the meeting room.

"So we're working with the cops now?" Isaac asked once Warren left.

"Not completely," Neil answered. He pushed off the desk and moved to a giant whiteboard in the front of the room. He drew a box on the board and then an identical box a foot away. "This is Bremerton, Emma's school."

"Your daughter?" Claire asked.

"Yeah."

"This shit is happening at a prep school?"

Neil silenced them with his hand. He put an X in the other box. "Most of the known cases have been outside of Bremerton. The file Warren briefed me with indicated three positive victims that spent time at Bremerton before getting wrapped up in this. By the time the police caught up with these girls, they were nineteen, twenty, and wanted nothing to do with leaving their pimps."

"How old were they when they were pulled in?"

"Two were sixteen, one was fifteen."

Claire could practically hear Neil's teeth grinding together.

"That's sick," Lars said.

Neil drew a line between the two boxes. "This is the school we're targeting, Auburn High."

"They're rival schools?" Claire asked.

"Not directly."

"Private schools and public schools don't compete as a rule," Lars said.

"True," Neil said. "But it isn't uncommon for kids to move out of the private schools and into the public schools when they show athletic ability. Especially if the private school doesn't have an organized team. As an example, Bremerton doesn't have a football team, Auburn does. Many parents cave to the pressure of letting their kids go to public schools so they can compete and possibly earn athletic scholarships for college. And therefore there are plenty of kids here . . ." He pointed to Emma's school. "Who know the more vulnerable kids here."

"Emma's too smart to let this kind of thing happen to her," Isaac assured him.

"This isn't about Emma." Neil dropped the marker.

"The hell it isn't." Claire flat-out called bullshit on Neil's words. "If there are dirtbags gunning for young girls at Emma's school, you either flush them out or send her off to a boarding school. Which everyone in this room knows doesn't guarantee safety." As Claire voiced her opinion, some of the reasons why Neil would even consider this assignment made sense.

Neil narrowed his eyes, stared directly at Claire. "This is about teenage rebellion being exploited and used for the purpose of financial gain for everyone but that teenager."

And Emma, Claire mouthed silently.

Cooper laughed. "If anyone so much as looked at Emma wrong, Neil would simply eliminate him."

Neil didn't confirm or deny that.

"You were the one who said you needed some excitement," Lars reminded Claire.

Yeah . . . that had happened yesterday.

Claire broke eye contact with Neil and glanced at Cooper and then Jax.

Jax shook her head. "Looks like we're going back to school."

CHAPTER THREE

"Do we really look young enough to pass for high school seniors?" Claire stood with a pool cue in her hand and waited while Cooper took his turn.

"I still get carded all the time," Jax said.

"Even if we look the part, we know next to nothing about American high schools."

The local bar was a dive. Dark corners and burned-out lights. But the place was clean, and the drinks were decent.

Jax took up space on a stool next to a high-top table that held their drinks.

"What's to know?" Cooper asked. "You have the cool kids, the mean kids, jocks, and geeks. You have the emo group and the out-casts. The party kids, the popular ones. And they're all on their phones twenty-four seven."

"Oh, damn, that's right." Claire and Jax were the exception to the twentysomething rule when it came to social media accounts. Claire didn't have her own cell phone until she moved to the States after her years at Richter. And once they started working for Neil, he made it clear that social media was contraindicated when you worked with him. Private security was just that, private. Social media didn't fit.

Cooper bounced his solid ball off the bumper, but missed the shot.

"We don't have accounts," Jax added.

"As soon as you get your identities, you're going to have to change that. It's the way kids communicate," Cooper said.

Claire walked around the table looking for a shot. "I wouldn't know what to post."

"Selfies," Jax said.

"How self-indulgent." She lined up her ball and pulled the cue back.

"Yeah, but no one will think twice if you're taking pictures all the time. And when we learn who the players are, we'll have images," Cooper said.

"I wonder how long this assignment is going to take."

Claire angled her shot and sunk the ball. "Takes time to earn people's trust and start knowing their secrets," she told Jax.

"It didn't sound like a quick job to me," Cooper said.

"I always thought I'd do undercover work, but didn't think that would mean I'm going back to high school," Claire said.

"I know, right? I saw myself on the coast of Italy following someone who jacked all of Neil's money."

"How does Neil have that bank account, anyway?" Jax asked Cooper. The man never seemed without funds. And in cases like this one, he had a steady stream of organizations that funneled money into worthy causes.

"I heard he invested a lot when he was a bodyguard for the Harrisons. And Gwen has family money."

"A *lot* of family money," Claire added.

"Why work, then?"

"Can you see Neil on a golf course enjoying retirement?" Cooper asked.

The image had them chuckling. Neil didn't idle well. None of them did.

"I guess not."

Claire and Cooper switched places at the pool table, and she changed the subject. "Are you glad to be back?" she asked him.

He stopped concentrating on the game and looked her in the eye. "Yeah. I am."

"So what did you do for six years? I'm surprised you didn't pay us a visit once in a while."

He blinked away, took a shot, and missed. "Neil had me busy. I helped set up the new team. Coordinated different things that will make it easier if we ever find ourselves with a Richter situation again."

The Richter Situation was a hell of a lot more than a "situation." Assassins and murder disguised as a military boarding school where the bad guy recruited kids to do his dirty work. Now that Claire had a moment to think about it, she realized it wasn't so different from the case they were about to dig into. People being manipulated and eventually blackmailed into doing something they didn't want to do. Only the punishment for murder was a hell of a lot more than for prostitution. Both would mess up a person no matter how you looked at it.

"Is it awful of me to look back on that and miss the adrenaline rush of it all?" Claire found herself asking.

"You wouldn't be a part of the team if you didn't."

She sighed.

"We're going to be seeing the inside of the classroom again, not jumping around on rooftops and crashing parties," Jax said.

Cooper went back to playing pool. "What self-respecting high school kid didn't crash a party or two?"

Claire and Jax looked at each other. "Never happened."

Jax shook her head. "Not once."

"Well, you're going to get your chance." Cooper took his aim and sunk a ball.

"Hey, wasn't it my turn?"

"No." Cooper narrowed his eyes, looked at the table.

"Yes, it was. You missed on the six ball."

He glanced at Jax, who pointed a thumb to Claire. "She's right."

"Whatever. Makes up for the cheap shot to the groin yesterday."

She placed a finger to his chest and pushed him away from the table. "Yesterday you were the bad guy running away with stolen gems. A knee to the goods is expected. And since you were wearing a cup, it doesn't count as a cheap shot."

"That was Sasha's suggestion."

Claire laughed. "We were taught by the same instructors."

"Nothing polite about a fistfight," Jax added, sending a fist bump to Claire.

"I'm not singing soprano today, so I'm thankful for the advice."

Claire winked before scooting one of the stripes into a corner pocket with her hand. "One free for me and the next two turns."

Cooper sent her an indignant look. "Changed the rules of the game while I was away?"

She pointed her cue at him. "Or we could call it and you just pay up your twenty bucks now?"

"Not in this lifetime, Yearling."

She winked and leaned over the pool table, pulled her pool cue back. Right as she took the shot, Cooper did his best to interrupt her concentration.

"You hold that stick like you enjoy it."

Her eyes moved to his, the smile that teased lingered on her face. "Wouldn't you like to know?"

~

Neil handed out driver's licenses and cell phones like he was dealing cards.

"You are no longer Claire Kelly, you're Claire Porter. Cooper Lockman is now Cooper Mitchel. Jax Simon is now Jax Livingston."

Claire looked at her driver's license. They'd done a good job of making her look like she was sixteen. The age she would have been if she'd been in California when she'd obtained her first license.

"Both your addresses are out of the area to coordinate with a new student transfer. We're working on a location that we'll use as a base. You will not be driving directly from your home to the school. Claire, your aunt is a flight attendant." He pointed to Sasha, who looked bored. "Jax, your parents are newly divorced, and your dad works nights." Lars waved. "These roles are contingent. The desire is to avoid parental involvement altogether, but we have it in place should we need it.

"Jax, you're the quiet one. Pissed your dad obtained custody. We want you blending with the kids that won't be missed if they don't show up for school. Claire, you're rebellious."

"Yes." Claire put both palms in the air.

Neil stared her down, completely unamused. "If you're done . . ."

She purposely frowned. "Sorry."

"Rebellion means your aunt is making you play a sport." He then pointed to Cooper. "Track."

"The school is working on your schedules now. You need the broadest range of contacts you can get. Be popular enough to be invited to parties, but blend enough so you don't stand out and have your covers blown," Neil told them.

"Your cheerleading aspirations will have to wait," Claire teased Jax.

She shook her head with a laugh.

Sasha handed out portfolios and continued where Neil left off. "Inside is a wide range of known victims. Along with their pictures are those of their friends. Study these and find potential patterns. Either with the victims or their friend base."

Claire looked at the first photograph. "Jesus, how old is she?"

"Fifteen," Jax said, waving her copy to show the details on the back.

At Claire's side, Cooper sighed. "This is disgusting."

As Claire sifted through the pages, the victims grew older. When she came to a girl that looked twenty, she turned the paper over and read the bio. Eighteen, but dropped out of school six months before graduating.

"Claire, you and Jax are leaving tomorrow for the Bay Area. You will go to the schools you transferred from, take pictures, and fill up your Instagram accounts."

"Can we hack Instagram to avoid the date stamp of the photos?"

"Not worth the effort," Sasha said. "Find an excuse for your parents to have taken you off of social media. Right before you transferred, you earned the phones and accounts back."

"In your packet, you'll find a case study done down in San Diego. Some of it is unique to that city and its proximity to the border, but most of it mimics what Warren and his team found before the area organized. Plenty of intel in those pages. Some of the main similarities are the victims themselves. Newly transferred in with a history of neglect and abuse." Neil stood up. "Jax, you are solo at Bremerton in the beginning. The last time you saw Emma was shortly after you moved in with Claire, and she doesn't remember you. Everyone else in this room she's more familiar with. She knows nothing about what we're doing. I'd like to keep it that way. I'm working on recruiting a second player now. You will take no risks. If you need backup, I will have a need to visit my daughter. Understood?"

Jax nodded.

"Good." He moved to the whiteboard. "Your main objective on campus: identify the biggest risk. The principal at Bremerton is the only administrator that knows you're there. I have personally vetted him, and he is not involved."

Claire chuckled. "Is that your way of saying you know the brand of toilet paper the man prefers?"

"It's Emma's high school," Neil said, deadpan.

Cooper leaned over. "That's his way of saying yes."

Neil continued. "I do not know how deep or fluid Detective Warren's staff is. They could be pushing a broom or be the resource officer. In each of your packets you have a list of current teachers and their tenure." He pointed to Claire. "Auburn High shuffles staff throughout the district, so you'll find plenty of new or newish teachers. What I don't have is all the ancillary staff information. These are district employees, which could easily fit into the profile of perpetrator."

". . . or undercover cop," Sasha pointed out.

"As far as I see this, no one on either campus has privacy until we are off this assignment. Both campuses have security cameras, and Sasha's working on access to Auburn High this week. There will be enough equipment available to plant audio in as many places as we need."

"At Bremerton, too?" Jax asked.

Neil stared at her.

Claire cleared her throat. "Emma," she said as she pretended to cough, guessing that Neil had already tapped into the audio at his daughter's school.

Jax shook her head. "Oh."

"This is fluid. I want you both tracked. Once we obtain decoy housing for you, audio and visual monitors will be in place in all areas but the bathrooms. When friendships are formed and deeper intel is needed, direct those conversations to your decoy home when you can. You will stay at your base if your cover is at risk of being blown. Otherwise go home."

That seemed reasonable to Claire.

"And for the duration of this assignment, surveillance is live in Tarzana."

Much as Claire didn't like the lack of privacy, she understood the need. "No audio," she told him.

For a second, Neil said nothing.

"Inside the house," she clarified.

She held her breath, fairly certain he was going to come back with a rebuttal.

"We'll install voice activation for audio." His words were measured.

Silently, Claire waved her hands in the air, doing her best jazz hands impression. Getting Neil to go along with her didn't happen very often.

Sasha handed her and Jax each an envelope. "Your flight leaves in the morning. Go shopping. Learn the areas. We don't want you tripping over geography or the weather. Spend a day in the city. Do what teens do. Get carded because of your behavior."

"Good idea," Claire muttered in Russian.

Sasha acknowledged her words with a nod.

"Cooper, I have you at Emma's school this week. I spoke with the head track coach. He'll bring you up to speed. He doesn't know why you're there. If nothing else, if something heats up at Bremerton we can move you," Neil said.

"You got it, Boss."

Neil pushed away from the wall. "Unless there are any questions, we're done."

They all started gathering their paperwork to leave.

"For the record, I'm not old enough to be Jax's dad," Lars said.

They laughed.

"That's debatable," Cooper dished out.

"Says the kid that didn't shave until last year."

Claire found her eyes lingering on Cooper's face. The extra facial hair he let peek out since he'd returned from Europe gave him a ruggedness that wasn't there before.

Cooper stood taller and rubbed his chin while looking at Lars. "You're just pissed because yours is turning gray."

"Just wait, buddy."

While he laughed, Cooper turned toward Claire. The laughter faded, but his smile stayed.

And for some strange reason, her stomach warmed. She liked the slight five o'clock shadow. Not to mention the way his jeans fit. Maybe Jax had something there.

Jax cleared her throat, breaking the silence that fell over the room.

Claire blinked out of her unexpected trance.

"Girls' trip," Jax said, grabbing her arm.

Claire fist-bumped Jax. "Frisco, baby."

Jax turned to Lars as she looped an arm over Claire's shoulder. "I won't be home tonight, *Dad*."

Lars groaned.

Right before they exited the room, Claire glanced over her shoulder and found Cooper quickly looking away.

She stared at his back, some of the humor faded.

Jax tugged her attention. "We have a plane to catch."

CHAPTER FOUR

"So what sport did you play in school?" Dale, the track team's head coach at Emma's private school, stood on the inside field with his arms crossed over his chest.

Cooper hadn't been sure what to expect, so he donned a pair of shorts and a T-shirt with simple running shoes for his crash course in coaching high school track.

"None," Cooper informed the man. "Joined the service the day after I graduated."

Dale nodded a few times, his eyes tracking several kids as they jogged the inside lanes. "I think Neil told me that. Not that the man elaborated."

"Talking isn't his strong point."

Just then two students walked up, both upperclassmen from the looks of them.

"Hey, Coach."

Dale patted the kid on his shoulder. "Get everyone stretched out and warmed up."

"You got it."

The student turned away and started to yell, gaining the attention of those on the track to circle up.

Dale started walking with Cooper in tow.

"Seniors love taking control of the field during practice, and since we have a small athletic department, I use them to mentor the younger kids."

"Makes sense."

Dale motioned toward the pole vault pit. "Do you have the basics of any of the field events?"

"Only what I learned in boot camp."

"Then we'll stick with relays and sprints."

Cooper could work with that.

They walked over to a stack of hurdles. "So, what's this all about with you coaching the Auburn kids, anyway?"

He wasn't about to give details. "What did Neil tell you?"

Dale placed a hand on one of the hurdles. "Let me see if I remember the conversation. 'Coach Levine. I have something I need ya to do for me.'" Dale lowered his voice to mimic Neil. "'Sure,' I said. Then he said, 'I have one of my men filling in on the Auburn track team, keeping an eye on one of the students.'" Dale nodded a couple of times. "Yup, that's all he told me."

"And that's all there is to it. Simple job," Cooper told the man.

"Huh. I didn't think any of the parents at Auburn had the money to hire anyone from Neil's line of work."

Cooper kept his expression steady. "You'd be surprised."

Dale shrugged his shoulders. "Hopefully it's nothing serious." He lifted a stack of hurdles and nodded to another stack for Cooper to grab.

"I doubt it."

Dale pointed to where the hurdles needed to be placed and then proceeded to lower the height of the contraptions. For the next hour and a half, Dale did his job with Cooper as a shadow. The kids knew what they had to do, for the most part. The coach's relationship with the students was more friend than mentor. Though when he had constructive criticism, the kids listened and worked harder to hear his praise.

As the practice neared its end, Cooper felt like he had some of the lingo down, and by the end of the week, he should be good to go.

The same students that led the warm-up finished the cooldown.

Slowly the kids peeled off the field when practice ended.

Dale handed Cooper a stack of papers. "This is how track meets are scored. Probably best you know this before you start your job at Auburn."

He scanned the papers. It seemed pretty straightforward. "Does your team rival Auburn?"

"Not really. We see each other at invitationals, mainly. The coaches there are straight up. Good guys who like kids and fell in love with the sport. I'm guessing you and I will see each other a few times this season."

One of the students called Dale from the opposite side of the field. "Yeah?"

"I can't find the keys to lock up the shed."

Dale lifted a hand, indicating he'd be there in a minute.

The phone in Cooper's jacket pocket started to vibrate.

"When we do see each other, I'd appreciate it if you keep my real vocation out of the conversation."

"Of course." Dale peered across the field. "I'll see ya tomorrow. And if you talk to Neil, thank him again."

Cooper tilted his head and questioned Dale with his eyes.

"For the new pole vault pit. Should be here in about a week. The kids are excited."

Cooper smiled. "I'll do that." As he walked away, the phone in his pocket buzzed again. He pulled it out to see who was texting him.

He smiled before he clicked on Claire's name.

Claire and Jax smiled at him with the Golden Gate Bridge framing the background.

Look who has the cushy job this week!

Cooper's fingers danced over the phone's keyboard. We'll see who's bragging next week when you have homework.

Claire followed up with a frowning face emoji.

For a moment, he stared at her image. She'd grown up since he moved away. Oh, she still had the snark that underlined nearly everything she said and did, but there was a calmness that hadn't been there before. He remembered the first time he saw her, fresh from the boarding school in Germany and only a hair past eighteen years of life. Much too young for him; or so he convinced himself at the time. Granted, he'd been younger, too. He'd casually flirted with her back then. In turn, she rolled her eyes and blew him off. "Put it away, buddy . . . you're much too old for me," she'd said to him on more than one occasion.

But when the initial drama of their first assignment waned, he had a hard time working with her side by side. She treated him like her best friend's off-limits brother. He told himself he was fine, that his infatuation would fade, until she walked into their headquarters one evening wearing what he referred to as a Sasha Special.

He was in the surveillance room keeping a selective eye on one of their Hollywood celebrity's cameras since the movie star was having a party. One of their team was at the party on the off chance something happened, and Cooper was the second set of eyes from miles away.

The door to the room opened behind him as he was running the license plates of the cars rolling through the valet.

The click of high heels suggested Sasha had walked in the room.

"You would think you'd get tired of wearing those pencil shoes," he said without looking over his shoulder.

"You're just jealous you can't."

With the sound of Claire's voice, his head swiveled, and his brain short-circuited. He blew out a breath as if someone had punched him in the gut. She wore a black, curve-hugging dress that stopped midthigh. Long legs stretched toward the ground where a pair of stiletto boots took over the entire look. Walking his gaze back up her frame, blonde hair draped over her shoulders and a dusting of makeup highlighted her girl-next-door features.

"Whoa."

Claire turned in a full circle, as if he needed more ammunition. "Do you think this is overdoing it?"

It was the kind of question meant for a girlfriend.

"Depends on what you're doing?"

"It's a first date," she said as she tossed a clutch purse in the seat beside his.

He swallowed and beat down the tinge of jealousy that sprouted from her words. Forcing his eyes off of her, he looked back at the camera footage. "Depends on how you want your date to end."

She sighed, almost like she was whining. "It's too much, isn't it?"

No, it was exactly right. And the lucky bastard that was taking her out . . . "Wait, who's the guy?" He turned back her way.

"From my school."

"A frat boy?" That just made him nauseated.

Claire narrowed her gaze. "You say that like it's a problem."

It was a huge problem. "I always took you for someone with better skills than beer pong."

She slid him a slight smile. "I'm sure there's more to him than drinking games."

"How long have you known him?" While Cooper quizzed her, he clicked the camera to focus on another license plate as the party on camera started to fill up.

"I don't really know him at all."

"Yet you're dressed like that for a first date."

"He said a nice dinner."

"Which is what? In-N-Out versus McDonald's?" She was dressed to rival the women in his field of vision from the party he was watching.

Cooper felt, more than heard, the silence stretched between them. When he looked over his shoulder at Claire, she was staring at him.

"What?" he asked.

"You . . . you sound jealous."

He immediately rolled his eyes and huffed. "Don't be ridiculous." He didn't sound like anything, he was feeling everything. "I'm just . . . concerned. You're still new here. You live alone, and even though I know you can kick serious ass, you don't have a wingman to fall on if this frat boy looks at that dress as an invitation."

Claire stepped between him and the vacant chair, leaned her hip on the desk. "Jax will be here in two months, so I won't be living alone for long. I might be new here, but I'm not some naive midwestern girl who doesn't know better than to not leave her drink alone with a first date. And yeah, I can ditch the heels and kick all kinds of ass if I need to. So your concern is almost insulting and something I'd expect from Neil, not you."

Cooper secretly wished his boss were there. He'd demand she change into jeans and a sweater. The man had taken Claire under his protection when he hired her on to the team. While she talked like Miss Independent, Claire thrived under the rules Neil had set out. Go to college, get good grades, report to work, and she had a home to live in with all her expenses taken care of. Neil treated her like a younger sister one day, and a daughter the next. And right now Cooper would give his next paycheck for Neil to walk in the door and tell Claire to go home and do her schoolwork.

"What? Nothing to say?" Claire crossed her arms over her chest.

"If you didn't want my opinion about the dress, or the guy, why did you come in here and ask me?"

The smugness of her chin slowly faded.

Her folded arms slid to her sides, and Cooper knew she was concentrating on her answer. "Because my wingman isn't here yet, and even though I can take care of myself, I'm smart enough to let someone know I'm going on a date."

"Why not tell Sasha?"

"She and AJ are in Colorado."

"Neil?"

It was Claire's turn to roll her eyes. "He'd try and stop me."

So that left Cooper.

Shoved into the friend zone.

And as much as he hated that position, he'd despise it more if Claire was left without anyone watching over her.

She pushed off the desk. "You know what, never mind. I can take care of myself."

He shot out his hand and grasped her forearm before she could storm away. It would have taken so little for her to get out of his hold, but instead she looked at his hand and then his face.

Cooper wanted to stand up next to her, have those blue eyes looking up at him. But that would be torture. She's eighteen, *his head screamed.*

Letting go, he swiveled around and walked to a cabinet filled with tracking equipment. Instead of handing it to her, he activated the device and put it in the purse she'd thrown on the chair. "What's his name?"

For a second she didn't reply.

"If Jax were here, would you tell her?"

He saw her swallow. "Miles Ketterman."

Cooper wanted to hate the name, but found it completely harmless. He handed the purse over and brushed his fingers against her in the exchange. Not trusting himself to say more, he sat back down and turned on one of the many screens in front of him to link up with Claire's tracker.

He should say something smug, something to express friendship and snark. But Cooper didn't have it in him.

Claire took a few steps toward the door and stopped.

"Thanks, Cooper."

"If you need backup . . ."

More footsteps and then the sound of the door opening.

Before she could walk away, he finally said what he couldn't hold in. "You look incredible." He kept staring forward, seeing her reflection in the monitors.

"Thanks," she mumbled again before letting the door close behind her.

The following week, Cooper and Neil had a long conversation about the help needed in the London office.

Only now he was back and Claire wasn't the eighteen-year-old off-limits girl she once was.

Cooper took one last look at the picture of her and Jax before tossing his phone in the passenger seat of his car and leaving the high school parking lot.

CHAPTER FIVE

Claire started her American high school experience in the principal's office.

"Miss Kelly. Please have a seat." The principal, Mrs. Hanley, indicated the chair opposite her desk and motioned to the office secretary to close the door behind her as she left.

Once alone in the office, Mrs. Hanley sighed before making her way around her desk. "The detective wasn't kidding when he said you would look young enough for the job."

Claire had thought the exact opposite before pulling into the school parking lot. "I suppose that's why I'm here," Claire told her.

Mrs. Hanley looked to be in her midfifties, a little on the short side, probably enjoyed one too many desserts on the weekends. Nothing about her appearance said she was anything but a career teacher who managed to work her way up the ranks to the office of high school principal. She lifted Claire's student profile and started to read. "You live with your aunt, who has legal custody?"

Claire sat back in her chair. "That's the story."

The principal grinned. "We have a large number of single-parent students on campus along with several who are being raised by a grandparent or a close family member."

"Then I'll blend right in."

"Got in a little trouble at your last school." She waved the paper in the air.

"Not too far from my real truth when I was eighteen."

Mrs. Hanley looked like she wanted details. Claire didn't oblige. "What is the dropout rate here?"

For a minute, Mrs. Hanley acted as if she didn't want to answer the question.

"It's part of the reason we're here, Mrs. Hanley."

"Right." She put Claire's profile down and folded her hands on top of her desk. "It varies with socioeconomic status and race. Overall we're sitting at seven percent, more males than females. But in the past three years we've seen a surprising number of younger female dropouts than we have in the past."

"Is there any commonality to the students that you've come in contact with that have dropped out?"

"Hard to say. In recent years, the counselors in our district have been used almost exclusively to direct students toward their future colleges and career aspirations. Unfortunately, that didn't leave a lot of time or energy for reaching out to at-risk kids unless they ended up on academic probation of some sort."

"Failing classes?" she asked to clarify.

"Exactly. But if they weren't failing, they never landed on our radar as potential dropouts."

"What is that percentage?"

"Less than one percent. But five years ago you'd be hard pressed to see a student doing well in school and with a somewhat stable home life just walk away from their high school diploma."

"Stable doesn't mean happy."

"Right. Obviously. My eyes were opened to that when Detective Warren's people were here. I thought they'd removed the teenage prostitution from the school."

"I read the profiles. It's called human trafficking, sex trafficking, for a reason, not simply prostitution."

Mrs. Hanley nodded. "Of course. If someone is exploiting these kids on my campus, I want to find them."

"That's why we're here."

The principal nodded and picked up her office phone. "I'm going to introduce you to Mr. Green. He and I are the only ones on campus that know you're here."

Two minutes later the vice principal walked in, eyed Claire, and then smiled at Mrs. Hanley. "New student?" he asked.

"One of the *special* students we talked about."

With that introduction, Mr. Green lost his smile and scanned Claire up and down. "You're kidding."

Claire looked at herself. Jeans and a T-shirt, flat sneakers that lots of teenage kids wore. She applied a little eyeliner and pale lipstick, but otherwise kept the makeup off. At her side, on the floor by her chair, was one of the secondhand backpacks she and Jax had gone out of their way to find so they didn't look like they'd just hit Target for back-to-school supplies.

Claire stood and extended her hand. "I'm Claire."

Mr. Green started to smile as he shook her hand.

They both took a seat.

Mrs. Hanley handed Claire's profile to him.

"Mr. Green is in charge of all disciplinary needs at Auburn High. Any kids caught skipping school, bringing illegal substances or paraphernalia, or engaging in possibly dangerous activities . . ."

"Unless it requires our local police." Mr. Green looked up from the paper. "Or you."

"I'm not a cop," Claire told him.

He looked confused.

"But you work with them," he said.

"Yes. But blowing our cover for anything that isn't directly related to our goal isn't an option for this detail."

"We have resource officers that work with the police," Mrs. Hanley directed.

"None of which know we're here. Once I walk out of this office, I'm Claire Porter, a teenager who's pretty pissed she had to relocate. You need to treat me like any other student. On or off campus."

"We can do that."

"Good."

Claire sat forward in her chair. "I'll find a reason to come in contact with one of you every week. If there are names of students you suspect as either a potential victim or perp, it will help that we know."

"All due respect, if we knew that, we wouldn't need *Twenty-One Jump Street* invading our school," Mr. Green said as he stared down his nose at her.

"Twenty-one what?"

He shook his head. "It was an old TV show."

"I don't watch a lot of TV."

"It was before your time," Mrs. Hanley told her.

Good, because a lot of American references were lost on her.

The morning bell rang, alerting them of the time.

Mrs. Hanley reached across the desk and handed Claire her schedule. "Our teachers give all incoming transfers time to catch up. Any issues with class placement will be shuffled in a couple of weeks. We'll accommodate what we can, but if you don't do some of the work, the teachers will request a change to give you the best opportunity to succeed. If you need help with anything, I'm here."

Claire glanced at the schedule before shoving it in her backpack. "I'm sure I can manage."

Mr. Green stood and indicated the door. "I'll show you to your homeroom."

As they walked into the halls of the school, students buzzed past as they hustled to their destinations.

The stares of students followed her as she walked down the hall. Reminding herself that she walked beside the disciplinary figure of the school, Claire attempted to appear aloof.

Rebel.

The word rolled in her head. *I'm a rebel!*

Reaching back in her memory of her years at Richter, she scanned the faces of those walking by.

Saw them.

Studied them.

Judged them.

Mr. Green walked her outside the administrative building and across a quad. "Your math and science classes are in C building. Literature and social studies are in B. Arts in A. Everything computer related is in E." As he explained the campus, he pointed toward different areas, although nothing he said was foreign to her. Did he really think she didn't look at a map before showing up for work?

"Got it."

"Most seniors have a limited schedule, but because you decided to skip most of your junior year, it looks like you have some making up to do."

Claire rolled her eyes.

Beside her, the vice principal chuckled. "You do that well," he said under his breath.

She didn't reply.

"Homeroom is twenty minutes at the start of second period. You're with a selective group."

"Selective?"

"Challenging."

The bell rang again, and the last of the kids scurrying in the halls funneled into rooms. "Challenging for the vice principal, you mean," she said.

He put his hand on the door, looked at her. "I know the name of every kid in this room and their reason for being placed there."

Copy that, she said to herself.

"Ready?"

She blew out a breath, looked at him, rolled her eyes . . . and ignored his smirk.

~

"This is the faculty lounge," Mrs. Hanley said as she showed Cooper around the administration building. Neil had arranged for knowledge of Cooper's presence at the school to be limited to the principal only. It wasn't that Mr. Green was a suspect so much as he just didn't need to know Cooper was there. Mrs. Hanley would deal with any problems Cooper experienced in the classroom. "Food tends to disappear from the refrigerator, so use at your own risk," she teased.

Cooper smiled and allowed her to introduce him to the few teachers that were in the space.

The administration building was filled with offices and reception desks. A scattering of chairs occupied a small waiting area, with very few people there. He was shown the nurse's office, where a nurse only came once a week. Next were the counseling offices, where the counselors split their time on campus and were available to the students by appointment only. The halls were bare of lockers, taken out at least twenty years before and the walls patched to erase that they'd ever been there. Students were given a set of books for home, and another was available in the classrooms, removing the need for lockers altogether. Sad, really . . . that kids who wanted to deal drugs and bring weapons to campus ruined the high school experience for so many.

Once Mrs. Hanley gave him the dime tour, they returned to her office.

"Mr. Diaz has left a class plan on your desk. He'll put together a month-long one by the end of the week."

"And if we need longer than that?" Cooper knew they would.

"Mr. Diaz will accommodate whatever you need. He was happy to take some paid leave time."

Cooper sat comfortably on the other side of her desk. "Who have you told that I'm here?"

"No one. Well, my husband, if I'm truthful, but no one here on campus."

"You're friends with the staff?"

"Of course. I've known some of the people here for many years. But I'm well trained at keeping secrets. The last group that came through brought that point home. I honestly felt safer with them on campus. I'm quite surprised it took this long for you to come back."

Cooper couldn't help but wonder if her words meant none of Warren's people were there any longer.

"Even your closest friends on staff know nothing?" Cooper prodded.

Mrs. Hanley laughed. "Goodness no. The students aren't the only ones who gossip around here. The superintendent made it clear what my role is."

Cooper watched the time. "I've been given information on the teaching staff, but if you could give me some insight on the ancillary staff, I'd appreciate it."

"What kind of information?"

"Names, ages, what their roles are, how long they've been on staff. The basics. I'll avoid coming to you directly as much as I can."

"I'm here to help," she offered.

"I'm sure you are. Your intentions are not what my focus is on. If I were to ask you about Sally, in the counseling office, and you and Sally spent your weekends together with your families, your bias will come through. Or you'll unintentionally treat Sally differently and spook her, or spark conversations."

"I understand."

"This isn't a two-way street. If you hear anything on campus about me or your new student, you need to let us know."

"I can do that."

Cooper stood. "I should get a feel for my room before everyone shows up," he said, reaching out a hand.

"Welcome to Auburn High," she said.

~

Auto shop?

How in the world did he qualify as a substitute teacher for auto shop?

Cooper searched the faces of the kids filing into the classroom that had a single wall between it and the shop filled with tools, lifts, cars . . . Yeah, he knew his way around the engine of a car, but what the hell did he know about teaching it?

He looked at the syllabus Mr. Diaz had mapped out. Third period was Auto 101. From the looks of the curriculum, it wasn't auto so much as small engines. Not one tire or exhaust to change out.

The kids took their seats. Most of them looked like they were twelve.

How bad could this be?

Ten minutes into class, his back was turned while he drew an illustration on the board, and something wet hit his neck.

If not for the laughter that followed, he would have thought the aging school had a leak.

Memories of his younger years surfaced.

Images flashed of him sitting back in his seat, acting like nothing happened. His friends all laughing along . . .

Cooper turned and watched as one by one the smiles slowly faded to snickers. The upright spines slid into chairs . . .

One student's eyes narrowed on his, the straight line of his lips shouted in their lack of expression.

As their eyes fixated, the room moaned in silence.

"What's your name?" Cooper asked.

At least one of the kids cut in with an audible *ohhhh*.

Cooper knew he had his man . . . or kid, as it stood.

The kid responded in Spanish . . . and with the delivery of his name, he added a slur he didn't expect Cooper to understand.

When Cooper narrowed his eyes, the kid laughed and looked around the room.

His friends, the ones who knew exactly what he said, started to laugh.

Cooper returned to his desk, crossed his arms over his chest, and stared.

The longer he did, the more silence cloaked the room.

Slowly, eyes shifted between each other until all darted back and forth from Cooper to the kid that smarted off.

"You got somethin' to say?" the kid challenged.

Cooper shrugged. "You and your friends obviously know the material. No need for me to teach it."

The kid tossed his pen on his desk and sat back.

The institutional-style clock on the wall ticked.

Each.

And.

Every.

Second.

Cooper waited until the bell rang.

"Mr. Diaz is out for the next three months . . . give or take. There's a test first thing tomorrow on today's material."

Cooper heard at least one f-bomb drop as the class grumbled in opposition.

As the one class funneled out, the next shuffled in.

Cooper silently apologized to every high school teacher he ever dissed, and moved into position to take his lashes of pushover substitute for the rest of the day.

CHAPTER SIX

One of the parts about being a graduate from a military school that had its students recruited for legit special forces units—and at the other end of the spectrum, criminal assassins—was extensive knowledge of communications.

Claire was fluent in English, German, Russian, and Mandarin and proficient in Italian and Spanish. Mandarin was the hardest one for her to tackle. It sounded like a mouthful to anyone from America. But since she'd spent years in Germany, German-English translation was easy, and her Italian wasn't half bad. Russian was her first challenge and then Mandarin made Russian look easy. She added Spanish to her American college studies. It seemed only appropriate with the number of Hispanics living in the States.

Once Mr. Green dropped her off at her homeroom, and she took one of the only seats left, which sadly was right in the front row, Claire removed a notebook she'd purposely and literally run over with her car, and started to doodle.

Mr. Eastman was the homeroom teacher. Claire's first impression: no nonsense. He called the students by their last names. Something retired military did. And her, if she was being honest. He was pleasant enough when Claire entered the room, but didn't single her out for just walking in the door.

The students were primarily male. Many of them muttered behind her. She caught some of what they said, but because she was sitting in the front, she didn't see who did the talking.

She doodled, or so it would look if anyone glanced over to see what she was doing. What she was actually doing was writing notes in the three languages she doubted anyone in the room could identify, let alone speak. To every voice she offered an adjective. Aggressive, vulgar, loud, chatty, rude. The handful of girls in the room she found an entirely different list of words to describe. Needy, shy, assertive . . . and all of that was assessed in the twenty minutes she had before the bell rang.

As the kids scurried out of the room, Mr. Eastman called her back, "Porter."

Rebel.

She turned to the call of her fake last name and lifted her chin. "Yeah?"

"Homeroom is meant for homework and a place to ask for help in any subjects giving you trouble."

She hiked her backpack on her shoulder a little higher. "First day," she told him. "I don't have any homework yet."

He looked her in the eye. "Right. You know where your next class is?"

Claire pulled the printed schedule from her pocket and glanced at the paper. "Shakespeare?" *Really?*

Mr. Eastman offered a half smile. "It's your English credit."

"So B building."

For a brief second, Mr. Eastman's gaze narrowed. Then he nodded. "Yeah."

Claire waved the paper in the air toward him and shoved it back in her jeans. "Great."

As she walked out the door, he spoke again. "Welcome to Auburn."

Instead of responding, she offered him her back and a wave of her hand. Just like a slightly rude, disrespectful teenager might do. Every step away from his room gave her a bit more confidence that she was blending in. Even though every kid she passed looked so young to her.

~

When the fifth period bell rang, signaling the end of Cooper's first day as substitute sucker, he sat behind his desk and rolled his shoulders back to ease some of the tension the day created. What a shit show. Each class seemed to have its own smart-ass, know-it-all, or clown. Three of his five classes had pop quizzes the next day, which meant he needed to come up with something relevant to test them on.

He gathered the syllabus the teacher had left him and the class roster he had scribbled notes on with the details of the power struggle he'd played a part in all day.

Looked like he had homework after all.

He walked through the shop and locked the place up.

As he turned off the last of the lights, the door leading from the classroom to the shop opened.

One of the seniors he recognized from his better-behaved class stood there.

"Mr. Mitchel?"

"Yeah." Cooper walked closer. "Sorry, I don't remember your name."

"It's Kyle."

"What can I do for you, Kyle?"

"Mr. Diaz usually opens the shop early on Tuesdays and Fridays so his trusted students can get some help with their cars. I've been his TA for two years now. Sometimes Mr. Diaz gets here a little late, and he's allowed me to open it for him."

Cooper nodded a few times. "I saw your first name penciled in on his schedule."

Kyle sighed. "Good."

"He was vague on the details."

Kyle's smile faded. "Oh, uhm . . . Can you get ahold of him? I'm sure he'd vouch for the early days. Especially if Mr. Diaz isn't gonna be back for a while."

"I see no problem with that. How many of you come in early?"

"Depends on whose car is sputtering."

Cooper smiled at that. "Let me put a call out to Diaz, ask the administration if there are any issues."

"Thanks. I appreciate it."

Cooper motioned out the door. "I need to lock up. I'm helping the track coach while I'm here."

Kyle walked with him. "I also help Mr. Diaz with grading papers and stuff like that."

Suddenly Cooper felt his homework load getting lighter. "What about creating pop quizzes?" he joked.

Kyle shook his head. "No, but he has a stack of old quizzes he makes the students do when they've been fuc . . . screwing around." The kid hesitated after nearly dropping an f-bomb.

"Any idea where those quizzes might be?"

Kyle nodded and pointed to one of the locked filing cabinets. "I make copies for him all the time. Especially after a sub has come in."

Armed with that, Cooper fiddled with the shop keys until he found the one needed for the cabinet. With Kyle's help, he found appropriate quizzes for the classes that challenged him, and gave Kyle the task of making copies.

With the promise of coming early the next day, Cooper left Kyle to the office printer and made his way to the track field.

Coach Bennett, or simply Coach, as everyone called him, stood in front of the team with Cooper at his side. As he addressed the students, they sat in various stages of stretches on the field.

"This is Coach Mitchel. He's going to be helping with sprints and hurdles starting on Monday. Today I'm having him circulate so he can get to know you and the team as a whole."

Unlike the classroom, the field was filled with kids that truly wanted to be there.

"You have two new teammates. Claire?"

Cooper tried not to smile when Claire raised her hand and the other kids turned to look at her.

"And Terrance."

The younger student raised his hand.

"I'll have Coach Mitchel circulate with the both of you through sprints and field events to see where you land. We have our invitational in less than a month. Any of you who haven't hit your parents up for donations, get on it unless you want to be schlepping candy bars for a buck a piece for the rest of the season."

There were lots of moans from the team.

"Okay, that's it. Seniors, get some stretching in and two laps before you split up."

With their dismissal, the students started talking while the seniors took over.

"Do they really have to sell candy bars?" Cooper asked.

"Haven't had to for years. Between the parent donations and the invitational, we get what we need. But you need to cattle-prod these kids and remind them of the alternative."

Coach Bennett walked him over to the sand pits and introduced him to the long- and triple-jump coach. As they stood there in small talk, the students started to run the track.

Cooper's eyes found the only student he knew as she kept pace with the high school kids in the pack.

She stayed right in the middle. Not overachieving, not lagging behind.

Yet she stuck out.

Maybe it was because Cooper knew Claire wasn't a high school senior.

Maybe it was because they worked together.

Or maybe it was because they were a pair of magnets that kept slipping by each other until the right parts could connect.

He tore his gaze away and stopped torturing himself.

". . . did you run, Cooper?"

Cooper found himself blinking, digging hard to find the question the jump coach had just asked.

He ended up shaking his head. "Sorry . . ."

Coach Bennett patted him on his back. "Yeah, they didn't look like that when we were in high school," the older man told him.

When they laughed, Cooper reminded himself that he was looking at Claire, who wasn't only age appropriate, she was equal in many other ways. What the coaches were looking at were several underage girls. That, somehow, put a thickness in his throat he didn't like.

"You were asking?" Cooper redirected the conversation.

"I wanted to know what your event was in track?"

"I didn't run track."

Coach Bennett narrowed his eyes. "Really? Most if not all of our coaches were runners at some point."

Cooper shrugged. "I was too busy running into trouble. Ever since I started subbing at the high school level, I realized I like this age group. Thinking about starting night classes to get my permanent teaching credentials and not just the emergency one."

Coach Bennett shook his head. "I don't know if I'd do it again. I've taught math for twenty years. Each year classes get bigger, regulations get thicker, and it feels like I'm not making a damn difference in most of these kids' lives. If it wasn't for track, I probably would have changed professions five years in."

"Good thing I volunteered out here, then," Cooper said.

Thankfully, any other personal questions were diverted when Claire and Terrance jogged over.

Cooper purposely avoided Claire's eyes.

Coach Bennett turned to the students. "Okay, you two . . . today you're concentrating on jumps. Tomorrow sprints. I don't care about form, I just want to see where you land. Unless you have a preference."

Terrance shrugged, and Claire blew out a breath.

"I'll take that as a no."

Again, neither of them spoke.

Coach Bennett looked at the jumps coach. "You got 'em, Mark?"

Mark offered a wave, and Bennett turned his attention to another spot on the field.

"Okay, kids. There are two key rules in long jump." He pointed to a white line. "Never start your jump after this line. Even a toe disqualifies it."

Cooper watched Claire as she nodded.

"Second, when you land, fall forward. Landing on your ass or falling back on a hand takes away inches if not feet from your jump." Mark pointed to the white line again. "On or behind the white line." He pointed at the sand. "Fall forward."

"That's it?" Claire asked. Her tone held a slight edge.

"For today, that's it." Mark pointed to Terrance. "You'll start."

Cooper and Claire took a few steps away from the pit while Mark worked at getting Terrance in the right position to run up and jump.

Cooper whispered Claire's way. "How did it go today?"

She looked to the side. "Happy hour at my place."

Terrance ran up and took his jump . . . and landed straight on his ass.

CHAPTER SEVEN

"It's like looking for a needle in a haystack." Claire sat on the edge of being annoyed as she spread out the notes she'd collected throughout the day.

In like fashion, Cooper looked over his lists of students and then worked to compile the athletes on the field. A half-eaten pizza and a couple of empty beer cans filled the space on the table that wasn't occupied with notes.

Jax took up the other end of the dining room table. "We need to put this into a spreadsheet."

Cooper and Claire both pointed at her at the same time.

"I pick you," Claire said.

"We have track," Cooper explained, waving his hand between the two of them.

Claire fisted her pointing finger and bumped knuckles with Cooper.

Jax rolled her eyes. "Fine." Her tone was anything *but* fine.

"Did you make any connections today?" Claire asked Jax.

"Not really. There were a few friendly smiles, but no one went out of their way to be welcoming."

"At least you didn't get hit with spit wads," Cooper pointed out.

Claire laughed.

"It's not funny," Cooper said with a glare.

"It's kinda funny."

"The headmistress would have had us in isolation if we did anything like that in school," Jax said.

"Last I looked, our headmistress did time for child endangerment," Claire clarified as she took a bite of her pepperoni with extra cheese.

"Which is crap, considering our parents knew what they were signing us up for."

Their boarding school was strict, in the military sense, and yes, parents knew the environment their kids were being exposed to. But in Claire's situation, it wasn't a parent that placed her there.

Jax must have realized what she was saying and quickly averted her eyes. "Sorry. That was insensitive of me."

Claire shook off her best friend's concern, put her pizza down. "Don't be. It's not your fault I was left on an orphanage doorstep by parents who didn't care. Much as I want to hate on those that eventually put me at Richter, I'm better for having been there."

The three of them exchanged looks, and when Claire diverted her attention to her papers, they got the hint to drop the subject. She'd spent so much time feeling sorry for herself, the last thing Claire wanted was her friends to worry on her behalf.

Jax moved from the kitchen table only to return with a laptop.

Claire shifted her homeroom roster notes to Jax. "Mr. Green gave me a list of students in my homeroom. They're the kids that spend time in detention, from what I was told."

Jax glanced at the notebook and grinned. "Back to our old tricks."

Claire nodded. "A mix of English, German, and Russian with enough doodling to make it look like I'm bored." Jax and Claire had passed similar notes with the mix of languages while attending Richter.

"There're no names with the notes."

"I got stuck in the front of the class. I'll rectify that tomorrow."

Cooper took her homeroom roster and scanned through his classes. "Looks like we have a few of the same names."

"Any of them spit-wad kid?" Claire asked.

"My back was turned, but if I had to guess . . ." Cooper starred a couple of names. "This kid spends time lifting weights, and this one eats too many burgers," he described.

"Find the rebels and we'll find the parties. It will be a lot easier to get a handle on these kids' agendas on a Friday or Saturday night than in homeroom."

Cooper ran a hand through his hair. "This assignment isn't going to give us much time for R and R."

"We'll make Neil give us a couple weeks in the Bahamas when it's all over," Claire suggested with a wink.

"Doesn't sound like Neil."

"He's softened up a little since you've been gone."

"Bahamas soft?"

Claire batted her eyelashes a few times. "I can talk him into it."

While Claire and Cooper talked about a vacation they had yet to earn, Jax typed away at her laptop. "What about the teaching staff? Anything to report there?" she asked them both.

"Nothing yet," Claire said.

Cooper, however, hesitated before he answered.

"What are you thinking?"

He shook his head. "Probably nothing."

"Let us determine that as a team."

Cooper looked Claire in the eye. "Coach Bennett."

Claire was surprised to hear that name. She hadn't gotten a vibe off him at all. "What did he do?"

"He didn't do anything. I was, uhm . . . watching you guys running laps, got distracted. Bennett made a comment about how the students didn't look that good when he was in school."

"That's fair, I guess. One of the throwers has a full beard and looks like he's thirty," Claire told him.

"Yeah, but that wasn't the vibe I got."

"So what, was he checking the students out?"

Cooper shook his head. "No, but it looked like I was, and neither Coach Bennett or Mark called me out. I don't know. It felt off."

"Hmmm, so you were checking out the girls—"

"No. I was . . ." Cooper squirmed. "I saw you run by and thought you blended in really well."

"So you were checking Claire out," Jax said with a snicker.

"No . . . well, yeah. I mean, that's what it looked like to them. But I know you're not a teenager, arguably that doesn't put me in the dirty-old-man category."

"But Bennett has to be in his late fifties, and Mark close to that."

Cooper lifted his hands in the air. "You see my point."

"Yeah. Not that it means anything. But certainly something to watch."

Jax stopped typing and turned her screen toward them. "I'm categorizing the students in three ways. Possible victims, accomplices, or leads. Leads can be gateways to parties or events where our victims might be lured. The adults are perpetrators or accomplices. I say we divide this up." She pointed to Cooper. "I see you doing happy hour with staff to learn their secrets, find the perps and accomplices."

"I can do that."

"I'm going to focus on victims. There wasn't any evidence that the perps were at Bremerton. Unless there's a staff member that Neil hadn't vetted," Jax said.

"I wouldn't be surprised if Neil has a home office storyboard with every teacher and staff member and what they had for dinner last night," Cooper teased.

Neither of the women disagreed.

"I'll be the brooding teen looking for love in the wrong places," Jax said.

"I'm going to focus on leads and accomplices this week. Try and get into the party crowd. I want to know who's peddling what on campus,"

Claire said. Drugs were a common denominator for the dirtbags getting the girls on board.

Jax pointed between the two of them. "I say we strike up a friendship and you feel sorry for me and I tag along."

Claire liked that idea.

"Also helps if you're ever seen in public together outside of school," Cooper pointed out.

Jax leaned back and stretched her arms over her head. "Well, I'm done."

"Go to bed, I'll clean this up." Seemed only fair, since Claire started school an hour later than Jax.

Jax took her computer with her after saying good night.

Cooper piled his papers together before grabbing the pizza box and taking it to the island in the kitchen.

"I can get that." Claire dropped the empty beer cans in the recycling bin.

"Takes two seconds," Cooper told her.

Claire removed a large resealable plastic bag from a drawer and handed it to him before heading back to the table to clean up their plates. A strange silence settled between them, and Claire felt the need to fill it. "You know, I think Neil picked us for the job because we're all single. Well, Jax is seeing someone."

"She is?"

"It's not serious."

"Hmm, well, I think Neil picked you guys because you're the closest to the age group we're targeting."

"I get that, but it would be harder to do if we were involved with someone."

Cooper glanced over at her before moving to the sink to wash his hands. "I guess it didn't work out with Miles Ketterman, then."

The name from her past had her staring. "You remember that guy?"

Cooper turned off the water, and she handed him a dish towel. "You asked me to be your wingman."

She crossed her arms over her chest and leaned against the counter. "I forgot all about him."

Her statement was followed by more silence.

When she looked up, she found Cooper staring.

"What about you?" she asked. "Anyone special in Europe? I thought for sure when you didn't come back there had to be a woman."

For the space of a heartbeat she thought he was going to deny her assumptions.

"One?" He puffed out his chest and ran his hands over his pecs. "Why deny so many of some good old American muscle?"

She pushed at his shoulder. "Such a liar."

He laughed. "What about you? Obviously Miles didn't do it for you."

"Miles had the attention span of a gnat. All he cared about was college sports and weekend parties."

"That might be helpful right about now," Cooper said.

"I'm pretty surprised you remember him."

"I remember everything." His words were slow and poignant as if they had more meaning than the obvious.

Words stopped, and both of them stared at the other.

The breath in her lungs felt as if it were being held hostage and she couldn't exhale.

Cooper shook out of it first. "I should go. Early morning tomorrow."

Claire closed her eyes. "Right. Auto shop."

She followed him to the front door and turned on the porch light.

He turned to her briefly as he opened the door. "I'll see you tomorrow."

"Good night."

He glanced at the keypad to the house alarm system. "Be sure and set that."

"Now you're starting to sound like Neil."

Instead of saying more, Cooper walked out the door and to his car.

When Claire closed the door between them, she leaned on the wall and stared at the alarm panel.

The lights from his car lit up the living room before fading away.

There was definitely something going on with Cooper, and she was a little afraid to find out what. Before she dug any further into her thoughts, Claire locked the deadbolt and set the alarm.

CHAPTER EIGHT

"Miss Porter, are you paying attention?"

It took a full second to realize the last name the teacher was saying was hers.

Claire popped the end of her pen in her mouth and sat back in her chair. "Yeah."

Mrs. Wallace placed a hand on her hip and stared. "You've been tapping your pen and doodling for almost thirty minutes of class." The woman walked up and lifted Claire's notes up in the air. A shake of her teacher's head made Claire thankful she'd been writing her notes in code.

"It's how I digest the knowledge you expound upon us."

When the other kids in the class started to laugh, Claire knew she'd gained some trust in them.

Mrs. Wallace didn't seem to like the spotlight and showed Claire's "doodling" to the class. "And what knowledge did you digest?"

Shit . . . What class was she in?

Shakespeare.

Romeo and Juliet . . . MacDeath . . .

Claire felt her pulse race, realized all eyes in the room were on her. *Be in the spotlight long enough to gain their trust and show you're one of them.*

She leaned back, just enough to show her disrespect, and took a chance. "You were asking if *Romeo and Juliet* was a romance or tragedy."

Mrs. Wallace closed her lips and tilted her chin.

Claire hesitated.

"I suppose it's not fair that I ask you as you've only been with us for a week—"

"It's stupid teenage drama."

A few students chuckled.

Claire looked to her left and her right and found the two guys in her class that she'd pegged as troublemakers, or at least the boys bad enough to know how to get in touch with the truly bad boys, and they were both smiling.

"Do you want to elaborate?" Mrs. Wallace asked.

Claire grabbed her notebook from the teacher's hand and slapped it on her desk. "Let me see if I got this right." She raised her voice an octave. "Waaah, my daddy doesn't like your daddy so we can't date." Claire lowered her voice. "But I love you, we can make it work." Her voice rose again. "How?"

Claire leveled her gaze to the teacher. "Romeo, wherefore art thou . . . you stupid asshole. I'll kill myself, but ha! Just kidding. Then Juliet comes along . . . Oh no"—Claire slapped her hands against her face for effect—"I'll kill myself, too. Then the boy toy wakes up . . . Oh no . . . the girl I love is dead and it's all my fault. I have to kill myself for real this time." Claire glared. "I think Shakespeare is a fucking joke and wouldn't be given a one o'clock time slot next to soap operas if he was a screenwriter today. The fact I have to sit through this stupid drivel is the true tragedy."

When the class erupted, Claire knew she had her audience.

～

Claire sat on the other side of Mr. Green's desk and waited until the door shut.

"'Shakespeare is a fucking joke'?" he asked as he started to laugh.

She chuckled. "If all it takes to be sent to your office is me cussing, I'll be in here a lot." Claire grabbed her notebook. "What can you tell me about Sean Fisher?"

~

Cooper was starting to question why he'd decided to leave his lax Europe-based job to work twelve hours a day, every day.

He rolled into the auto shop early Friday morning to find Kyle bent over the hood of a car, the shop doors rolled up, and a half a dozen guys drinking coffee and eating donuts.

"Good morning," Cooper said as he walked into the shop.

"Hey, Mr. Mitchel." The greetings came from at least two voices.

Cooper offered a wave and glanced at the pink box filled with sugar. "What's this?"

Kyle glanced up from whatever he was working on. "What self-respecting auto shop doesn't have donuts on a Friday?"

Cooper picked up a chocolate glazed and bit into it. "You won't see me complaining."

Kyle stood back from the car, wiped his hands on a shop towel. "This is Tony. Graduated last year but comes in once in a while to help out."

Tony could easily pass for twenty-one. Big guy, more facial hair than anyone Cooper knew at that age. Of course he had been enlisted at that time, and extra hair wasn't accepted.

Tony stepped forward, reached out a hand. "Nice to meet you."

"Likewise." Cooper glanced at Kyle's project. "What are you working on?"

"It was supposed to be simple spark plugs, but the damn things are rusted in." Kyle went right back to work as he spoke.

"You shouldn't have bought a Jeep that originated in Michigan," Tony told him.

Cooper looked around. Another set of his senior students had a car on a lift and were doing a brake job. "Anyone need any help?" he called out.

"Got it."

"We're good."

Cooper waved his donut in the air. "In that case, I'll be at my desk."

"Thanks for letting us come in," Kyle said.

"We're good." He indicated the classroom. "You know where I am." As Cooper left the shop, he popped an AirPod in his ear and removed his phone from his back pocket. What looked like he was listening to music was actually him eavesdropping on the shop conversation as he left the room.

"He seems cool," Tony said right as Cooper cleared the door.

"So far so good," Kyle said.

Kyle's words made Cooper pause.

From that point on it was rust this and plug that. Nothing incriminating.

It wasn't until he stepped on the track field that he felt anything else that needed recording. None of which had anything to do with the case, and had everything to do with Claire.

He arrived late, which was expected on Fridays until the track meets started.

Claire was poised and ready in the last hundred yards of a relay race. She watched as the third runner pumped arms and feet as she rounded the corner.

Claire's hand reached back, her legs bouncing.

Cooper walked to the side of the field to Coach Bennett. "Hey."

Bennett shook his head. In each hand he held a stopwatch. "Watch this."

"Watch wha—"

Bennett interrupted with the lift of his right hand toward the track. The second Claire started to move, Bennett leaned forward.

The baton passed, and Bennett clicked one of his timers.

Claire took off, and the other teammates stopped to stare.

Cooper knew she could move, had watched her more than once, not to mention the last time she tackled him to the ground.

His lips pulled into a grin.

She was a powerhouse that didn't let up until she was well past the finish line and Bennett was staring at both of his stopwatches with a huge smile. "We just found our last leg in our Varsity Girls Relay."

The grin on Cooper's face spread ear to ear.

And as he watched Claire catch her breath and walk off the track with her teammates patting her back, he realized the fine line they were treading.

Get enough attention, but not too much.

He was afraid Claire had just pushed over the line.

Cooper walked beside Coach Bennett as he made his way to Claire's side.

She was hunched over, hands on her knees as she caught her breath.

"Not bad, young lady," Bennett said.

Her attention found Cooper first and quickly moved on to the coach. "Thanks."

"I'm putting you in this position for our invitational."

"What?" Claire lost her smile and found Cooper's eyes. "Really?"

"Maybe the one hundred, too."

The coach diverted his attention and walked away.

Cooper glanced around, then leaned closer. "That's not good."

She stood tall and wiped her forearm over her brow. "I was holding back."

Just then, two of the other girls from the relay bounced up to Claire and put their arms over her shoulders.

"You just flew!"

"So cool."

Claire placed a fake smile on her lips and stared at Cooper. "I didn't know I had it in me."

CHAPTER NINE

Wearing a T-shirt and jeans every day had Claire searching for something a little different when she wasn't at school.

With Jax at her side, they walked into headquarters at eight thirty for their nine o'clock meeting Saturday morning. Most days, Jax would drive separately, not seeing the need to arrive early, but Lewis was meeting her around the corner for lunch, and the plan was to stay with him until Sunday. The poor guy had been put on the back burner since their assignment began.

Jax stayed in the situation room, and Claire moved on to the surveillance room searching for coffee.

"Hey," she said as she crossed through the doors.

She went straight to the coffeepot and was surprised to smell something fresh.

"Oh, hi."

She glanced up to find an unfamiliar face watching the monitors. "Sorry, you must be new."

And youngish. Late twenties, maybe early thirties. Looked like the typical Neil recruit. Still had the military haircut and shoulders that filled out a shirt. Easy smile, a good seven out of ten on the attractive scale.

"I'm Manuel," he said, leaning over to shake her hand.

Claire moved the coffeepot to her other hand to shake his. "Claire," she told him.

"You work for Neil?" he asked.

"Yeah. We have a nine o'clock briefing."

Manuel didn't offer more than a nod.

"This smells fresh." She lifted the coffeepot.

"I made it about a half hour ago. I can't stand stale coffee."

Claire found herself smiling. "Finally, someone in this office that has taste buds."

Her new coworker laughed and turned back to the monitors while she fished out a clean mug and poured herself her second cup for the day.

"Nice meeting you," she said as she backed out of the room.

"You, too."

At the whiteboard in the situation room, Jax was laying out their notes and pictures of some of the possible players they'd managed to identify.

Lars arrived next, and before the door shut, Cooper and Neil stepped in together.

"Wow, why are you girls all dolled up?" Lars asked before he sat down.

"Jax has a date," Claire announced.

Neil came to a stop. "Not with one of the students."

Jax made a motion as if she was going to be ill.

Claire laughed.

"What's your excuse?" Cooper asked. "Do you have a date, too?" His eyes walked up and down her body. She was wearing a dress, which she didn't often do unless she was painting the town with her best friend.

But sometimes, when she'd been cooped up too long and hadn't been able to shop or let her hair down, or be something other than a girl trapped in a world she didn't want . . . yeah, at those times she needed to get out. It was her release valve.

Jax started to laugh.

And laugh.

Claire followed Cooper's gaze in Jax's direction.

"Claire doesn't date!"

The hair on her neck started to stand on end.

"I date."

Jax leaned her head back and laughed. "No, what you do doesn't classify as dating."

Much as Claire wanted to disagree, she knew her friend spoke the truth. It wasn't that she had an aversion to dating, there just didn't seem to be enough datable guys out there.

"What the hell does that mean?" Cooper's tone was anything but happy as he asked the question.

Claire was about to ask why he cared when Neil stepped forward. "Are we done with the chitchat and ready to work?"

"Technically this is my day off, and since I have homework, not even that."

Neil's expression told Claire he wasn't amused.

Cooper looked like he had more to say, but kept his lips shut.

Lars patted Cooper on the back as he walked by. "I need coffee."

"There's a fresh pot in the surveillance room," Claire informed him.

"We start in ten," Neil said before heading to his office.

Once the door was closed, Cooper slid beside Claire. "Mind elaborating about this 'doesn't date' thing?"

She slowly looked at him, took a sip of her coffee. "Why deny all the men?" she asked, tossing back the words he'd used on her only a week before.

"You're lying."

Any amusement in her faded with the seriousness of his voice. "Why are you so interested?" And why was Cooper standing so close and watching her as if an expression was going to give something away?

When his eyes dropped to her lips, her belly did a little twist.

It was then that her brain started to short-circuit and the coffee felt bitter in the back of her throat.

There were two reasons a man stared at a woman's lips.

The first was if they were a family member or possibly a gay friend that wanted to comment on the shade of lipstick.

And the second . . . he wanted to kiss her.

Holy shit!

She blinked several times.

Cooper wanted to taste her.

The realization of that fact had her head spinning. Then, because she couldn't stop herself from looking, she took in his lips, and then the expression on his face.

So many things clicked together. With them, a thousand questions.

Lars pushed through the door from the surveillance room talking and had Cooper taking a step back. "Have you met the new guy?"

Claire's eyes stayed on Cooper. "Yes, I have."

Cooper blinked and turned away. "I have not."

A few more steps and Cooper walked into the other room.

"What the actual hell?" Claire asked the universe out loud.

Lars walked by, oblivious to what had just happened. "What?"

Claire glanced over at Jax to see her soft smile.

In German, Claire asked, "Did you see that?"

"I felt the static in the room," Jax replied.

"You know it's rude to speak in a different language, right?" Lars said.

Jax shook her head and went back to writing on the whiteboard. "Sorry," she replied in English.

~

Cooper listened, participated, reported his end of Operation High School, and did everything in his power to not look Claire's way.

He'd blown it. Got caught salivating over her as if she was ice cream on a hot summer day.

Put it out of your mind, dude.

Manuel had joined them and was brought up to speed.

"And what exactly do you plan on doing to get out of participating in the track competitions?" Neil asked when the conversation came up about Claire having the fourth position in the relay.

"Cooper and I talked about this. I can always throw a race or two and then fake an injury or fail a class and be prohibited from competing." Claire looked at Cooper.

"I like the idea of an injury, but want to wait until the first meet. Right now Claire is popular enough with the team, and I think we should cement that before we take her away."

"If she's injured, does she drop track?" Neil asked.

"No." Cooper shook his head. "She has to come along to the meets and the practices, even if it's just to time other students. If there's an academic probation, she's likely to lose favor with the coaches and her fellow students. Which might be something we pull later if we need to."

Neil nodded in agreement. "I like that. Lars, what do you have?"

"Both decoy residences are up and running," he told them.

"Good, because I've struck up a couple of 'friendships' with the promise of study dates," Claire said.

Jax pointed between the two of them "We *met* last week, and together we'll start to narrow our search. We'll bring the students I've struck friendships up with from Bremerton together with the Auburn kids. There is a surprisingly large number of kids that are close with those from the other school."

"Which of these players are involved?" Neil nodded to the whiteboard.

"Elsie is Kyle's girlfriend. She doesn't fit the profile as victim or perp, but because of Kyle's comments, we thought she needed flushing out," Claire told Neil. "We're meeting at Jax's place, because her dad is working late. And my aunt is home."

"Yeah, and there's a new student at Bremerton, Ally. She's living with her grandmother, parents lost custody and think the best place for her is a prep school. A couple conversations and I can already tell she's looking for trouble. Parties, sneaks out at night."

Neil narrowed his eyes. "What about this guy?" He pointed to one of the names and photographs on the board.

"Sean is the class bad boy at Auburn," Claire said. "Spends a lot of time with the vice principal and barely makes the grade. But he drives a brand-new car and yet lives with his single mom and older brother. Something there doesn't add up."

"Maybe the absent dad feels guilty and buys big toys," Lars suggested.

"We need to get to know him in order to find out. The decoy houses are the safest places to talk," Claire pointed out. "Where is Sasha, anyway?"

Lars answered instead of Neil. "Sasha's chasing a lead in Seattle. We've been spending time looking into the dropouts over the past few years."

"All the way up in Washington?" Jax asked.

"If this is as organized as Warren suggested, moving girls away from people they know would be key for going unnoticed."

"Warren said he's had deep undercover work going on at Auburn for several years and is convinced there's something sinister lurking they couldn't dig up."

"But not Bremerton?" Claire glanced at Cooper when she asked the question.

"If Warren had undercover cops there, the principal wasn't aware. Which is exactly how we are playing it with Manuel. He's the school's new resource officer. There shouldn't be a reason you don't get to know Bremerton's problem kids."

"Are the principals at either school suspects?" Manuel asked.

"Burke passed inspection, but we have no idea if he talks to his teachers at Bremerton. So the less he knows, the better. Hanley and Green seem to be exactly who they say they are. Backgrounds check out."

"Mrs. Hanley is a middle-aged woman, not exactly the profile fit for this behavior," Cooper added.

Claire cleared her throat. "Never underestimate a middle-aged school administrator."

Cooper found her gaze and was brought back to a moment in time shortly after they'd met when they were infiltrating Richter and learning just how sinister middle-aged women could be. "Right," he said, acknowledging her thoughts without them being spoken.

Jax broke the silence. "If anyone at either school knows we're there, I can't imagine them doing anything so long as we're on campus."

"I'll pass these names on to Warren, and if he objects to any of them, I'll let you know." He looked around. "Anything else?"

They collectively shook their heads.

"Okay, then. We'll meet back here next week. I want to see more intel on staff. We'll start switching schedules around."

Jax bounced out of her seat. "See you on campus, Manuel." She then turned her attention to Claire. "I won't be home tonight."

"I know."

With her purse over her shoulder, Jax hustled out of the office.

Lars abandoned the room along with Neil and Manuel, leaving Claire and Cooper alone.

Instead of running off, Claire folded her arms over her chest, stood in front of Cooper, and waited.

Did he play dumb?

Did he blow off what had happened as brotherly concern?

Or did he just stare back?

That's what he did.

And like any game of chicken, one of them would have to cave.

It was Claire.

She unfolded her arms, grabbed her purse, and stormed out the door.

"That went well."

~

"Don't you look lovely?" Gwen MacBain greeted Claire with a kiss to both cheeks before standing back and taking her in again. "It seems every time we have one of our lunches you look more grown up than the last."

"You say that every time, Gwen."

"Because it's true."

The maître d' pulled out Claire's chair and quickly moved to Gwen's before she could adjust it herself. They were just off Rodeo Drive in an upscale restaurant that Claire only knew because of Neil's wife. Every eight to ten weeks, Gwen insisted on a private lunch, which was often followed by a shopping trip, so she could keep tabs on Claire's life. The life she had outside of MacBain Security and Solutions. If Neil was a surrogate father, Gwen took the role of mother.

When Claire had first moved to California, these lunches were more frequent, and the shopping trips were up there with Little Orphan Annie and Daddy Warbucks going to the mall. No matter how much Claire insisted she didn't need a lot, Gwen acted as if she didn't hear her. Sasha did the same, but never at the same time. One look in Claire's closet and you'd never know she was an orphan.

"I'm glad I could squeeze in some of your time before this new assignment consumes you," Gwen started.

"I have a feeling this one is going to take a while."

Gwen sat politely across the table, her hands in her lap. The woman was regal. Always turning heads whenever they walked into a room. Today was no different. Even though the restaurant was filled with a larger number of women than men, that didn't stop those masculine eyes from shifting her way.

"When Neil told me you'd be working nights and weekends, in addition to the school hours, I told him it was too much."

Claire grinned. "Let me guess, he gave you *the look* and walked away." They both knew *the look*. It said: *I know what I'm doing. We're not talking about this. The subject is now closed.* All in one.

"That look doesn't work with me."

"Doesn't stop him from trying." Claire reached for the sparkling water already poured in her glass and took a drink.

"When he told me Cooper was back and on the case with you, I felt a bit better."

Just the mention of Cooper's name had Claire thinking of the lip stare. "It's good to have another set of eyes on campus."

When Gwen didn't comment, Claire looked over at her. The quiet lasted a bit longer than expected.

"He's changed since he was here last," Claire said.

Gwen smiled. "I can't say I've noticed, since we've seen him from time to time in Europe."

"He seems to have slipped right back in with the group. Makes me wonder why he left in the first place."

Gwen broke eye contact and picked up her menu. "I'm sure he had his reasons."

Claire wondered what the diversion was about. "Do you think this case had something to do with him returning?"

"I couldn't tell you. I know Neil wanted as many hands on this as he could spare. The whole idea that these awful things are happening where Emma goes to school . . . I don't have to tell you how he is. I thought for sure he was going to insist on Emma changing schools."

"There would be no way to know if the same thing isn't happening elsewhere."

"Exactly what I told him," Gwen said, smiling. "I know my husband, though. If the team isn't successful, he'll figure out a way to homeschool."

That had Claire laughing. "I can't see him as a teacher."

"Goodness, no. We'd hire someone. But that isn't fair to Em."

"That's true. I wouldn't worry. We'll find out what we're there to uncover."

"I hope so. Neil might not show it at work, but I know this is eating at him." She put the menu aside. "He's compared this trafficking to the fate of some of your classmates from Richter. Forcing kids to do things they wouldn't otherwise until they can't see their way out. I realized then that on the surface it looks like he's evolved because of Emma, but in reality, it's penance for what could have been you."

She'd never considered that. "Has he always had this soft spot?" Claire asked.

Gwen laughed. "Don't let him hear you say that. And yes . . . I saw it from the beginning, although our mutual friends didn't. He's certainly opened up through the years."

Claire couldn't help it. She busted out a laugh. "There is nothing open about Neil."

The waiter arrived, took their order, and left them alone again.

"How is it being back in school?"

She sat back. "Awkward. But I think I'm getting the hang of it. I don't get the impression that anyone is clued in to the truth."

"That doesn't surprise me. I always knew you'd excel in whatever you put your mind to."

When Claire heard words like that, she was quickly reminded why she looked to Gwen as a motherly figure. Although she'd had to have been pretty young to be Claire's biological mother.

"Can you hint to Neil, the next time we go undercover, to pick something in the south of France?" she asked, joking.

"You want to study French?"

Claire shook her head. "Never mind. Make it Italy."

Gwen said something to her in French that Claire didn't understand, and Claire replied in Italian. Even though the Italian sounded rusty to her ears.

When they stopped laughing, Gwen took her napkin and spread it on her lap. "Now that we have work out of the way, let's talk about your love life."

"It's always the same with you."

"Would you rather I tell you about mine?"

Claire found herself squeezing her eyes shut. The image of Neil and Gwen . . . If she needed any more proof as to the roles they had taken in her life, picturing them naked cemented it.

"What if I told you that Neil was—"

Claire lifted a hand. "Nope. I'm good. Thank you for keeping the details to yourself."

"So?"

Claire erased the image from her mind. "There is nothing to tell." And as she said the words, the image of Cooper popped up in her head. His eyes lingering on her lips.

"Are you certain?" It was Gwen's turn to give *the look*. But hers said something entirely different from her husband's. Gwen's look meant *You're not telling me everything, and I'll just be quiet until you do.*

Only this time, Claire wasn't falling for it. "When is Neil going to let Emma date?"

One question, and Claire's love life was cleared from the conversation.

By the time they were finished with lunch and took a short walk through a few shops, Claire left Beverly Hills feeling refueled. There wasn't a day that went by that she wasn't grateful that she met Sasha and AJ, and in turn Neil and his family.

She pulled into her driveway and was reminded that Jax wouldn't be home. Her next thought was to call Cooper, maybe grab some takeout.

Then she remembered the lip stare.

Instead of takeout, she settled on a pasta dish she shoved in the microwave and a glass of red. With that, she settled in front of the TV and clicked through the streaming services looking for something to binge-watch.

CHAPTER TEN

"Porter? A word, please."

Claire held back as the rest of her homeroom filed out the door.

Mr. Eastman waited until they were alone. "You've been with us for almost two weeks."

"Yeah, so?"

"I understand you've been sent to Mr. Green's office at least twice for using profanity."

"Yeah, so?" Her tone alone would have gotten her in serious trouble in her high school.

He held her gaze. "I also understand that your teachers all think there's a lot of intelligence under that attitude you carry around."

"A lot of smart people cuss."

Eastman didn't miss a beat. "In fact, the only staff on campus that don't have an issue with this attitude seem to be your coaches."

Claire shrugged. "That's because they want something out of me."

He paused, took a breath. "Maybe. But if you want to continue running track, you're going to have to leave the profanity off campus."

Claire blinked a few times and put a mental checkmark next to Eastman's name as a possible good guy. She doubted teachers correcting her desire to cuss would be the same ones pulling kids into the sex trade. But was he the mole? "I'm going to be late for Shakespeare. We both know how much I'll be using iambic pentameter in my future. So if you don't mind . . ."

Eastman cracked a smile and nodded toward the door.

As Claire made her way out of his classroom, she texted Cooper. **Find a reason to get Eastman out of his classroom after the last bell and before track.**

Cooper's reply was a check.

In fact, all of Cooper's responses were just like that. One word. One graphic. One something.

It had been four days since the lip stare, and it didn't appear either one of them was going to bring it up.

And as Claire dragged her feet in the halls of a high school, ignoring a boy suddenly felt very adolescent. They needed to talk, and not about work.

As she pulled her phone out to tell him just that, the bell rang, reminding her she was late. Students rushed past as she opened the classroom door.

Her teacher stared her down and pointed to her watch.

"Yell at Mr. Eastman. He kept me late."

"Don't think I won't check on that."

Claire plopped down in her chair. "You do that."

~

Claire waited outside Mr. Eastman's classroom door, in the shadows of one of the other buildings. With her backpack flung over one shoulder, she appeared to anyone watching like someone texting on her phone.

Movement out of the corner of her eye showed Eastman closing his classroom door behind him. He walked away from where she stood, and toward the field. She waited until Cooper sent a signal, and when he did she slid out a couple of tools as she angled to the door. It took less than ten seconds to pick the flimsy lock and push her way inside.

Behind his desk, she woke his computer and went straight to work. Thanks to some coaching from Sasha, Claire had learned a few tricks about hacking into the school's intranet. Through a back door, she linked Eastman's information to Cooper's classroom. Thankfully, the computers weren't ancient, and accessing audio without letting the person staring at the screen know they were being heard took less than ten minutes.

Still, the clock on the wall told her every minute she was in there was a minute closer to being caught.

With that work done, she did a quick look through Eastman's desk. She wasn't sure what she would find, but rifled through it anyway.

When she found the bottom drawer locked, she considered picking it as well.

The time told her she was pressing her luck.

Careful to put everything back the way it was before she came in, she opened the door, looked twice, and left.

~

Cooper glanced at the time after he texted Claire that Mr. Eastman was on the field.

Eastman couldn't have been much older than him. He wore slacks and one of the high school shirts that had the mascot logo on one side, and "Auburn Pride" written on the other. One of the students pointed Cooper's way, directing the other man.

"Cooper Mitchel?" he asked when he approached.

Cooper smiled, extended a hand. "Mr. Eastman."

"It's Leo."

Cooper indicated another spot on the field. One, so no one could hear their conversation, and two, so he could see when Claire walked onto the field.

"I'm glad you messaged me," Leo said as they walked. "I was about to do the same to you."

"Really? About Claire Porter?" Cooper's message to Leo was to discuss Claire.

Leo offered a single nod. "She's a bright girl."

If only you knew how bright. "And pretty fast on her feet, too."

"So I heard. Does she have an attitude out here?"

Cooper shook his head. "Nothing that I've seen. I was surprised when Mr. Green told me she's spent time in his office."

"My homeroom is full of kids with chips on their shoulders. I don't buy into a lot of their drama, but when I see someone with potential acting out, I try and learn what makes them happy and use it to help them focus."

"And you think that's track?"

"I'm asking you."

"The kids seem to like her, she doesn't have that chip out here," Cooper said.

Leo looked around them. "I'm hoping we can work together and keep her focused. I'd hate to see her attitude keep her from competing. I told her that today."

Cooper tried to act surprised. "I'll certainly talk to her, see if there's something causing her anger that we can mitigate."

Leo nodded a few times. "So was there something you wanted to talk with me about?"

"You covered most of it. I've reached out to a couple of her teachers when Green told me she needed to shape up." Then, because Cooper needed to stall, he asked, "Is there a behavior you've noticed with her?"

"In homeroom, she seems annoyed to be there. But I've heard she likes to challenge her teachers and say *fuck* a lot."

Cooper couldn't stop his laugh.

"I know. But a lot of the teachers get up in their ass about those things."

"Seems stupid to treat seventeen-year-olds like they're five."

"Hard habit for many teachers to break, I'm afraid."

"I see Claire hanging around Sean Fisher. Anything you can share about him?"

Leo shook his head as if he had plenty to say. "Sean's parents are both in the business . . ."

"Hollywood?"

Leo's nod was the answer. "His parents are uninvolved. Plenty of rumors on campus that if there was a drug you wanted, he could help with that. I had a conversation with his mother early in the year. I hinted about drugs . . . Her response was that 'pot is legal now'."

"Ouch."

"I know."

"I have him in my auto class, he doesn't appear strung out on anything to me."

"He's had plenty of Mondays where he doesn't get to school on time. I think he cleaned up a little after the holidays. Hard to tell. His grades are marginal, reminds me that his parents didn't go to college and they do just fine."

"Maybe Claire will have a good influence on him. I don't see her as the party type."

Leo laughed. "Oh, she parties. I guarantee it. Let's just hope she sticks with the simple shit and Ubers. There's a safe ride program with the school, too."

"How often is that used?"

"Not as much as it should be." Leo looked around the field. "Sports help, so I'm glad Claire is here."

The buzz in Cooper's pocket distracted him. A glance at his home screen said Claire was on her way. "I'll talk with Claire. We don't want to see her dropping track."

"Is she really that good?"

"I'm new to coaching, but Bennett thinks she's a contender for state."

Leo held out his hand. "Let's use that to keep her focused."

"Great talking to you," Cooper said.

"We should grab a beer sometime. I have a few of your kids, would like to know what makes them tick. Maybe direct them toward trade schools."

Cooper nodded. "That would be great. We'll hit happy hour."

"Next Thursday?"

The kids started running their warm-up laps. "You're on."

Cooper waved as Leo walked away and moved to where the kids dropped their backpacks. It wasn't long before Claire showed up.

He walked up, ignored how good she looked in her running shorts and tank top. "Did you get what you wanted?"

She dropped her backpack next to the others, lifted one leg up on the short fence, and stretched over it. "I got in. Now I need your computer to funnel the details out of the intranet and into my home computer."

"We can do that. Not sure why. The man seems legit. Worried you're searching for drama and will get lost."

"I think he's our mole."

"Warren's man?"

Claire switched legs. "Think so. I sincerely doubt he knows we're here. I won't know for sure until we can do some recon."

"Sounds like a good plan," Cooper said, looking behind him.

Claire stopped stretching, turned to him, and smiled.

She had the most expressive eyes. Coral blue with long lashes. Cooper's chest pulled, and he dropped his gaze.

She started to walk away.

Not really thinking, he reached out and grasped her arm. For a second, he just looked at where he touched her before meeting her eyes again. His mind never moved far from the Saturday meeting, and since then they'd only been polite or talked exclusively about the case. "I think we should talk," he whispered.

Her smile slowly melted and her eyes drifted closed. "I think so, too."

Cooper's neck tingled and he dropped his hand, looked around. He saw Leo Eastman turning in the direction of the parking lot and walking away.

"Not here," he said.

She pulled one knee into her chest and then the other. "Of course not."

He watched her as she jogged away and caught up with the kids running the track.

Now what the hell was he going to say?

CHAPTER ELEVEN

Claire and Jax roamed around the decoy apartment set up by Lars.

It was perfect. It looked like a bachelor pad attempting to be a family home. Hard surfaces of glass and fake leather. A big-screen TV. No real knickknacks. No family photos. The kitchen had essentials, and someone had brewed a pot of coffee and left half the coffee in the pot and grounds in the filter. Lars must have gone through the effort of making a meal and leaving the mess. Even the dish towels were stained.

"Make sure you know where everything is in the kitchen," Claire said, opening and closing the cupboards and looking for herself.

Jax started to laugh. "Even the dishes are chipped. Well done, guys." Her words were meant for whoever was at headquarters listening in on the conversation.

Claire meandered into Jax's fake bedroom, flipped back the blankets on the bed, jumped inside, tossed and turned, then kicked the sheets away. In the bathroom she brushed her hair and pulled what was left in the brush free and dropped it in the wastebasket. After that she pulled away a few tissues, blotted her lipstick, and tossed that away, too. Under the sink she found the usual suspects . . . tampons, extra toilet paper, and acne cleansers and creams.

Jax walked past her and emptied a plastic bag full of dirty clothes in the corner of the room. Next was a handful of cosmetics she no longer used and a vanity mirror. She sat at the pretend desk, rifled through them. "Looks like they thought of almost everything," Jax said.

Even the dresser had clothes tossed in with no apparent order. A closer look might clue in a detective that the style didn't exactly match Jax, but a glance would certainly pass as teenage crap. "I bet Neil took a picture of Emma's room and told Lars to match it." As Claire spoke, she looked up at the camera that was disguised as a smoke alarm. "You did, didn't you?"

The camera didn't answer back.

Then again, there was no guarantee Neil was on the other end. Cooper, on the other hand, was likely there watching.

The doorbell to the apartment rang.

Jax turned Claire's direction. "Someone is early."

"Probably the pizza."

Jax jumped up and hustled down the hall.

As she did, Claire tossed the bags they'd brought stuff from home in into the trash.

"It's the pizza," Jax yelled from the living room.

A peek in Lars's so-called bedroom confirmed that the setup was pretty complete. A bedside drawer check was missing one thing. "A man might have condoms," she said for the cameras.

Her phone buzzed in her pocket.

A text message from the office stated, A man with new custody of his teenage daughter isn't having sex in his own bed.

She laughed. "Good point."

And even though she didn't like where her thoughts led, she wondered if Cooper was the one responding. The second thought was . . . Did he have condoms next to his?

Claire shook her head.

Not going there.

Just because he'd looked at her lips and had been acting different ever since he returned didn't mean a damn thing.

They would talk about it and clear the air.

And everything would go back to normal.

Claire worked her way into the living room of the apartment. Jax was spreading her world out. Backpack sprawled on the floor, notebooks on the coffee table. "It's like we're back in Richter all over again, minus the pizza," Claire said.

Jax started to laugh. "If the headmistress could see us now."

"She'd be shitting her pants."

The doorbell rang.

Claire stopped laughing, looked at Jax. "Showtime."

Jax offered Claire a fist bump before opening the door.

"Oh, hi . . . is this a—" It was Elsie's voice.

"Hey, Elsie." Claire bounced off the couch and peeked her head around the corner through the front door. "You found the place."

"Yeah."

Jax stood back, let Elsie in.

"Elsie, this is Jax."

Jax waved her hand, closed the door behind her. "Nice to meet you."

"Thanks for having me over," Elsie said.

Elsie's backpack met the other two on the floor.

"It's cool. I need to meet new people." Jax pulled a pillow off the couch and set it on the floor before she sat on it.

"Claire said you go to Bremerton."

Jax rolled her eyes. "My dad's idea of parenting is sending me to the strictest school he could find so he could ignore my existence."

Elsie sat next to Claire on the couch.

"At least he lets you have your friends over."

Jax laughed. "As long as I clean it up after. He's such a pig, I don't think he'd know if I didn't."

Claire couldn't help but notice how easily Jax slipped into an American accent. It was like she'd never been to Germany, let alone grown up there.

The doorbell rang again.

Claire leaned forward and grabbed a piece of pizza. "Dig in," she whispered. "Jax's dad gives her guilt money."

"I sometimes wish my parents would get divorced so I can have some of that," Elsie said, reaching for a slice.

Jax walked around the corner with a petite girl who was undoubtedly the youngest one in the room, yet wore the most makeup. By her side was a woman in her sixties.

"Hi, girls," the older woman said. "I'm Ally's grandmother."

Claire waved with her pizza. "Hey."

"I told you everything was cool." Ally's jaw was tight, her eyes said she wasn't happy with Grandma walking her in.

The grandmother seemed to take in the whole room. "Do all of you go to Bremerton?"

"Just me," Jax said.

"We go to Auburn High," Elsie told her, waving a finger between her and Claire.

Grandma looked down in that disapproving way some adults could manage. "Are any boys coming over?"

Ally grunted. "Grandma!"

"Hey, I'm gonna ask."

"You're so embarrassing." Ally marched into the room and placed her backpack to the side of the coffee table.

"My dad would kill me if we had boys over," Jax assured her, polite smile firmly in place.

That made the older woman soften. "Is your dad here?"

Jax shook her head. "No, but if you want to talk to him, I can call him. He's at work, but he picks up if it's me."

"Grandma!" Ally glared.

"No. That's okay." She turned to her granddaughter. "Call me when you're ready to leave."

"I told you someone could give me a ride home."

That was news. "I can," Claire volunteered.

"Not this time." Grandma turned toward the door. "You girls have fun."

Ally wanted nothing to do with it. "Goodbye!"

Claire waited until the door closed before she started to laugh. "She's worse than my aunt."

Ally dropped her head back on the chair. "So annoying. I can't wait to get my driver's license."

"Jax said you're a junior," Claire said.

"I am, but my mom wouldn't pay for the class, and my grandma said I needed to get Cs in all of my classes before she'll do it."

Claire took a bite of her pizza. "I get it."

"I don't. So stupid. She blows money on a stupid private school instead of a car."

Jax and Claire exchanged glances. She seemed to remember Jax complaining of the same thing when they were at Richter.

"Do you live with your grandma?" Elsie asked.

"Sadly. My mom has a few *problems*. So I'm living with the old bat."

Claire couldn't help but think a "few problems" were more than Ally was suggesting.

"I'm Elsie, by the way."

"Claire," Claire said, with her mouth completely full of pizza.

Jax sat back on the pillow. "Sorry, guess I should have introduced you."

"Whatever." Ally grabbed a slice of pizza.

Jax bounced up almost as soon as her butt sat down. "Want something to drink? I think my dad went shopping." She headed toward the kitchen.

"Do you have soda?" Ally's voice grew louder.

"Think so."

Ally leaned over and picked up her backpack.

"Found some," Jax called from the kitchen.

Claire looked over her shoulder to see Jax waving a two-liter bottle of cola.

"Good, it will work with this." Ally waved a plastic water bottle in the air.

"What's that?" Elsie asked.

Ally's lips pulled into a Cheshire-cat grin. "The old bat should really put a better lock on the liquor cabinet." She handed the bottle to Claire, who took the lid off and sniffed.

"Whiskey."

"Yep. And good stuff, too. Not that cheap Jack that my mom always drinks."

Elsie started laughing. "Now that's the way to study!"

Oh, God. Underage drinking. Where did that fall in the investigation?

"Ally, I thought you were failing algebra," Jax said, looking at Claire.

Yeah, they were both thinking the same thing. And it sucked. In reality, Claire couldn't care less about a little adolescent fun, had drunk several times before she turned twenty-one. Then again, she'd turned eighteen while in Germany, and it was legal there.

Elsie set her half-eaten pizza down and moved into the kitchen. "Where's the glasses?"

Jax hesitated. "You get the ice."

"I can help." Ally jumped up and moved into the kitchen.

"Hey, Jax, we need music."

Jax left the kitchen while the other two scurried around in the kitchen opening cupboards.

"Well?" Claire said under her breath.

"My dad uses some country station on the TV," Jax said, a little loud. Her eyes opened wide with a *what the hell do we do now* expression.

"Veto on country."

Claire noticed an Echo on a side table. She told it to turn on and play.

"You're the rebel and I'm at home," Jax said quietly in Russian.

Yeah, they were kinda screwed.

Claire shrugged. There were plenty of ways to pretend to drink, not that she had to in an apartment that had several eyes watching them. The concern of something being slipped into the drink wasn't there, and there was backup in case that did happen.

"Elsie, did you drive here?" Jax asked.

"Yeah, but I can call Kyle to pick me up and tell my parents I had car trouble."

"You sure?" Claire asked.

Jax sighed with relief.

The girls walked into the living room and handed out the drinks. "To new friends," Elsie said.

Claire could smell the liquor before she put the glass to her lips. "Wow, that's strong."

Ally nodded several times. "Yeah!" she said with a smile.

Jax looked at Ally. "What about algebra?"

Ally knocked back a pretty good size swallow. "Mr. Cummings looks at my tits, I'm sure I can sweet-talk my way into a C."

And with comments like that, Claire knew their study date was the right choice. "Cheers." She took a sip of her drink.

CHAPTER TWELVE

Cooper waited outside a bar in Valley Village, where Claire and Jax had taken an Uber. Since Cooper was the one watching the monitors, he was put in charge of getting them home.

He kept an eye on the parking lot while they went into the bar. After ten minutes, he was certain no one had followed them, and he sent Claire a text.

Once they were in his car, they both started to giggle.

The sound was infectious.

"That was highly entertaining," Cooper said as he pulled out of the parking space.

He'd never eavesdropped on a teenage girls' party without actually being there.

"Ally can seriously drink," Claire said from the passenger seat.

"I noticed."

"One drink and Elsie was done." Jax sat in the back seat and leaned forward. "Do you know the guy Kyle came with to pick her up?" she asked Cooper.

"He was too far outside of range of the front-door cameras." Cooper merged onto the freeway leading to their place.

"We need to fix that, then."

Cooper had thought the same thing. "I already scheduled an adjustment."

Claire smiled at him before turning around in her seat to include Jax in the conversation. "Not a lot on Kyle tonight, but Ally sure paid off. And that thing she has for Sean Fisher. I bet we can learn more about him through her, too."

Cooper looked in the rearview mirror at Jax. "Do you know this Mr. Cummings?"

"No. But I'll make a point to run into him tomorrow." Jax sounded half-asleep.

"It's hard to say how much of what Ally says is sensationalized for drama, or truth," Claire said. "She has a hard shell."

"I knew she lived with her grandmother, and assumed it wasn't a great parent relationship, but after tonight, it sounds worse than I thought. She has an attitude at school, but isn't at all like we saw tonight."

"Lots of kids her age drink like that to get attention," Claire said.

"That drinking gets them into trouble." Cooper switched lanes.

"We're all guilty of teenage drinking, and sometimes the purpose was the trouble." Claire swiveled back around. "God, I'm tired."

"Me too."

Cooper glanced between the two of them. "It didn't look like you guys drank that much."

"Just enough to not drive," Claire said. With her eyes closed, she reached over and placed a hand on his arm. "Thanks for picking us up."

They'd put the plan in place to Uber to a drop-off or pick-up place away from the Tarzana home to avoid any tails. Not that it was clearly needed yet, but there was no reason to take chances this early in the game. Two girls Ubering to a bar with fake IDs was easier to explain than the assistant track coach picking up two teenage girls.

"No problem."

Claire didn't pull her hand back immediately, instead it kind of slid off and onto the center console. Cooper glanced over to see her eyes unfocused on the road in front of them. "We scored a party invite for Saturday."

Jax groaned. "Lewis is gonna be ticked."

"If he doesn't understand your work, you might wanna get rid of the guy."

Cooper felt a bit like a chauffeur listening in on the paying clients who were both half-asleep and half-drunk.

"He's getting clingy. I didn't think that would happen until he finished law school."

"Your boyfriend is a lawyer?" Cooper asked.

Jax lifted a hand, eyes still closed, and yawned. "Almost a lawyer."

"He's not the guy for you, Jax. We've talked about this." Claire took that moment to open her eyes. When she did, she pulled her hand away from his side of the car as if she didn't realize it was there.

Cooper turned off at their exit and drove through the dark streets to their home. One look in the rearview mirror suggested Jax had fallen asleep.

With Claire quiet at his side, he didn't think she was far behind.

He lowered his voice. "I take it you don't like the boyfriend."

Claire leaned her head against the window. "He's fine. Just not the right guy. Jax has adventure inside of her, and he has an agenda."

"What agenda?"

"My family has money and connections," Jax said from the back seat.

Claire laughed, pointed a thumb toward her friend. "What she said."

"And he wants those things?" Cooper asked.

"According to Claire."

Cooper met Claire's eyes.

She nodded.

"What do you think?" Cooper asked Jax.

Jax sighed. "Claire's right."

Okay, now he was confused. "Then why are you with him?"

Both Claire and Jax offered tired laughs.

"The sex is good," Jax confessed.

Ooookay then.

Cooper pulled into their driveway, and Jax pushed out of the back seat. "'Night, Cooper. Thanks again."

"No problem."

When Claire didn't follow her friend's lead, his nerves started to fire. He watched as Jax walked up the path to the front door, and Claire twisted in her seat and looked straight at him.

Getting the hint, Cooper turned off the engine.

"You've been different since you've been back," Claire started.

Was he ready for this conversation?

"Well, I've put on a good five pounds." He smiled and patted his stomach.

Claire reached out and stopped his hand.

"That's not what I mean, and you know it."

Did she understand how warm her fingertips felt on his skin?

He took a deep breath, blew it out slowly. "Damn it, Claire."

"See, right there. That's different. Where's 'Yearling,' or 'Sasha wannabe'? You never say my name, and now you have to take a massive breath before you talk."

They were sitting in a car, in the dark . . . in a driveway. "Maybe we should go inside."

She shook her head. "You know as well as I do that the house is completely wired with eyes and ears everywhere. You can't sneeze without someone from headquarters phoning in to say gesundheit."

He laughed, despite the feeling of his gut stirring.

"Talk to me, Cooper. I thought we were buddies."

God, he hated that word. "You're wrong."

"About what?"

He looked her in the eye, pulled the humor out of the conversation. "I say your name. I said it a lot when I was in London. Even more when I visited Berlin the first time." He remembered standing in front of the Brandenburg Gate. "I asked myself, 'What did Claire think the first time she saw the Berlin Wall?' 'What did it feel like to be Claire escaping the prisonlike walls of Richter with no money and no plan?'" Cooper saw understanding seep into her eyes. "But most of the time I'd say your name when I asked myself what you were doing. Were you kicking ass in America, or breaking hearts?"

Her jaw dropped, but no words came. Her breathing increased, and the rapid rise and fall of her chest told him exactly what her heart was doing.

"We're friends. You could have called and asked me those questions."

He shook his head. "No, Claire. I couldn't do that. I didn't have it in me."

"Why?"

He didn't answer . . . "Remember when we were in Texas and you told Neil you needed some trigger time so you could think?"

She blinked. "Yeah."

He smiled at the memory of that day. "You walked into the weapon room determined. I tried to hold you back, told you all the weapons were loaded. You marched past me, grabbed an AR, did a weapons check, tossed it over your shoulder, and moved on to the next."

Claire smiled all the way to her eyes. "Yeah. And you stepped back and told me, 'That was hot!'"

It had been. "And do you remember what you told me?"

"I told you to put it away, I was too young for you. I said that a lot back then."

The muscles in Cooper's throat started to constrict.

Silence hovered.

"I had to put it away, Claire." His words came out slowly.

He felt her fingernails push into his forearm where her hand was still resting.

"What?" Her one-word question was asked with a quiver in her voice.

"You were eighteen."

"Oh, God."

"Eighteen and Neil stepped in as father figure."

"Eighteen and able to make my own decisions," she told him.

"You needed to grow up."

Claire's hand pulled away. "And did I? Am I grown up now?"

Even dressed like a teenager, she wasn't one. "Yes."

"Is that why you're back now? I'm old enough for this conversation?" Her words were crisp and her smile was replaced with a thin line.

"I needed to stop pretending I was happy in Europe. I needed to stop getting information about you by asking coy questions to the team."

Her eyes narrowed. "So you talked to the team about this, but not me?"

"It wasn't like that."

She twisted even further in her seat, hands fisted by her lap. "We were friends!"

He hated that she put that in past tense. "Of course."

"You were crushing on me, so you left?"

Crushing wasn't the right word. "You were eighteen."

She ran a hand through her hair. "I was an adult."

"You had the nickname Yearling."

She lifted a finger in his face. "No. You don't get to call me that anymore. My friend called me that because I could outshoot, outrun, and hold my own with him. You called me Yearling as a way to pretend I wasn't qualified to work with this team when we all knew I was."

No, she had that wrong. "I called you Yearling to remind myself that no matter how hot you were making a target your bitch, no matter how sexy hearing you talk to Sasha in some foreign tongue was, and no matter how much I wanted to feel you pressed against me . . . You. Were. Eighteen!"

Claire's eyes shifted rapidly between his, her lower lip started to quiver, and her nose flared as she pulled in each staccato breath.

She scrambled to get out of the car.

Cooper didn't think, he just made sure he got out of the car faster and caught up with her as she reached the front door.

He stopped her hand before she could twist the knob.

Only now she was standing in front of him, his body pressed close to her back.

"Let me go," she whispered. He heard the tears in the back of her throat.

Cooper closed his eyes and briefly lowered his forehead to the back of her head. He'd ruined their friendship with his confession. And that hurt more than he thought possible. He loosened his hold on her hand, and she slammed the door between them.

With his palm resting against the house, he heard another door inside slam.

"Damn it."

CHAPTER THIRTEEN

First thing Monday morning, Mr. Eastman stood in front of his white-board with several algebra equations scribbled on it.

As Claire filed into the room, and took her normal spot toward the back, she heard several students grumble.

"What's this?" Sean flung a hand gesture at the board as he turned his chair around and straddled it.

The last of the students walked through the door when the bell rang.

"I've been told that several of you are having trouble in Dunnan's class, so I thought it would be a good idea to spend our time reviewing some of the basics."

One of the girls raised her hand. "Angie and I are taking geometry."

Eastman smiled. "Then maybe you guys can tutor some of your classmates who are struggling."

Claire lowered her head in her hands with an audible moan.

"Do you have a problem, Miss Porter?"

"Too much whiskey last night," Sean muttered so quietly under his breath, only those closest to him heard what he'd said.

She snarled at the guy. He obviously had spoken to Elsie or Kyle. Good gossip spread in a high school faster than a venereal disease in a brothel.

"Mind sharing?" Eastman asked.

Claire glanced around the room. It was time to ramp up her reputation. "Yeah, I have a problem."

He lifted both hands to the classroom. "You have all of our attention."

"I'm hungover and I'm not going to math today." She used *math* as if it were a verb.

The class erupted in laughter.

Eastman tapped the whiteboard pen against his palm.

"Hungover?" he stated.

"Hey, I'm here, aren't I?" Truth was, the conversation with Cooper had zapped all the alcohol from her system the second his words were out. Her hangover was from crying and avoiding Jax's questions all night. She'd managed three hours' sleep and she felt it.

"So is that going to be your excuse when you have a job and can't perform the next day?" he asked.

"I can do the job," she challenged him. "I said I'm not going to."

"Ohhh . . ."

Claire was surprised there weren't cell phones out and filming the way the class was chattering among themselves.

Without warning, Eastman tossed the whiteboard pen in the air.

She caught it on instinct.

"Prove it."

She leaned back in the chair, tossed the pen back. "What's in it for me?"

He looked at the board, then to her. "Free pass from homeroom for a week."

That brought an excited rumble from the students.

She realized, in that moment, that she'd grab all the clout she needed from this class of troublemakers. Party invites would be in the bag for the rest of the semester. People would talk to her, and maybe they could wrap this assignment up sooner so she could find that beach in the Bahamas and truly get drunk.

When she slid out from behind the desk, the class went back to whispering.

Claire walked up to Eastman, plucked the pen from his hand.

For a moment, she looked at the board and growled.

Several voices said she couldn't do it.

But what the class didn't understand was that algebra was in fact a useful math that needed to be mastered before the computer classes at Richter were allowed. And Claire loved hacking into computers.

She scratched her head for drama and pulled the cap off the pen.

The first equation was like putting ten divided by two on the board for a CPA to get right. She wrote the answer and moved to the next.

"Show your work."

She rolled her eyes, erased the answer, and spelled out the process of solving for x.

She stopped, glared at Eastman, and waited for his nod.

The second equation required fractions, the basics. She skipped over the board, spelled out her answer, and proceeded to finish the last two before capping the pen and tossing it at Eastman.

Without asking if she was right, she returned to her chair, grabbed her backpack, and walked to the door.

"Peace," she said with two fingers flying in the air as the door closed behind her.

~

As the day inched by, one class at a time, Claire heard her name spoken by people she didn't know.

Elsie jumped up behind her between classes, full of energy. "Here's the girl who's the talk of the school."

"Et tu, Brute?"

Her snark was lost on Elsie. "What?"

Claire shook her head. "Never mind."

"Did you really tell Eastman off?"

She was about to correct the girl. "If we wait an hour, the school gossip mill will have me punching the man."

"So cool," Elsie laughed.

"Who did you hear it from?"

"Sean told Kyle. The whole school is talking about it."

"Great." She really could use something for her headache.

"Is it true you told him you were hungover?"

"What's he gonna do? Call my mommy and tell on me?" As the words left Claire's mouth, she realized she'd said them before. Back when she would act out at that age. She didn't have a mom then any more than she had one now.

"He could tell your aunt."

"My aunt doesn't care. She can't wait until I'm out of her hair."

"That's so cool. My parents would flip."

They walked into class together.

Claire rubbed the space between her eyes. She had one more class before she was faced with Cooper. And she wasn't ready for that.

She and Elsie sat in their usual chairs. "Do you have an aspirin or something?"

The bell rang as Elsie reached into her purse. "I might."

Claire looked and found Mr. Dunnan, with his receding hairline and blustery red nose, staring down at her. On the board were almost identical questions to those that had been on Eastman's.

"Oh, shit." Claire moaned.

"I can't find anything," Elsie whispered.

Dunnan walked down the aisle of desks. "I understand we have a protégé in our class."

Not today . . . not again.

Claire reached for her backpack and stood.

"Where are you going, Claire?" Dunnan asked.

Because she was there on an assignment, and because she knew walking out without some cooperation from the teacher would likely cause more problems, Claire suffered a breath. "I don't feel well."

"Heard that, too. So unfortunate." Dunnan wasn't amused. "Have a seat."

"Fine."

He turned back around.

"Does anyone have an Advil or something?" Claire asked the entire room.

Someone laughed.

"Students are not allowed to take any medication on campus unless they're in the nurse's office," Dunnan explained.

Claire grabbed her backpack and was halfway to the door before Dunnan stopped her.

"Excuse me!"

"You said go to the nurse's office." She used his words against him.

"That was not what I said."

She looked him in the eye. "All due respect, Mr. Dunnan, but I have a bitch of a headache and I'm on my period. So unless you want me moaning *and* bleeding all over your classroom, I suggest you allow me to go to the nurse's office."

Nothing shut a man up faster than the period card.

"Go." His nose deepened in color when he was mad.

~

News of Claire's shenanigans caught up with the track team.

Cooper wasn't sure if it was strategy on her part or because of what he'd told her the night before. A combo of both, he assumed.

He searched the team as they slowly made their way on the field, looking for her.

They needed to keep it together.

Coach Bennett approached him. "Afternoon," he said.

"Hello."

"I heard our new sprinter is pushing the limits in the classroom."

"You mean Claire?"

"You heard about it, too?"

Cooper nodded.

"Yeah. Listen, I don't want to lose her. Varsity girls need a solid runner."

"I'll talk to her," Cooper said.

"No, I'll do the talking. After, I want you to run that attitude out of her."

Damn.

He wanted to text her, send a warning.

"Here she is. I'll let them stretch and then pull her aside. No reason to give her an audience. I heard she likes that."

Cooper tried to make eye contact with Claire, but she was doing her best to look anywhere but at him.

When the stretching was done and the kids took the field, Coach Bennett waved Claire his way. A look over his shoulder and he asked Cooper to join them.

"Do you know why we called you over?" Bennett asked.

Her eyes caught Cooper's for two seconds.

"Yeah."

"I like you, Claire. You fit on the team, the coaches like you. But the classroom has to come first. If you mess up out there, fail your classes . . . track is history."

"I'm not failing." The attitude she used on campus seeped out.

"Do you want to be out here?" Bennett asked.

Claire looked from the coach to Cooper. "Yeah."

"Then clean up the bullshit. I can't stop you from doing what you wanna do when you're not in school, but if you bring it on campus, I won't have any choice but to cut you."

"Fine."

"Good."

She started to walk away.

"And, Claire?"

She turned around.

"I asked Mr. Green to switch you into my algebra class. Mr. Dunnan seems to think he bores you and you need a challenge."

"You what?"

"See you tomorrow." Bennett smiled, completely amused.

Claire shook her head and started her laps.

"Did you volunteer to take her?" Cooper asked.

He shook his head. "Dunnan wanted me to cut her from the team. I negotiated to take her off his hands."

"Smart."

"She's going to hate it."

"Why?"

"Because I'm going to make her work. Dunnan lets kids skate. Should have retired five years ago. When you demand excellence, you get it. When you accept mediocrity, you get it. Remember that, if you decide to fall into the trap of being a full-time teacher."

"I'll do that."

Claire ran by.

"You got it from here?" Bennett asked.

"Yeah."

"I want to see her sweating. If she's partying, she better not bring it on my field."

Any previous conclusions that Bennett was one of the bad guys vanished.

CHAPTER FOURTEEN

Claire collapsed onto the living room sofa the second she walked in the door. Not only had she suffered a headache the entire day, Cooper ran her like a trainer working an Ironman competitor.

"That sounds like a bad day," Jax said as she walked around the corner of the kitchen.

"You don't want to know."

Claire flung an arm over her eyes to block out the sun.

She heard Jax walk in the room and then exhale as she sat down. "You're right. I don't give a crap what happened in school, unless it involved Cooper. What I want is the details of last night after I got out of the car."

Before Cooper picked them up, Claire and Jax had agreed that Jax would give them a few minutes to have a private conversation. Now Claire regretted that plan.

"The long story, or the short story?" Claire asked.

"Whatever one you want to deliver."

Claire's arms slid off her head, and she pushed herself into a sitting position.

"Cooper has a thing for me."

Jax sat silent, blinked a few times. "Okay, and?"

"What do you mean, 'okay, and?'"

"Sorry, Claire, but that's obvious. I think you'd have to be an idiot to not see it. Even the guys on the team see it."

"What? Are they talking about—"

Jax stopped her with a shake of the head. "Of course not. But you can tell by how they look at the two of you that they know there's an attraction."

Claire pointed to her chest. "I'm not doing anything, it's him."

"Maybe it's *more* him."

She kept shaking her head. "No, it's *all* him. I'm not instigating anything."

"You flirt with him all the time."

"I do not," Claire huffed.

One look from Jax and she rescinded her statement. "Okay, we banter. But it's always been like that. I have the pool stick, he makes some kind of phallic joke. It's banter. Not flirting."

Jax sat back, crossed her arms over her chest.

"You know when I'm flirting, you've seen it. Remember Blane in the stacks at Richter? That was flirting. And Steve last year in Vegas? That was flirting."

"That's a flower calling a bumblebee to mate. It's called getting laid, not what you and Cooper are doing."

Claire couldn't believe her best friend was calling her out. "We're friends. And last night he ruined that by telling me he's had a thing for me since we met. Told me he left sunny California for dreary London because I was too young and naive to handle him when I first got here."

Jax narrowed her eyes. "Is that really how he said that?"

Claire's headache was coming back. "No. He said I was a child."

"A child?"

Claire stood up from the couch, started for the kitchen. "He kept repeating that I was eighteen back then."

Jax followed behind. "Which is true."

Claire yanked open the fridge, pulled out a beer. "Whose side are you on?"

"Yours. Always. But I just don't see where all the fire is about this. Cooper owns up to the flirting comments and puppy-dog looks he gives you, and you're pissed because he walked away six years ago. Walked away because you were barely eighteen and he was what? Twenty-four, twenty-five? Think about that, Claire. We're back in high school, the kids there . . . Do you look at any of them and think, *Well, maybe?*"

She shook her head. "Of course not."

"Okay . . . but what if you did?"

"I wouldn't."

"So fast-forward six years, you see that guy again . . ."

Jax was starting to make sense.

"It's different."

"Why?"

Claire twisted off the cap of her beer, took a sip. "Because Cooper and I are friends. He was the only one on the team that treated me close to an equal."

Jax grabbed the beer from Claire's grasp and took a drink. She handed it back and said, "That's because you're the closest in age. And guess what, you're not eighteen any longer. He's not too old, and you're not too young. There is zero ick factor to the two of you getting together."

Like picking a lock, the pieces slid into place and finally started to click. "But he's my friend."

"Trying to say you've never thought of him as more?"

"No." Her denial was quick.

Jax started to smile. "You've never checked out his ass? The guy can fill out a pair of jeans."

Some of the anger she'd harbored all day eased. "That's true."

"And that smile. When he's belly laughing he has the tiniest dimples."

Claire closed her eyes, pictured his smile. She hadn't noticed the dimples, but now that she thought about it . . . She opened her eyes to find Jax staring at her.

"Sounds like you have a thing for him," Claire said.

"Wouldn't matter if I did, and I don't, by the way, but it wouldn't matter. The guy can't stop looking at you."

Claire put her beer down, leaned against the kitchen counter. "I don't know what to do."

Jax moved across from her. "Where did you leave things last night?"

"I was shocked. The man uprooted his whole life because of me, and I had no idea. And here I thought I was the smart one."

"Okay."

Claire looked up. "I ran. I didn't know what to say, so I bolted."

"What about today? You saw him at track."

Claire found a smile for the first time that day. "I ran again. Only he was holding the whip."

"What?"

"Claire Porter got into some trouble. Well, not trouble so much as showed off for a couple of teachers. I bragged about being hungover, then shoved Eastman's algebra equations down his throat. Petty of me, but it felt kinda good. Then in Dunnan's class, I did it again. Which probably worked to my advantage since I've already made my connection with Elsie in that group, and should move on."

"So what did all that have to do with Cooper and a whip?" Jax asked.

Claire let out a laugh, the first one all day. "Coach Bennett told Cooper to run the attitude out of me."

When Jax started laughing, Claire caught the giggles.

"Cooper must have been dying."

Claire squeezed her eyes shut, thought of the look on Cooper's face when he said he had to make her work hard. "After the first mile, which none of the sprinters like to do, I passed him and asked if he was enjoying himself."

"Ouch. Now you're acting like an eighteen-year-old."

The mention of the age brought the humor out of the conversation. "God, what am I going to do with him?"

"I don't think you have to *do* anything. It's not like he asked you out and you said no and now it's awkward."

"You're right. It's worse than that."

"You're overthinking it." Jax pushed off the counter. "You know what, let's gussy up a little and hit a proper happy hour. We'll talk in German and pretend we don't speak English and shamelessly flirt. All this high school crap is making us act like we're truly back there. Time to remind ourselves that we're grown-ass women who are kicking butt and taking names."

Claire abandoned her beer. "Now that is exactly what I need to do and get my mind off of boys."

"Yeah. Flirt with other boys."

~

This was the last place Cooper wanted to be and the last person he wanted to be there with.

"What a shitty day." Leo Eastman bent over his draft beer while Cooper did the same.

They sat at one end of a crowded bar with happy hour in full swing. The time and date had been dictated by Cooper, the place picked by Leo. It worked out fine since Cooper's apartment wasn't far away. He could have a beer, pick the man's brain, and slither home where he could work up the nerve to call or text Claire and apologize for making her run like she was escaping the reaper.

"You can say that again."

"We don't get paid enough."

Cooper chuckled. "Hey, you get paid more than the lowly auto shop sub. And I volunteered for the drama in track." Actually, Cooper wasn't getting paid anything for the teaching. It was all part of the operation.

"I take it you heard about Claire's latest today," Leo said.

"Oh yeah."

Leo started laughing, throwing Cooper off. "What's funny?"

"I should have put harder problems on the board."

Cooper studied his beer, found his smile.

"The minute she asked what was in it for her, I knew I was screwed. You should have seen her. Sass and attitude as she damn near flipped me off walking out the room. She impresses me almost as much as she aggravates me."

Cooper lifted his beer. "You have no idea."

"I never have understood why smart kids act dumb."

"It's all about reputation."

"How so?" Leo asked.

"Oh, c'mon, you remember high school. You're what, thirty-five?"

"Thirty-four, but high school feels like a lifetime ago."

"It's no different for them than it was for us. In order to stand out, you have to be the best at something. You have to be the quarterback and not the benchwarmer claiming someone else's fame. No one remembers the person who was second-in-line for valedictorian. Hell, I don't even remember number one."

Leo nodded in agreement. "Our Claire wants to be a badass."

"Number-one badass," Cooper corrected.

"Have you met any of her family?"

He immediately thought of Neil. "I heard she lives with her aunt. Hoping I can meet her at a track meet."

"I'm sure there's more to that story. So many kids are getting the fucked-up end of bad parental choices." Leo sucked down a generous amount of beer.

"Are you married? Have kids?"

There was a moment of hesitation. "Did that once. Have a four-year-old I'm allowed to see a couple weekends a month."

Cooper hadn't found that bit of information on the man.

"That sucks."

"Just another parent fucking up their kid."

"Lots of kids grow up fine with divorced parents."

Leo looked over at him. "Your parents still together?"

"Yeah."

"You're lucky. Divorced for twenty years and my parents still bicker about each other any chance they get. I don't want my kid growing up hearing those things." He stopped talking long enough to finish his beer and signal the bartender for another one. "You know why I ask for the troublemakers at Auburn?"

"No."

"Because I want to identify the kids that are really screwed up. The kind that walk onto campus with an AK and light it up. I want to stop a kid from being the one that will never be forgotten because of an adolescent mistake."

That, Cooper wasn't expecting.

"No guarantee you're going to pick that kid out of a crowd."

Leo turned in his seat, lifted his fresh beer. "Not going to stop me from trying."

Cooper touched his glass with his. "If it makes you feel any better, I don't think that kid is Claire."

"I have a feeling she's going to light up the school, just not with a gun."

Cooper couldn't help but laugh. "She's definitely that girl." He tilted his beer back and looked across the bar.

Beer slid down the wrong pipe when his eyes collided with hers.

CHAPTER FIFTEEN

This was exactly what Claire needed.

Loud music and a crowded bar that she and Jax had never gone to before. It proved difficult to pretend you didn't speak English if you went to an old haunt.

They ordered drinks with a thick German accent, and purposely screwed up the names of their cocktails. Their parlor trick was always the best way to have a private conversation in a crowded room. And if the right guy came along, they could speak enough English to have a conversation.

Still, it had been a while since they went out on a random weekday for happy hour, and Claire realized she missed it. "Lewis has distracted you these last six months," Claire told her in German.

Jax sipped her fuzzy navel while Claire drank a proper martini with two olives. If there was one thing about being tutored on the finer things by Sasha, it was ordering the right drinks. Anytime Claire tried to order some fruity stuff like Jax's, Sasha would send it back and order something else.

Sasha scolded in Russian.

Claire found it endearing.

"I know. He's been nagging about going to visit my parents," Jax said.

"He obviously didn't listen when you told him your parents weren't high on your list."

"He seems to think he can mend fences."

"Fences that surrounded Richter and the parents that put their children there don't come down easy." Claire plucked one of the olives out of her drink. With it halfway to her mouth, tall, dark, and not-so-handsome slid up to her.

"Well, hello," he slurred.

"Talk about subtle," she said to Jax in German.

"Oh, what are you speaking?"

Jax offered her flirting smile, the one that called the man an asshole before she opened her mouth. "From Germany," she said in broken English.

"I've never been to Germany." He stared down at Claire's drink.

"He's never been outside of the valley." She smiled and sipped her drink as if she'd just offered some kind of a compliment.

He took it as an invitation. "What's your name, beautiful?"

It took everything in her to not laugh. He was trying way too hard, and she was in no way interested.

Jax spoke for both of them. "Our English not very good."

"I understood that."

"How long has this guy been in here drinking?" Claire asked Jax.

"Smells like a half a liter in."

Mr. Not Getting the Hint reached out and touched Claire's shoulder and asked her name again.

She moved away from him. "No touching."

"How about another drink?" He raised his hand for the bartender.

Claire waved over her drink. "No. One only."

When he touched her a second time, she was close to ending the charade.

"I'm going to dump this drink on him," Claire told Jax.

The bartender walked over, and both Claire and Jax waved off the offer of drinks by Mr. Pushy. "Doesn't look like the ladies want another round."

Claire smiled at the bartender, said thank you in German, then again in English. She lifted her drink and looked anywhere but at the guy who wasn't getting the hint.

With the glass to her lips, she looked over the rim and gasped.

There, on the other side of the bar, Cooper sat staring at her.

Next thing she knew, he was coughing and someone was handing him a bar napkin. When the profile of the man became clear, Claire nearly shrieked. "Ah, fuck." Without warning, Claire grabbed Jax's arm and pushed her into the barstool she was on so her back was to Cooper and her homeroom teacher.

"What the hell?" Jax asked.

Mr. Pushy smiled. "You're cute, too."

"Go away," Claire demanded in English, then she tossed out an expletive in Russian.

The guy lifted his hands in the air, called them a nasty name of his own, and walked away.

"Look over my right shoulder, slowly," Claire coaxed Jax.

Jax switched their drinks around and did just that. "Cooper's here."

"Do you see who he's with?" Claire felt panic rising in the back of her throat.

"A friend?"

Claire grabbed her glass, downed the drink, and started searching the bar for an exit. "My homeroom teacher."

Jax's eyes grew wide. "Oh, no . . ."

"Is he looking over?"

"No, the bartender is setting down another drink and handing Cooper napkins."

"I've got to get out of here." But to get to the front door, they'd have to walk right by Cooper and Mr. Eastman.

"Front door is too risky," Jax stated the obvious.

"Always back doors in kitchens."

"I'll create a diversion," she said as she undid another button on her blouse. "Have the car running."

Claire reached in her purse, dropped a twenty-dollar bill on the bar. A wink and a fist bump to her best friend, and she waited.

Jax stood and walked a straight line toward Cooper.

Claire waited until Jax was standing at Cooper's side, leaning over the bar. Cleavage did what it does when heterosexual men are around, and gave Claire an exit.

When Eastman scooted around in his seat, Claire made her move. Quickly but not to the point of attracting attention, she inched out of their line of sight and walked right past the "Employees Only" sign. The obtrusive bright lights of the kitchen had her blinking.

"The bathroom's not back here," someone said behind the grill.

Claire shook her head, pointed toward the bar. "Abusive ex-boy-friend. I need the back door."

Without questions, the man pointed behind him.

"Thank you."

Claire's shoes clicked on the tile floor as she rushed outside.

Once she was inside her car, engine running, Claire texted Jax.

Two minutes later, as they rushed out of the parking lot, Claire was happy Neil had taught her to back into every parking space she ever used.

Jax watched from behind. "Go."

Three blocks from the bar and the adrenaline that had been pumping finally fled Claire's system, and she started to laugh.

"Damn, that was close."

Jax was laughing so hard she snorted, and that had Claire doubled over the steering wheel.

"Guess we're drinking at home for the duration."

Within ten minutes of their arrival at home, Cooper was walking through their front door.

Claire had ditched her fancy shoes and mixed new drinks.

"All the bars in the world, and you had to walk into mine." He was all smiles and relief.

Much as it was hard to see Cooper walking through her house and tossing his keys on the island in the kitchen where she and Jax hovered, it was also a comfort.

"What are the odds?" Jax asked.

Cooper looked directly at Claire, his eyes softened. "What are you drinking?"

"Vodka martinis."

"What do I have to do to get one?"

Normally, that charged question would have a snarky remark on its tail. Something slightly sexual and inappropriate. She settled for something else. "Don't tell my homeroom teacher I was out drinking tonight."

Claire moved around the kitchen to mix another one, pulled a glass out of the cupboard.

"He didn't see Claire, did he?"

"No indication he did. How long were you guys sitting there?"

"Not long. Thirty minutes, maybe," Jax answered.

"Long enough for Mr. Clueless to hit on us," Claire said as she poured a generous amount of vodka.

"I missed that," Cooper said.

"Good thing. I was about to make a serious scene. One that Eastman wouldn't have missed." Claire shook the tumbler several times before dumping the liquid into a glass. She reached for her jar of olives.

"I don't need that."

Claire glanced over her shoulder and, without looking, picked an olive out of the jar and plopped it in the glass. "A martini without an olive is just vodka."

He smiled, and it was then she realized that he didn't have to be belly laughing for his dimples to show up.

"What on earth made you pick a bar on that side of town?" Cooper asked, accepting the martini.

Claire and Jax exchanged glances. "Should we tell him?" Claire said in German.

Jax shrugged.

"Is that 'told' or 'tell'?" Cooper asked.

Claire's smile fell. "You . . . wait, you understood that?"

There was a moment when Cooper just grinned. "I didn't spend all my time in London when I was overseas."

"Seriously? *Du hast Deutsch gelernt?*" Claire asked.

"I'm not sure you can call it *studying* German. I spent a lot of time outside of the bigger cities so I could learn it. I'm pretty sure most of the people I came in contact with were horrified at how I butchered their language. But I can hold a fairly decent conversation about day-to-day things."

She couldn't stop smiling. As brownie points were earned, Cooper stacked his deck with that one.

"Why?"

Their eyes locked. "I would think that would be obvious at this point."

His words did what his previous confession had failed to do. It made Claire look deeper in Cooper's eyes and see an emotion she hadn't noticed before.

"Uhm . . . I can leave the room," Jax teased.

Claire offered Cooper a sincere smile and shook her head. "I'm in the mood for Chinese food."

"Sounds perfect." Cooper smiled and sipped his drink.

CHAPTER SIXTEEN

He'd been ready to quit. Call Neil and tell him the minute the assignment was over he'd be looking for another job. Someplace where he didn't have to see Claire constantly and mourn the loss of their friendship. Worse, moon over her like a lovesick puppy.

Instead, Claire offered an olive branch by way of Chinese takeout and martinis.

The three of them ate and drank, and talked about the case. He told them what he'd learned about Eastman. As of yet, the man wasn't putting stuff on his class computer to indicate that he was anything other than a high school teacher with good intentions. According to the employee record, he'd transferred into Auburn that year, which lined up with the divorce he'd spoken to Cooper about.

"Expect harder questions if you plan on putting Eastman in his place again," Cooper warned Claire.

He could tell by the look in her eyes she was buzzed from the alcohol.

"I might have to actually study. I don't remember everything."

"More than me," Cooper said.

Jax changed the subject. "After tonight, we're going to have to map out the teachers' homes. Get a general idea of their stomping ground."

Claire leaned her head back on the sofa. "It feels like this assignment is taking forever."

"I'm not sure that's going to change anytime soon," Cooper said.

"We have back-to-back parties the next two weekends. Hopefully we can find a solid lead."

"Any weight to Mr. Cummings?" Cooper asked Jax.

"He has the reputation of staring at chests." Jax hoisted her breasts with both hands. "These are a little hard to miss, I'll see if he notices."

"You have to wear a uniform."

Jax frowned at Claire. "Never stopped us at Richter."

"True."

"Cummings is short, balding, typical dad body. Reminds you of the guy who lost his virginity at thirty. Easy to label him as the dirty old man. School gossip may just be assumptions."

"You just described Dunnan," Claire told her. "Only he has the reputation of hating his job."

"That's exactly what Bennett said," Cooper added.

"The invitational is coming up. Maybe something will evolve."

"Still thinking of throwing a race?" Jax asked.

Claire shrugged. "Not sure that's the best thing right now. Bennett is working hard to keep me on the team."

"That's because you're good." Cooper nudged her foot with his. He was rewarded with a smile.

"I'm also several years older than my teammates. It's not exactly fair."

"As soon as this case is over, your wins will be removed. Second place becomes first."

"Fine, for the individual races, but the relay will screw with three other girls. And if the team loses after a win . . . that just sucks for them."

Claire had obviously been thinking about this a lot. "A moral dilemma, no doubt, but what we're doing there is bigger than a track meet."

"I know. It just sucks, that's all I'm saying. Do we even know why being placed on the track team was a thing? So far all I see is relatively well-adjusted kids competing and coaches that like their jobs."

Cooper had thought the same thing. "A question for our next briefing."

Jax sat up from her lounging position. "I suggest we bring Manuel in on our next impromptu huddle."

"How is that working out?"

"Fine. I've only seen him on campus twice. Both times he completely ignored me."

"If you're not causing trouble, that would be the case," Cooper suggested.

Jax stretched as she stood. "I have a book report due in the morning."

"And you're doing it?"

Jax looked at Claire like she was crazy. "No." She shook her head, then started to nod. "I don't know how to slack."

Claire laughed harder.

"Are you telling me you're not doing any homework?"

"I have a report due tomorrow on *Macbeth*."

"And?"

Claire cleared her throat. "*Macbeth*, by Claire Porter . . . They all die. The End."

The laughter in the room didn't ebb until Jax climbed the stairs and left Cooper alone with Claire.

"I probably don't need to remind you that failing a class isn't an option until we cut track out of our agenda."

"That won't happen. I have it covered."

"No doubt you do." For the space of ten seconds they sat there staring at each other.

When Claire started to fidget, it was time to leave.

He placed both hands on his knees and pushed off the sofa. "Thank you for the drink."

She stood with him. "Thanks for paying for dinner."

"Least I could do." He patted the front pockets of his jeans, searching for his car keys.

Claire pointed behind them. "Kitchen, I think."

She followed him, an awkward silence took the place of easy conversation. Waving the car keys in his hand, he said, "Got 'em."

He was two steps toward the door when she stopped him.

"Cooper?"

He looked up, found those fidgeting fingers clasped in front of her. "I handled last night poorly."

"I—"

"No," she interrupted. "No one has ever said anything like that to me. I wasn't expecting it. I mean, I've noticed a few things since you've been back, but I told myself I was wrong. I need time to process it."

Air filled his lungs, and he beat back a smile that threatened. "I can live with that."

"I hope so. Because I don't want to lose this . . . tonight, kicking back with a quick meal and comfortable conversation." She rolled her shoulders. "I don't want this tension or to feel the need to fill the awkward gaps in conversation."

"I don't want that either, Claire."

"Good."

"Good," he repeated.

"So we'll talk about awkward stuff, laugh at it, okay?"

"I can do that."

"I don't know if we can be . . . you know. If we can ever be more. I didn't think about it . . . then last night." She closed her eyes, took a deep breath. "Now I can't think about anything else. And I know that's going to screw up my work. And we don't want that."

He was smiling. He couldn't help himself. "We don't want that."

She finally looked up at him. Her eyes glistened just a little. "Why are you smiling?" she asked.

He paused. "Because you're not saying no."

She pushed at his shoulder. "I'm not saying yes either."

He took a step closer, waited until their eyes met and her fidgeting stopped. Cooper placed a hand to the side of her face, traced her cheek, and relished in her tiny gasp at his touch. "But you're not saying no."

Her chest rose and fell a little quicker, and unlike the night before, it wasn't anger fueling her change in heart rate. That, Cooper could tell by the way she slightly bit her lips together as if not doing so could possibly be an invitation. "I should go."

"Yes, you should."

He looked at his palm on her skin and soaked in the feeling a moment longer.

Reluctantly, he let his hand drop. "I'm going." He heard Claire's footsteps behind him as he walked to the front door.

Hand on the knob, he turned back. "I'm sorry I made you run hard today."

Claire's cheeks blushed with her smile. "Don't worry. I'll pay you back."

Cooper clenched his chest. "Don't I know it."

She reached around him, opened the door, and gave him a playful shove. "Goodbye, Cooper."

"We're good, right?" he asked, knowing they were but needing to hear it from her beautiful lips.

"We're good."

He practically skipped to his car, a chorus to a song tapping in his head. And when he looked up, he found Claire watching him.

～

The party was hosted by a student at Bremerton. That's all they knew up until thirty minutes before it started. There was no way for the team to work out any details until the address was posted. On Instagram, of all places.

Ally had the connection, and since the algebra-study-session-turned-girl-party had procured the invite, with the encouragement to invite others, it looked like Elsie had done just that.

Wearing tight jeans and a spaghetti-strap top that stopped above her belly button, Claire was teenage party ready. Jax took it up a notch, as any kid in a private school forced to wear a uniform would, in a tight miniskirt and a top that boasted her ample D cups. They both wore their hair bone straight and in exactly the same style. They wore hidden earpieces, the devices so tiny you would have to be looking for them to find them. They worked as microphone and earphone. Jax wore a pendant necklace equipped with a tiny camera. Claire's smart watch had a similar function. Their cell phones were a constant uplink of the entire experience to a mobile headquarters, otherwise referred to as the *creeper van*, which was parked a few blocks away.

Sasha, Cooper, and Manuel were in the van. Their mics tuned in to Claire's and Jax's.

Neil was back at headquarters watching it all.

Teenagers, and several not so teen, were strolling toward the bump of the music and mix of voices like bugs to light.

Claire and Jax had parked just far enough away so that they could leave without a lot of eyes on their car.

"Let's do a mic check," Cooper said in their ears.

"This is Yoda, one, two, three."

"Sounds good. Claire?"

"Loki. It's Loki to you. One, two, three."

Someone chuckled.

"Your turn," Claire instructed.

Each person in the van said their name and counted.

Nearly at the edge of the driveway, they did a sweep of the area. "Do we have the details on who owns this place?"

"Working on it," Sasha said.

"It's a nice neighborhood, average list price in the three million and up range, I'm guessing," Claire said.

"North of that. Find the residents so we can get a clear picture of them." The request came from Neil.

"Copy that," Jax said.

The closer they came to the front door, the louder the music screamed.

"Let's do this." Claire reached out a fist and bumped Jax's as they walked inside.

CHAPTER SEVENTEEN

The party had just gotten started, and the crush of teens was staggering.

"Start talking so we can zero in on your voices," Cooper told them.

Jax started. "I can't believe I've only been in LA for a couple months and I'm at a huge party. This place is massive. What parent tells a kid they can have full run of the house? Even this would be too much for my dad. It's crazy—"

"Got it. You're fine-tuned, Yoda."

Claire liked that Cooper obliged them by using their nicknames.

"Stick with me, Jax, I'll get you invited to all the parties. Lots of party kids at Auburn."

"You're good, Loki."

Claire smiled at the faces of kids she didn't know as she walked by. A few of the guys looked her up and down the way they do.

"There's Ally." Jax pointed to the far end of the living room.

Three guys surrounded the younger girl, one Claire recognized from Auburn.

"We need to get drinks in our hands," Jax reminded her.

The music was a little easier on their ears when they walked into the kitchen. On the massive island was a host of alcohol and mixers with a cooler filled with ice that sat by the side.

Claire nodded toward the open French doors that led to the back-yard. There were teens gathered around a beer keg in the outdoor kitchen where Claire and Jax took their place in line.

"Hey! Aren't you in my homeroom?"

Claire turned and smiled. "Yeah. It's Todd, right?"

"Right. Man, what you did the other day with Eastman, that's some epic shit."

"Eastman's an asshole," Claire said.

The kid took a drink out of his red cup. "I know. Total douche. How do you know Russell?"

"Who?"

"The guy who lives here."

"I don't," Claire said.

Jax leaned in to talk over the music. "My friend Ally invited us. We go to Bremerton."

They took a step forward in line.

"Are you coming to the big party Nunez is talking about?"

"Free beer? I'll be there."

In Claire's ear, she heard Sasha's voice. *"Get him to point out Russell."*

"Which one is Russell?" Jax asked.

Todd did a three-sixty. "I don't . . . wait, yeah, he's over there."

Claire followed the pointing finger to see a huddled group of eight to ten people. Couple of them looked a little older than the high school group. "He's the big guy."

"They're all big," Jax said with a flip of her hair.

"He's cool."

They stepped up to the keg, and Claire filled two red cups.

"Does he have these parties a lot?" Jax asked.

"He and his friends rotate. Keeps the cops from showing up."

"The parties in my old neighborhood always got busted when they were this big." Claire handed Jax a beer.

The three of them stepped away from the keg. "I was at Brandon's last one. Cops showed up at midnight. No one got busted or anything, they just told everyone to leave."

Claire had no idea who Brandon was. She nodded toward the group of guys that apparently included Russell when Elsie and Kyle intercepted them. Elsie walked in, arms open. "Is this cool or what?"

There were hugs, hellos, and introductions. Elsie said something about Jax's outfit, the compliment was returned.

The line to the keg kept growing, so they moved away.

Twice she tried to redirect the conversation to the people giving the party, both times she was interrupted.

"There's a lot of Auburn kids here."

"Hey, we go to every Bremerton party we can. They have better booze," Todd told her.

"Well, if it isn't the algebra protégé."

Claire turned to see Sean Fisher and two of his sidekicks flanking him.

"Hey, Sean."

From the gleam in Sean's eyes, it appeared that he'd either been pregaming for the party or he'd been there longer than everyone else.

Todd and Sean did a little fist bump. "That was some crazy shit you did in Eastman's room."

So crazy it seemed that's all anyone wanted to talk about.

"Jax, move to Claire's left, look behind Sean." Cooper's voice added a layer of distraction.

"I wish I had seen it."

"Epic, ballsy shit."

Claire listened while the small group she stood with yammered on and on.

"Did you really get pulled out of Dunnan's class?" Kyle asked.

"Coach Bennett made it happen."

"Sucks. I had Bennett last year. He's the hardest math teacher at Auburn."

"Did you have him for algebra?"

"Physics."

"A little more to the left, Jax." Cooper's voice was a whisper in her ear.

Claire kept the conversation going. "That's pretty advanced math."

"I want to get into USC."

Elsie leaned into her boyfriend's arm. "You'll get in."

"Got what we need, Jax."

"There you guys are!" Ally came bouncing into their circle. "Is this awesome or what?" She slid up next to Sean, smiled.

"It's—"

"I need a drink, do you need a drink?" Ally couldn't stand still. The nystagmus in her eyes was off the charts.

"I do. We were headed to the keg and ran into—"

Ally didn't let her finish. "You don't want beer. C'mon," she said, pulling on Elsie's arm.

"Hey, babe. Go easy, okay. Your parents . . . ," Kyle tried.

"Parents? Who cares?" And Ally pulled her away.

"Wow! What did she take?" Jax asked.

"Never know with Ally," Sean said.

Claire turned to him. "You know her? She doesn't go to Auburn."

"Not anymore, no. We went to the same junior high and sopho-more year at Auburn, before her mom ended up in some rehab and she went to her grandmother's. Even back then she seemed to always know where the parties were."

Claire and Jax exchanged glances. "Any idea what her mom was taking?"

"Heroin, I think. That was the mom rumor anyway." Wasn't Sean a wealth of information?

"Mom rumor?"

"My friend's mom was the PTA mom from hell. She always talked about everyone's parents."

"I can't picture a woman taking heroin being on any PTA," Claire told Sean.

"I read an article a couple years ago that heroin was on the rise with the soccer moms. I think that's what the paper called 'em. Heroin Soccer Moms," Kyle told them.

"Why heroin?" The question was asked by one of Sean's friends.

"Because Dr. Feel-Good stopped handing them oxy. And heroin is cheap."

Sean was right. As street drugs went, heroin wasn't hard to come by. "Aren't you the knower of all things drugs. Something you're not telling me, Sean?" Claire prodded.

Sean took a drink of whatever was in his cup. "I'm smarter than I appear. I mean, I won't be handing Eastman his ass anytime soon, but I know shit."

Kyle kept watching the back door. "I'm gonna go find Elsie."

Claire thought that was a great idea.

"Do you need the bathroom?" Jax asked.

Claire looked into her completely full cup. "Yeah, I need to empty the one out to put more in."

The two of them left the guys and worked their way inside.

"Do you need to go?" Claire asked.

Jax shook her head. "I noticed the guys in the back split up and start mingling."

"Let's find Russell."

"Any clue which one that was?"

Claire shook her head. "No, but I have an idea." Back inside, they moved into the living room, which had completely packed out. She pointed up the staircase, saw a few family photos on the walls.

Leaving her red cup on a table with twenty empty ones, she and Jax bumped around kids and took in the images on the walls.

"Jax, stop."

Cooper halted them in front of what looked like brothers. All of them in their mid-to-late twenties, early thirties.

And that was about it.

Two girls squeezed behind them. "Is there a bathroom up here?" one of them asked.

"That's what we're looking for."

They followed the others until they found a line. "Get what you need?" Claire asked.

"Yup."

Both she and Jax reached for the phones buzzing in their pockets.

"Wait until you're alone to check your phones," Sasha told them.

Claire opened her camera, put an arm around Jax's shoulders, and took a selfie.

The first person in line pounded on the bathroom door. "C'mon."

Five seconds later a couple came out and two girls went in.

When it was their turn, they went in laughing. Once the bathroom door closed behind them, they both opened their messages.

The house belongs to Mr. John Sanders. No wife on title. Looks like the house might be a rental. This is a picture of Russell Mirkin from the Bremerton files.

"Slavic or Russian?" Claire asked.

"We'll work that out later. Let's meet the party throwers," Cooper said.

"Copy."

Another flush of the toilet, and then a quick wash of their hands, and they left the bathroom giggling. "He is really cute. I saw the way he was looking at you." They walked down the crowded hall, heads together like teenage girls do.

They roamed the house, said hi to a few of the kids they knew, then meandered to the backyard again. A mixture of cigarette smoke and pot formed a haze as the temperature outside dropped. A gas firepit lit up a corner of the yard. Around it were three guys who looked old enough to be the ones that bought the liquor. One of them might pass for one of the guys in the hall picture.

Claire jumped right in. "Hey, is one of you Russell?"

"Who's asking?"

Jax giggled. "We heard Russell was throwing the party, and we wanted to thank him."

Claire rolled her eyes. "She doesn't get out much."

Closer now, it was easy to see that these guys were not teenagers. Easily late twenties, maybe flirting with their thirties, and two of them were drinking out of crystal highball glasses.

"You're welcome." The guy that looked like an older version of the photographs in the hall sat back, all smiles.

"You're Russell?"

"Milo, his uncle. Why don't you ladies have a seat?" Milo was a good-looking guy and he knew it. The other two he was with were a bit bulkier, not unattractive.

Jax tugged on her miniskirt as she sat down.

Claire took a seat beside her and said, "Nice place you guys have here."

Milo nodded. "It's okay."

Claire pointed behind her. "You know it's a mess in there, right?"

"We pay people to clean it up." Yup, the guy talked like a baller.

"My dad would never let me have a party like this." Jax played the innocent girl really well.

Milo leaned forward. "Where do you girls go to school?"

They both answered at the same time and then laughed.

"I'm Jax."

"Claire," she said, pointing to her chest.

"Welcome to my home. This is Brian and Gorge."

Brian and Gorge were sitting back in their chairs, arms spread, smiles wide. Claire made sure to swipe at an imaginary bug so her watch faced the other guys. Jax's necklace was the perfect magnet in the V of her breasts.

"You guys seniors?"

"Yeah," Claire answered.

"Eighteen?" Milo asked.

"Next month," Claire answered.

"My birthday is in July."

Milo nodded a few times. "That's cool. You ladies could pass for twenty-one. Do you have fake IDs?"

"Keep him talking," Sasha told them.

"Of course," Claire told him. The rebel would.

Jax shook her head. "No. I wouldn't know where to find one."

"I could help you out with that." Milo reached for a pack of cigarettes at his side, pulled one out.

Jax's eyes lit up. "Really?"

Milo bent his head, lit his cigarette. The action of him lighting up a cigarette added to the whole package. Claire made a mental note to adapt that skill.

Milo blew smoke between his lips. "Yeah. You seem like you're all right. No reason not to help out a friend. Besides, I was seventeen once."

"That would be really awesome."

"Wait, what's it gonna cost her?" Claire played bad cop.

Milo tilted his head. "Aren't you the suspicious one?"

"Shut up, Claire." Jax turned back to Milo. "I can pay you. I mean, I can come up with—"

Milo shook his head. "A girl as pretty as you doesn't have to pay for anything."

"Bingo!" Claire heard Cooper in her ear.

"Now what are you ladies drinking?" Milo pointed to Brian and Gorge. "Go get the good stuff, none of that shit the kids are drinking in there."

"Neil is sending in a diversion," Cooper said.

There was no way they'd be sipping what Milo's boys were bringing.

"Have you been to one of our parties before?" Milo asked Jax.

Claire wasn't oblivious to the fact that Milo wasn't asking her.

Jax smiled, blushed as if on cue. "My parents just got divorced, now I'm living with my dad."

"That's tough."

Jax shrugged. "New school, bunch of kids I don't know. Sucks."

Milo sat forward, a flirty smile on his lips. "You're meeting new people."

"I guess."

It took a lot not to laugh. Jax had never been that passive in her life.

"Holding on diversion until your drinks are delivered. Bring them with you."

"I guess?" Claire nudged Jax.

The two of them went back and forth for a few minutes.

A good ten minutes passed.

"Took long enough," Milo told his boys. And that's how Claire saw it. Milo was the leader, the others were ancillary.

Brian handed Jax and Claire crystal glasses.

"What are we drinking?" Claire asked, stalling.

Jax sniffed her glass.

"I enjoy a good whiskey. The kind that doesn't need a lot of help."

Jax smiled, flirted. "You mean it's straight?"

Brian set the bottle on the side of the firepit, poured liquid into his glass.

In her ear Claire heard Cooper's voice. *"Five, four . . ."*

"A good whiskey doesn't need any fillers."

". . . three, two . . ."

Sirens filled the air.

Two things struck Claire at the same time.

Milo looked utterly shocked while sitting still.

Second, his friends stood tall, flanking Milo as if protecting the boss.

"Cops?" Jax asked.

"We got this," Milo said.

Claire grabbed Jax's arm. "We need to bounce."

"My dad will kill me."

Claire looked at Milo. "Is there a way out back here?"

Milo huffed, sat back in his chair, and pointed to the far end of the yard.

Claire and Jax started to go.

Jax turned. "I had a good time. We're still good on the ID?"

"I'll have Russell hook you up."

Jax bit her lip. "Thanks."

And they ran.

CHAPTER EIGHTEEN

Five of them shoved in the back of the surveillance van was rather tight, not that Cooper would complain with Claire at his side.

Sasha bagged the glasses and bottled what was left in them for testing and prints.

Claire and Cooper worked together to ID every kid at the party that they knew from Auburn, while Jax and Manuel did the same for Bremerton.

Cooper enhanced an early image of Milo standing with his two friends and a few others.

Manuel pointed to the screen. "This guy could be Russell. Hard to tell from this angle, but I've seen him at Bremerton."

"Troublemaker?" Cooper asked.

"Not that I've noticed. I've seen him leave campus at noon, not sure if he comes back."

"Put a trace on his car," Sasha said from the front of the van.

"Easy enough. Seniors have assigned parking spots," Manuel said.

Cooper circled a half-hidden face in the crowd. "This guy looks familiar."

Claire shook her head. "He looks too old to be a student."

Jax leaned back, scratched her head. "This is unusual, right? A big party like this with a huge mix of kids from private and public schools?"

"If this was a neighborhood party, I'd say no. But Bremerton's students come from all over, and most of the kids at Auburn had a decent drive to get here."

"The question is, why?" Sasha asked.

Claire turned around to look at Sasha. "I think that's obvious. We're looking for a link between the schools, and we may have found it."

Sasha shook her head. "You've found nothing incriminating. We have a rich man entertaining his nephew, who is showing off for his friends." She lifted the plastic evidence bags. "If these come back tainted, then we have a little more, but not much. In Seattle, I chased a lead. The girl is now nineteen. Marie Nickerson, she ran cross-country for Auburn. She wasn't good. We know she dropped out of school her junior year. Warren's investigation revealed this girl as having met an older man she never introduced to her friends or family. She started to attend parties, skip school, and within a month of finding trouble, she disappeared. The first hit in the system signaled Warren. Until now, there was no way to know if she was simply a runaway or a victim."

"Sounds exactly like the profile we're looking for. What happened in Seattle?" Claire asked.

Sasha lifted a finger in the air. "One prostitution bust. One. Then nothing. Disappeared again."

"They're moving the girls around." Cooper glanced at Claire.

"Keeping it underground. I take it we don't know who the guy was she was dating," Claire said.

Sasha shook her head. "All we have is a car description, no plates. And that is a three-year-old lead."

Manuel cleared his throat. "What about the john? The man Marie was caught with?"

"Booked and released. Pleaded not guilty. Said he was answering an ad for a professional massage."

Cooper shook his head. "Yeah, right."

"But now we have a name and a positive ID of a student at Auburn." Sasha turned to Claire. "Remember where we met? And what I was doing?"

Claire smiled. "In the library at Richter and you were going over old yearbooks."

"Guess where you're going to be on Monday. It's only been three years that she's been missing. Many of her teachers will likely still be at Auburn."

"Why not go to the administration and pull an old schedule?" Cooper asked.

Claire and Sasha exchanged looks. "Because we don't know if we can trust them."

"The less people that know what we're learning the better," Sasha said.

"Even Warren?" Cooper asked.

"Leave Warren to me." Neil's voice came from a single speaker in the van.

Claire jumped.

Cooper placed his hand over hers. "Damn, Boss. We forgot you were even there."

"Neil is always listening," Sasha reminded them.

And when Sasha's eyes didn't leave Cooper's, an uneasy pitch in his stomach had him wondering just how much Neil listened to.

~

Claire went into the next week with a completely new agenda. She arrived to school early and went straight to the library. Unlike Richter, the library at Auburn seemed to house more computers than books, and a quick search uncovered that the library didn't have a stash of old yearbooks. Those could be found with Mrs. Appleton, the yearbook committee director.

No way Claire Porter would want to be on that kind of thing. That left Claire only a couple of ways to get the books. She could break into the classroom and steal them, or break into the classroom and hack Mrs. Appleton's computer and hope the old files were in there.

Much as Claire loved a good computer hack, she doubted she'd have enough time to find what she needed and get out unnoticed.

When Mrs. Appleton wasn't dealing with the yearbook, she was teaching English in the room that adjoined Mrs. Wallace's, which was a lot less conspicuous to break into from than a hallway filled with students walking by.

A plan formulated as Claire walked into Shakespeare and took her usual seat.

Instead of her normal attitude, she paid attention to the lesson and wrote a few notes.

When the bell rang, Claire held back.

"Mrs. Wallace?"

The older woman looked over the rim of her reading glasses, her expression unamused.

"About my book report . . ."

Mrs. Wallace removed her glasses and pointed them at Claire. "We can't call that a book report."

"Oh, so you read it already."

"Let me see if I remember it clearly. 'Everybody dies. The End.'"

Claire lowered her eyes. "Yeah—"

"I especially liked the postscript. 'Five acts for any play is three acts too many.' Bravo, Claire. Your best work to date."

Claire huffed out a breath. "I just don't get it. And last week I had a ton of work and I didn't actually read anything but CliffsNotes until this weekend. And I'm still not . . ."

Mrs. Wallace kept watching her as if she didn't believe a word Claire was saying. The woman was smart like that.

"When I try to write down the meaning of the play, I just get all tied up."

"Then ask for help." Mrs. Wallace started to soften.

"That's what I'm doing." Claire laid on the sad face, the one that used to get her a hall pass from Checkpoint Charlie at Richter.

Students for the next period started to enter the room.

"Okay, come in at your lunch."

"I can't. Coach Bennett has me at lunch for algebra."

For the first time, Mrs. Wallace cracked a smile. "I'm surprised he doesn't own your nights and weekends."

"How about after school? I can ask to show up a little late for track. The coaches did say my schoolwork had to come first," Claire said, smiling.

It took Mrs. Wallace a few seconds to answer. "Fine."

The bell rang, and Claire turned toward the door.

"Miss Porter?"

"Yeah?"

Mrs. Wallace scribbled on a notepad. "A pass for being late."

Claire took it, waved it in the air. "Thanks."

Instead of finding third period, she worked her way to the auto shop.

The metal roll-up doors were all the way to the top, and twenty or so students were working on small engines on various tables set up beyond the car lifts.

Cooper was bent over, showing a handful of kids something in the engine.

For a few seconds, Claire stared and listened. Jax was right, Cooper filled out a pair of jeans really well. And his laugh, the richness of it, had started to become something she wanted to hear often.

One of the students looked up, and then nudged Cooper and pointed her way. "Uhm, Mr. Mitchel."

He turned and saw her, and those dimples she had just started to notice appeared on his cheeks.

"Sorry to interrupt, Coooach. Can I, ah . . . t-talk to you for a minute?" Claire nearly called him Cooper and stuttered.

"Yeah." He wiped his hand on a shop towel and patted one of the kids on his back. "You got this. Try again."

"I have to be late for track today," Claire said loud enough for anyone listening to hear.

"Oh?" Cooper opened the door to the empty classroom. "What's up?"

Claire lowered her voice to a whisper. "Yearbooks aren't in the library. I need to get into Mrs. Appleton's room. I've arranged to meet Mrs. Wallace after school. Their rooms connect. I need you to check up on me and distract her."

"How much time?"

"I don't know where she keeps them, ten minutes?"

"That's a long distraction."

"I'm not going to get another chance, so make it work." Claire gave him a knowing grin. "Flirt with her. I know you know how."

"Seriously?"

"Don't try and tell me you haven't flirted with older women."

Cooper's gaze moved to her lips. "And younger women." His words were slow.

"You're killin' me." Claire ignored the heat rising in her face.

"I certainly hope so." His words were charged, the look in his eyes matched.

"Cooper," she said his name between clenched teeth. "Save it for Mrs. Wallace."

"Sorry." He closed his eyes, shook his head. "Better now."

Claire took a step back, put out her palm.

"What?"

"I need a hall pass. I'm pretty sure Mrs. Wallace's expired after the first fifteen minutes."

Cooper started to laugh. "What's in it for me?"

She had a hard time not laughing. "C'mon." She pushed at his shoulder.

Cooper found the notepad and handed her a pass. "You could have just texted me this info."

"And spend my time in World Affairs? Where is the fun in that?"

"You just wanted to see me."

His words made her pause. Probably because he was partially right. Or maybe more than partially.

CHAPTER NINETEEN

Jax sat in the tiered quad, her uniform sweater under her butt to keep her skirt from getting wet. If there was one thing about this assignment she didn't like, it was plaid. She'd burned her Richter uniform, every version of it, down to the socks. To her, there was nothing worse than a strict uniform code making all the students look exactly alike.

With a sandwich in one hand and book in the other, she ate and watched.

If it wasn't for Ally and her connections to the party crowd, Jax was starting to think her presence on Bremerton's campus was a waste of time.

Her phone rang, pulling her out of her thoughts.

Lewis's initials flashed.

"Hey. I'm a . . . I can't talk long."

"How about a simple hello?"

Jax closed her eyes. "Sorry. I don't want you upset if I have to hang up." She glanced around, found no one watching her.

"You sound like you're outside."

"I am." Lewis had no idea where she was, only that she was part of a group investigating human trafficking. She told him that if he saw her anywhere, even if she was with Claire, to ignore her and walk on by.

"Where?"

"You know I can't tell you that."

"I'm starting to think you're living a double life."

"Technically, I am," she said with a slight laugh.

"Hmm." He wasn't amused.

"You're calling midday, so something's up." Jax put her sandwich down, no longer interested in it.

"Me and a few of my friends are renting a big Airbnb in Santa Barbara over the long weekend, blow off some steam."

She knew without asking what he was going to say next. "I'm sure you need it."

"We all do."

She was quiet.

"I want you to come."

Jax picked at the grass. "I'm not sure I can."

"You can't work seven days a week."

"Actually, I can." She looked to her side. "I can't talk about this right now."

"Really, why?"

"Lewis." His name was a warning.

"I hear voices. Like you're in a park." He sounded angry.

"I'll call you later."

He huffed. "Just tell me something."

This conversation had gone on too long. "What?"

". . . is there someone else?"

"What? No." It was her turn to be pissed. "I told you—"

"Yeah, that you're working. But we both know you don't have to work. And since you've reduced me to once a week, I'm starting to think it's all bullshit."

"I do have to *work*." She whispered the last word and spat it at him at the same time. "I have to go."

From behind her, her name came out in a girlish scream. "Jaaax!" Next thing she knew, Ally was practically jumping on her before plopping at her side. "I've been looking for the party girl all day."

"What the—"

"Goodbye," she told Lewis before hanging up the phone.

"Ewww, that sounded bad."

Jax rolled her eyes. "My dad is so annoying."

"Did he find out about the party?"

"I stayed with Claire so he wouldn't, but he's suspicious."

"That sucks." Ally laid on the grass. "Saturday was epic. I think I was drunk until Sunday afternoon."

"You didn't seem drunk. You were bouncing."

"I know." She sat up, rested on her elbow. "I think I was roofied," she said, smiling.

Jax wanted to deny that. "Did you pass out?"

"No. I didn't at all that night. Crashed big time Sunday afternoon."

"So you didn't take anything on purpose?"

Ally shook her head. "Not my thing."

The girl was sixteen, she didn't know what her thing was. Nevertheless, Jax was happy to hear she wasn't seeking drugs on purpose. "Who would put drugs in your drink?"

"I don't know. Maybe it was just the tequila . . . or vodka."

The bell rang and they both stood. "Next time, stick with me," Jax told her. "I'll keep anyone from spiking your drink."

Ally put her arm around Jax's shoulders. "Yeah, we girls need to stick together."

Jax tossed her uneaten lunch in the trash can as they walked by. "Hey, if you see Russell, can you point him out?"

"Sure, why?"

"His uncle is gonna hook me up with a fake ID," she whispered.

Ally jumped in front of her and stopped. "Get the fuck out. No way."

"That's what he said. I mean, before the party broke up."

"Dude! I want one."

Jax's first thought was, Ally wouldn't pass for twenty-one with a fake ID. "Okay. I mean, I don't know if he'll do it. But we can ask."

They started walking again. "I probably shouldn't go bursting up to him and asking about an ID."

"Probably not."

"I wonder if he'll be at the Nunez party."

Jax felt tired just thinking about it. "I heard it might be canceled."

Ally pouted. "That would suck."

The warning bell rang. "Shit, I can't be late to Mr. Levin's class."

Jax waved the other girl away.

Instead of heading for her class, she walked toward the girls' bathroom and texted headquarters.

By the time she made it to the administration building, her pass to leave campus was stamped and she was headed toward the parking lot.

Manuel leaned on the side of a security car, eating a burger.

She walked up to him and handed him her pass. "Any luck with the car?"

"Didn't show up for school."

"I'm ducking out early." She needed to deal with Lewis before he did something stupid and blew her cover.

"Copy that." Manuel looked beyond her as if bored.

"If you see Ally jumping in any cars, make note of the plates."

"Got it."

"See ya," she said under her breath before heading to her car.

～

Claire stood outside B building after the final bell and waited for Mrs. Appleton to walk out before she made her way inside.

"I was starting to wonder if you were coming."

"I was on the other side of campus, sorry."

Mrs. Wallace indicated one of the front seats, and Claire sat down. "Before we get started, I have to tell you . . . your behavior in this classroom has been nothing short of appalling."

Time for a lecture. "I know."

"Why?"

"Can I be honest?" Claire asked.

"If you can keep the profanity out of it."

Claire squeezed her eyes as if in pain. "It's so freaking boring! I mean, not you. Shakespeare."

"How can you say that about *Macbeth*? There's high drama . . ."

"And endless death. It's predictable. After you get through the singsong way he phrases everything, as if iambic pentameter makes it better. It doesn't, it puts you to sleep like a children's lullaby."

Claire kept talking, purposely giving Mrs. Wallace things to chew on so when Cooper arrived she'd be just flustered enough to need a few minutes to digest everything Claire was saying. From Claire's experience with teachers, nothing excited them more than when a student has a light bulb moment of clarity.

"Yes, but—"

"You know what reading *Macbeth* did for me?" Claire didn't let her answer. "It made me look up good old Bill's daily life. Who were his people? Cuz there had to be some serious story in there. Sure enough, he had siblings die, as in several. Kinda the norm back then, but then he had his own kid bite it because of the plague."

By now Mrs. Wallace was sitting back and listening.

"And why didn't he write a play about marrying a cougar at eighteen after knocking her up? Now that play I might try and suffer through, even if it's written like a musical without actual songs."

"Well—"

"And a hypocrite to his deathbed. Or at least his tombstone. *'Good friend for Jesus sake forbeare, To digg the dust encloased heare: Bleste be ye man yt spares thes stones, And curst be he yt moves my bones.'* " Claire took a breath. "In one breath he says he's a godly man and the next he's cursing you if you loot his grave. Those two things are a contradiction, don't you think?"

Where the hell is Cooper?

"Certainly—"

"And his poor wife . . . he dies and leaves his wife a *bed*? And he dies a month after signing his will. I have to tell ya, I wouldn't put it past Anne to reenact *Macbeth* and kill him herself once she realized she'd get nothing when he bit it. Was he faithful? I bet—"

There was a knock on the door.

Claire finally took a breath. *About time!*

Cooper walked into the room, his eyes collided with Claire's.

"You *are* here," he said as if surprised.

Claire brought her attitude back. "I told you Mrs. Wallace was giving me extra help."

"You'll have to forgive my lack of trust, you haven't exactly been completely honest lately."

With her arms crossed over her chest, Claire turned to Mrs. Wallace. "I've been here the whole time, right?"

Mrs. Wallace smiled. "She has been. It's Mr. Mitchel, right?"

Cooper turned a full-wattage smile toward Mrs. Wallace, and damned if her face didn't perk up.

"That's right."

"It does appear as if Claire is attempting to get on track with her studies."

Cooper nodded a couple of times. "Can I have just a moment?" He opened the door.

Claire's hand slid into her pocket and fiddled with lock picks.

"Certainly."

Claire huffed as if annoyed, and waited until Cooper closed the door before bolting from her seat.

CHAPTER TWENTY

"Thank you," Cooper said as he kept walking to draw Mrs. Wallace farther away from the classroom. Once they reached the double doors leading into the hall, he stopped and glanced at his watch. "You have no idea how glad I am to see Claire in your room, Mrs. Wallace."

"It's Louise."

He put a hand to his chest. "Call me Cooper. I feel like I haven't met a third of the staff."

"If you're here long enough, you'll learn the names."

"I'm sure. Anyway, I need to know how bad Claire is doing in your class."

Louise lifted her eyebrows and shook her head. "If you'd come to me last week, I'd tell you she's failing."

He shook his head as if disappointed.

"But after everything she just told me, I honestly couldn't possibly fail her. Education is meant to teach a subject, yes . . . but it's also meant to open the eyes of the student. Make that student look for their own answers to life's big questions. And that is exactly what Shakespeare is doing for her." The woman looked like a proud parent.

"You mean Claire likes the class?"

"Quite the opposite, I think she hates it. Hates it enough to study the man and not his work. But you cannot do one without the other and truly understand."

Wow, this lady really loved Shakespeare. "So Claire is doing the work?"

Louise shook her head. "Not really."

Cooper glanced at his watch.

Louise started to chuckle. "She turned in a book report on *Macbeth*. You'll never believe what she wrote."

Actually . . . "Do I really want to know?"

She leaned a little closer. "Everybody dies. The End."

Cooper closed his eyes, tried not to laugh.

When Louise's giggles grew, Cooper joined her. "What a little shit," he said.

"I know. She's not wrong."

"Maybe not, but still . . ."

"I think I can get her back on track so she can keep running for the team," Louise said.

"I hope so." He looked at his watch, still two minutes to go. "Maybe with Coach Bennett moving her to his algebra class, the girl will be able to graduate."

"He will shape her up. And if she's still struggling, Mr. Dunnan has several tutors he can recommend. I'm told they're young and speak teenager."

"I'll make a note of that." Cooper felt his pocket buzz. Looked like he didn't need to flirt with the woman after all. "I won't keep you. And thank you for giving her a chance."

"I like the girl. I'd just like to see her be less of a . . ."

"Pain in the ass?" Cooper finished for her.

"Well, yes."

He walked Louise back down the hall and opened the door.

Claire sat slouched behind a desk, cell phone in her hand. She really knew how to play her role.

"Well, Claire, it appears that Louise . . . Mrs. Wallace, is willing to help you out. Although after that book report, I'm surprised."

Claire rolled her eyes, attempting not to grin.

"I'm excusing you from track today . . ."

"But Coach Bennett—"

"I will talk with Bennett. You go home, do your homework, and get a good night's sleep. And when you come back to school tomorrow, we all need to see some improvements." Cooper saw her trying so hard not to smile.

"Okay, Coach."

"Good." He redirected his attention. "Louise, thank you again."

~

"I broke up with Lewis."

Jax's announcement met Claire the second she cleared the front door. "You what?"

"I was waiting for him at his apartment door when he came home, I handed him his box of crap he'd started leaving here, and I said goodbye."

Claire dropped her backpack, dumped her purse on top of it, walked over to the couch, and pulled her friend in for a hug.

Jax sniffled and hugged her back.

When Claire leaned away, she looked hard in Jax's eyes. "Is this an ice cream breakup, a tequila breakup, or a trip to Vegas breakup?"

Jax wiped a tear from her eye. "Vegas sounds perfect, but we both have school tomorrow."

That was laughable.

"So, tequila?"

"Make it wine . . . no, champagne."

"Bubbles?"

"Yeah."

Claire pushed off the couch to fill her request. When she returned, Jax had curled back up on the couch with a blanket over her legs. Claire handed her a glass and joined her.

"Okay, tell me everything."

Twenty minutes later the story was out, and Claire was refilling Jax's glass.

"You know what really made me do it?" Jax asked.

"You had so many reasons."

"The part about him saying I didn't have to work. I mean, for God's sake, has he listened to nothing I've told him in the last six months?"

"You know what he heard? 'Blah, blah, blah . . . level up . . . blah, oh, sex . . . blah, blah, level up, connections . . . and more sex.'"

Jax released a long breath. "I know. I shouldn't have ever told him about my family. Then it would have been 'Blah, blah, blah . . . sex, sex, sex. Blah, blah.'"

Claire smiled when Jax did.

"He even started telling me he loved me."

Claire almost spat out her bubbles. "He what?"

"It happened right after we started this assignment. I think he saw me getting excited about work and felt cockblocked."

"He wouldn't be wrong about the cockblocking. Do we even have groceries?"

Jax laughed until it dwindled to a chuckle. "Damn."

Claire watched while reality settled.

"Am I going to be one of those people who has to hide their family?"

Claire bit her lip to keep her thoughts from becoming words. *At least you have a family to hide.* "I don't know," she said instead.

"I'm wallowing."

Claire reached for the bottle. "You're allowed. You just broke up with a guy. It's a free pass for feeling sorry for yourself."

Jax tilted the glass back. "You know what really bugged me about Lewis?"

All Claire had to do was be silent to get the answer.

"My parents would have *loved* if I brought Lewis home. It wouldn't matter if he was a decent guy. Wouldn't matter if he really loved me. He has the right pedigree."

"And that makes you a mare."

Jax lifted her head from the couch, sat up. "All I've ever been to my family is a burden. If I marry well and bring them something, I am something. Bringing Lewis is exactly what they want."

They both took a heavy pull from their glasses. Some of that wallowing dissipated. In all the things Claire had to think and worry about, disappointing a mother or a father wasn't one of them. Wanting their love . . . yeah, she wanted that. Her mere existence disappointed them enough to leave her the moment she took her first breath.

"Good thing we're not living our lives for someone else's approval."

"Amen!" Jax grabbed the bottle, refilled glasses.

~

Claire tucked Jax into bed, reminded her she was her own woman, and left her snoring friend.

She sent a message to Neil and the team. Told them Jax was taking the next day off.

After a shower and slipping into a simple baggy T-shirt to sleep in, Claire pulled one of the yearbooks from her backpack and started flipping pages.

Her eyes kept sliding to the digital clock on her nightstand.

She put her AirPods in her ears to keep at least half of the conversation from anyone who may be listening. She trusted Neil with her safety . . . privacy, not so much.

Cooper picked up on the first ring.

"Go home and do your homework?"

Claire curled up in bed, a water bottle in her hand.

"Hey, I'm an upstanding staff member. I need to start talking like one." Cooper answered as if they were in the middle of a conversation.

"You know, I think you like bossing me around." Claire flipped the page.

Cooper was silent for a moment.

"What?" Claire asked.

"I'm not commenting on that one."

"Dangerous ground?" she asked, teasing.

His silence made her laugh.

"Jax broke up with Lewis tonight."

"Ohhh . . . is that a bad thing?"

"No. Still sucks. He called her and started giving her crap about not being around for him. She was at school. Ally was there. He was never right for her."

"How is she?"

"I poured her into bed. Taking tomorrow off."

Cooper chuckled. "That's fair."

She turned a page, looked past all the pictures of previous Auburn seniors.

"What are you doing right now?" he asked.

"I'm doing homework, in bed."

Silence.

She stopped leafing through the pages. "And don't ask what I'm wearing."

He moaned. "That was mean."

"Oh, was it?" It was good to laugh.

"Yeah. Now I want to know exactly what you wear to bed."

"I'm not going to tell you."

Was that Cooper growling?

Claire closed the yearbook and rubbed her eyes. "This is weird, Cooper."

He paused. "Weird good or weird bad?"

"I don't know, just weird. It's like the rules changed overnight. And now, every comment, every joke, every look is charged, you know?"

"And that's bad." His voice sounded strangled.

Claire tried to grasp on to her feelings, which was never an easy thing for her. "Not bad," she decided out loud. "Weird. Upended. That's what it is. I'll feel turned around and not sure which way to step or what to say."

"That doesn't sound like you."

"I know."

"How about going with your gut. Instead of thinking, just step or turn. Move forward."

She shoved the yearbook off her lap and kicked the covers off her legs. "For the first time since I left Richter, I'm worried I'll make a wrong move and regret it."

"Will you do me a favor?" he asked.

"Depends on what it is."

"I'm probably shooting my own foot, but when you stop thinking and start feeling, will you act on that?"

"That could go wrong." *In so many ways.*

"Maybe, but it's your truth. When I joined the service, I just jumped, went with my gut. Six months in I was like *What the hell did I do?*"

Claire laughed at that.

"But that didn't last long. Yeah, I wanted out after four years, but I came out a different person. When I signed up to work for Neil, I knew it was the right choice. It filled that part of me that I joined the service for, without tying my hands the way the service did. I thought I was the luckiest bastard in the world. I got paid doing the shit I love to do with enough of an adrenaline rush to make me feel alive."

"I know exactly what that feels like."

"I know you do. We all do, even Sasha, who tries so hard to act indifferent. We're all cut from the same cloth, as my mom would say. And if going with my gut hasn't led me down an irreversible path, then maybe that will work for you, too."

"Go with my gut?"

"You did that when you hopped the fence at Richter. How did that turn out?"

Claire looked around the bedroom she called hers. In a home that felt like she belonged. "Not bad."

"Damn good, if you ask me."

She was smiling again. "Pretty damn good."

"There's the spark in your voice I'm used to."

She liked how easy their conversation flowed. "I've been wondering about something . . . ," she started.

"About what?"

"All that time in Europe . . . Did you ever come back?"

"Yeah. I visited my parents a couple times. Mainly during the holidays."

"I don't remember where they live."

"Rural Michigan. Which was a huge reason why I joined the service to start with. Winters suck, summers are too short."

Claire tried to scrape together her memories of Cooper's conversations about his parents. "You have a brother, right?"

"You remember."

"Barely. Back when I first moved here I didn't pay a lot of attention to anyone else's family unless I met them."

"I don't think any of us went out of our way to talk about our families. Didn't seem right since you didn't exactly have one."

She couldn't argue there. "It doesn't feel that way now."

"Hmmm, you'd like my parents. My dad works heavy construction. Mom works in a dental office as a receptionist. Pretty boring and normal. Mom was nervous when I joined the military but got over it. She thinks I'm a bodyguard, now."

"A job you've done a few times."

"If I told her about our time at Richter, she'd do that worry thing all over again. It's best I just keep that to myself."

In all the ways Neil and his wife, and Sasha and her husband, had filled the holes in Claire's life, having them worry about her wasn't part of that. They all knew what their jobs were and understood how to execute them and stay safe. She supposed that didn't stop them from being concerned from time to time, but they'd never once tried to change Claire's mind about working for Neil. "Did you ever think of flying back here to visit?"

"All the time. I didn't trust myself."

"I guess that's my fault." She didn't like the thought of being to blame for him staying abroad all those years.

"My choice. I went with my gut to leave, and had to own my feelings so I could come back."

"You can't tell me that you've been pining over me for six years."

He paused. "I wasn't a monk, if that's what you're suggesting. But I did try and put you out of my head."

"Did that work?"

"Yes," he said a little too quickly.

"Really?"

Another pause. "No. I flew back to the States and kept lying to myself. But this lady I know pinned me down, kicked me in the groin, and woke me up."

Claire took a deep breath and curled her knees into her chest. "She sounds badass."

"She is."

They both stopped talking.

"Claire?"

She still wasn't used to him calling her by her first name.

"Yeah?"

"Are you feeling less weird?"

She laughed away the last of her tension. "I am."

"Good. Now do your homework and go to bed."

"Good night . . . Cooper."

"'Night, Claire."

CHAPTER TWENTY-ONE

A nagging ping in Claire's head pulled her out of a dream. She rolled over, curled up on herself, but the ping didn't stop. Her eyes opened. It was still completely dark outside. A glance at the clock said she'd only been asleep for thirty minutes.

The ping came from her cell phone. Neil's number lit up her screen.

She sat up in bed, ran a hand over her face. "What's going on?" she answered.

"We have a situation."

Twenty minutes later she was standing in the surveillance room at headquarters.

Neil was sucking on a cup of coffee, Sasha looked like she'd just walked off a fashion runway, and Cooper mirrored Claire's appearance as having been pulled out of bed in the middle of the night. All they'd been told was that there was activity at her decoy house and to prepare accordingly.

Claire walked directly to the monitors. "What's going on?"

"You have a visitor." Neil ran the footage.

She expected to see Elsie or maybe someone from the house party.

A shadow swept by the first camera, too dark to really see anything other than darkness on the screen.

Cooper pushed a cup of black coffee in her hands.

She smiled her thanks.

The infrared cameras turned on and the blur came into focus. The image jolted her awake, more than the taste of stale coffee. "Mr. Eastman?"

"What's he doing?" Cooper asked, peering closer.

"Checking to see if anyone is home," Sasha told them.

Claire's eyes kept glued to the monitors. "How long did he stay?"

Neil leaned forward, advanced the time of the film. Eastman walked around the small half of the duplex, stuck to the shadows, and glanced in the windows. He didn't linger. The camera stayed on him as he walked out of the yard and continued across the street to get in a car. Neil stopped the image.

"How long was that?"

Neil shook his head, pointed to the live feed. "He's still there."

Claire looked up at Cooper, who was standing over her. "He's making sure I live there."

"Why?"

"To know that, we need to know exactly who he is." Sasha did this part really well. "We can rule out that he's a concerned staff member worried about his student."

"He's either the link to the organization who feeds them children—" Neil started.

"Sorry, Boss. I'm not seeing that," Cooper countered.

". . . or one of Warren's men."

Claire pressed a button, watched him casing the yard again. "So he's a cop. And he's onto me."

"At what angle?" Cooper asked. "Let's say he's clean. Claire shows up, he profiles her as a possible risk. That's reason to keep watch on her house."

Claire listened, rewound the tape again. "If he's a good cop, wouldn't he phone in for someone else to do this? A little risky poking his head into my bedroom window when I know what he looks like."

"If he's a bad cop, he isn't going to phone in anything." Cooper placed a hand on Claire's shoulder.

She knew Cooper's feelings on Eastman. Neither one of them wanted to see him coming out of this with dirt on his hands.

"Good cop who is watching out for new players and he's made me as one," Claire suggested.

". . . or someone you are in contact with as one." Sasha directed her look at Cooper.

Claire felt Cooper's hand squeeze her shoulder. "We have very minimal contact on campus, most of which is on the track."

Neil cleared his throat and focused their attention on another monitor.

Claire recognized the front of her house. In the frame, Cooper was pulling into the driveway after the sun had set. When Jax jumped out of the back seat, Claire knew what was coming. Neil fast-forwarded until she'd run from the car.

He stopped the image with Cooper standing behind her, his body well inside her physical space.

Claire glanced over and found Neil looking between them.

At her side, Sasha was silent.

"Eastman has seen something," Neil told them.

Cooper spoke for both of them. "There is nothing more to see than this."

Sasha made a clicking noise. "Emotion is felt."

Claire sometimes hated that Sasha was sharper than a samurai's sword.

Neil was pinning his eyes on Cooper. Tension in the room simmered.

Claire reached up, touched the hand on her shoulder, and held it firmly in place. They'd done nothing to compromise this case. "Then we need to flush Eastman out. He's at the decoy house because that's what's on file. Gathering Cooper's address isn't as easily obtained." She turned back to the monitors, reran the images of Eastman walking around.

"What are you looking for?" Sasha asked.

"If I was a cop, good or bad, I'd plant some kind of bug so I could sleep at night."

Cooper set his coffee beside hers and pointed. "There."

Claire backed up the image, frame by frame. A tiny flash of light reflecting was all they needed. Something was in the bushes.

"Looks like I'm moving in." Which did not make her happy.

"Do we have a tail on Eastman?" Cooper asked.

"AJ is on him now. We'll have wherever he's staying staked out and online within twenty-four hours." Sasha's husband, AJ, was an occasional helper to the team.

Claire patted Cooper's hand and scooted back in the rolling chair to stand.

"Sasha is coming with you," Neil said. "You're not alone in the house until we understand the danger level."

Claire nodded.

They all started to leave the room.

Neil stopped Claire and Cooper. "You have a few minutes in private to work out whatever is going on here," he said to both of them. "But it stays here and not out there unless it can work to our advantage."

Claire and Cooper stayed back, watching the other two walk away and close the door behind them.

"This is on me," Cooper said the second they were alone.

"We don't know that."

He turned her to face him. Shook his head. "My thoughts are less than pure when I see you on the field. If Eastman is watching, or someone reporting to him is . . ."

She smiled, looked up. "Don't kick yourself too hard. I might have been checking out your ass when you were elbow deep in that engine today."

He rubbed his hands up and down her arms, and instead of feeling the need to pull away, she wanted him to pull her close.

"I knew I felt heat on my backside," he teased.

Claire placed one hand on his chest. For several seconds she looked at her fingers and enjoyed the strength of the man under them.

Cooper placed a hand to her cheek and tilted her head.

She felt her lips pulling into a smile and her gut suggesting she move in closer. Instead of questioning, she reached for his neck and met him halfway.

His lips were warm and soft, gentle with the first taste.

Inside she felt her gut celebrating their first kiss, telling her she was doing the right thing.

Cooper wrapped one arm around her back and pressed their bodies close from knees to lips. Then reason took a back seat to the desire that started to churn. Mouths opened and her tongue pressed against his. All the wonder of what it would be like to be kissed by this man fled with the reality that it was spectacular. Both hot and sweet and nothing like anything she'd ever felt before. Probably because she knew the man kissing her more than any other in the past.

She felt his kiss soften and his hands grip her harder right before he ended their first taste.

Her breath came fast and her eyes opened slowly to find him staring down. "I guess that answers that," she said in a whisper.

Cooper closed his eyes, and wrapped her close for a hug. "Thank God," he said against her ear.

They walked out of the surveillance room holding hands.

Sasha stood in a flight attendant uniform, the appropriate luggage at her side. Her expression completely neutral.

Neil's jaw, on the other hand, was tight.

"Are you ready?" Sasha asked in Russian.

Claire nodded. And with a squeeze of her hand holding Cooper's, reluctantly let go.

~

Cooper watched her leave, and for the first time since they met, hope flared so brightly inside of him he wanted to scream. The cruel irony that their first kiss was going to be their last until . . . he had no idea how long . . . was the only thing biting at his joy.

"Remove that expression from your face before I'm forced to remove it for you." Neil's words were measured.

Yeah, even that didn't dim Cooper's sunshine. "Are you telling me you don't approve?" he asked Neil flat out.

His boss, and friend, was slow to respond. "Why do you think I sent you away?"

Cooper remembered their conversation. It had been short and clipped.

"I see what is going on. Do I need to remind you how old she is?"

"Eighteen going on thirty."

"Stop at eighteen. And under my protection."

Cooper had already concluded his attraction wasn't appropriate and was doing everything he could to stay away. But he loved his job and couldn't imagine finding work somewhere else.

"Everyone here is my second family."

Neil looked him dead in the eye. "Second. We are her first."

"What do you want me to do, quit?"

Neil shook his head. "I'm expanding in Europe. Many of our clients have second homes there. My wife's family . . . Richter proved there is need. I'd like you to head the operation."

"You're sending me to Europe."

"I'm suggesting you request a transfer."

Which was better than being fired.

"You need distance and she needs an opportunity to figure out what is best for her without distractions."

Much as Cooper had wanted to argue the point, Neil had been right. And his solution made sense.

Cooper pushed his memories aside. "I requested the transfer." He looked Neil in the eye, saw some of the tension fade.

"I would have fired you if I didn't approve and wouldn't have let you come back if I thought Claire wasn't . . ." Neil didn't finish his thought. "Just don't rub it in my face."

Cooper wanted to laugh so hard it hurt. "She's a daughter to you."

Neil wasn't one to overtly show his emotions, but he was failing that self-imposed rule with Claire.

"We're the only family she has."

Cooper couldn't stop smiling. "You're a giant teddy bear." He knew he was pushing Neil's buttons. There wasn't a soft anything on the man's body.

Any teasing, if you could call it that from Neil, was gone from his next message. "If you hurt her, I'll be forced to hurt you."

Cooper could accept that.

With a moment of quiet understanding, he broke up the heavy air with one question. "Does this mean I can call you Dad from now on?"

And Neil grinned.

~

Claire sat in silent reflection as Sasha drove to the decoy house. Much as she would've loved to be thinking about the case, the only thoughts in her head involved Cooper and the churning he'd caused in her body.

She glanced at Sasha, who hadn't uttered a word.

"Aren't you curious?"

Still there was silence.

"Surprised?"

Claire leaned her head back and broke up the quiet. "I was. Did you know Cooper went to Europe to stay away from me? How was I so clueless?"

"You're not clueless now," Sasha finally said.

Claire ran her fingertips along her mouth, still felt the press of his lips. "Am I making a mistake?"

"I'm not the one to deliver advice on personal relationships." Sasha made a turn off the freeway.

"That doesn't stop you from having an opinion."

When it seemed Sasha wasn't going to say anything, Claire pushed. "C'mon, Sasha. You're a sister to me."

That title had grown on the other woman in the past six years. When Claire used it, she usually got what she wanted.

"I was preoccupied at the time Cooper left for Europe. The time I spent overseas and the few occasions Cooper and I worked together, his questions centered on you. It was easy to deduce why. Him leaving was the right thing to do."

"I'm still not so sure about that."

"Time and wisdom will change that opinion," Sasha said.

"You still haven't said if you like the idea."

Sasha glanced over and a smile crested her lips.

That was all the approval Claire needed.

"Now, I have a question for you."

These moments with Sasha were rare. Claire ate them up. "Go for it."

"How is the sex?"

She blurted out a laugh. Not at all surprised about the question. If there was one thing Sasha had taught her, it was to be open about her sexuality and what her needs were. "I don't know."

"Excuse me?"

"We haven't." She cleared her throat. "Cooper wasn't lying when he said we had done nothing to create suspicion. In fact, tonight was the first time we kissed."

Sasha was smiling. "And how was that?"

Claire curled up in the front seat. "Freaking amazing."

They pulled down the street that Claire needed to become more familiar with, very quickly. "What about Neil? What does he think?"

Sasha shook her head. "Neil is a man. And protective about you."

"He's not happy."

Sasha shrugged. "Let me know if Cooper is bruised tomorrow and I'll talk to him."

Claire lost her smile. "You don't really think he'd do—"

"I've brought him off a ledge more than once these past years. The man loves you as his own, even if he never says it."

That had unexpected tears filling the back of her eyes.

Gwen had told Claire that more than once, but to hear it from Sasha made it more real.

"Thanks, Sasha. We don't do this enough," Claire said.

"It appears that is about to change." Sasha turned the corner. Neither of them looked directly at the car that had a man watching in the shadows, but both of them saw it.

Sasha signaled a garage door opener with her phone.

"Burst out of the car and yell at me and slam the door into the house. Make sure he sees you but don't give him a target."

Claire smiled. "Showtime."

CHAPTER TWENTY-TWO

Leo Eastman lived in a gated apartment complex. Or at least, the man posing as Leo Eastman lived there. Lars followed Eastman until he pulled into the employee parking lot at the school. And Cooper took charge of planting a tracer on Eastman's car.

While Claire experienced her first day back in homeroom, the apartment above Eastman's experienced an unexpected odor that required a team to identify and fix the issue. By the time Claire was delivering her revised report on *Macbeth*, Eastman couldn't so much as burp in his apartment without someone at headquarters hearing or seeing it.

With a renewed desire to see the case find some resolution, Claire systematically spent time in the principal's and vice principal's offices, and Coach Bennett's classroom, long enough to plant an audio device in each of them.

By track practice, Claire was linked in and listening to clips of conversations.

Her first glimpse of Cooper was on the field. It took colossal effort to avoid searching him out and looking at him. But in doing so, she found a rhythm in watching everyone else.

The sprinters, which she was technically a part of, stayed together. They stretched together, ran together, and gossiped together. As age and grade tended to be a hierarchy, and only permeated by a younger student if their skills stood out, it was easy to identify the students like Marie Nickerson.

She texted Cooper from across the field, didn't look his way. **Find a way to make me run with the distance runners today.**

He didn't text back, but she could tell the message had been received.

Without shifting her routine, she joined the three girls she ran the relay with and started her warm-up stretches. The girls were talking about prom dresses and hairstyles. Considering Claire hadn't had a senior prom, she found herself wrapped up in their excitement, even though the prom was over two months away.

They moved from stretching to warm-up laps, and the conversation never stopped. "What about you, Claire? Anyone ask you yet?"

"Why does the guy have to ask?" she responded.

"Right? That's what I've been saying."

And so the conversation circled.

When they stopped to catch their breath, and the team started to segregate, Claire found herself face-to-face with Cooper for the first time since he reminded her what it felt like to be kissed. Thankfully she was flush from the run, and any blush while looking at him wouldn't look out of place.

She found herself squinting to see if there was in fact any bruising on the man.

Coach Bennett clasped his hands, Cooper at his side.

Bennett huddled them up. Most of them sat in the grass, stretching. "We're going to run full relays today. I want to see clean starts and smooth passes. The invitational is a week from Saturday, our first competition of the season. This will set the pace for the year. We have some strong teams. Solid teams. Chelsea, I want you taking Claire's place as anchor today."

A hush went over the group. Chelsea wasn't on their normal relay.

"Why?" Claire asked, speaking out.

Coach Bennett stared her down, his lips a thin line. "Because she needs to practice in case your English grade doesn't pull up and you let your teammates down."

Claire dropped her shoulders and looked at her team. "What do you want me to do, then?" she asked.

He pointed across the field. "Distance runners are doing a five-mile loop."

Several sprinters groaned.

"That sucks," one of the guys muttered. Sprinters hated distance runs.

One of the girls mouthed the word *sorry*.

Claire stood and dusted off her shorts. "No, it's fair," she said to them. She turned to Chelsea. "You totally got this." She extended her hand and fist-bumped the other girl.

"I can help you in English," Leah offered.

Bennett and Cooper exchanged smiles. "That's the kind of teamwork I like to see."

Claire took a few steps.

"And, Claire?" Coach Bennett said.

"Yeah?"

"Keep pace and come in pushing the leaders."

That she didn't expect. The back of the pack was where she wanted to be.

She turned and had to double her pace to catch up.

"Let's get to work." Cooper's words fueled her legs.

~

It didn't take long, or much, to catch up to the back of the pack. Most were sophomores and freshmen and built like beanpoles. The boys weren't shaving yet, and the girls had half a foot on the boys, which put many of them at perfect boob height.

She caught up with the first cluster, surprised them from the back. "Hey," she said.

"What are you doing?" Terrance was the kid she'd run through her first circuit with. He settled for distance.

"I'm failing English," she said, hoping to get them to talk, even a little.

"Really?"

"Currently. I mean, I won't."

The three other kids he ran with puffed out their chests, wore big smiles.

Okay, this won't work.

She picked up her pace. "See ya."

One of them said she was hot when he thought she was far enough away not to hear.

Up on a pack of girls. And that's how they ran, in a pack and chattering. Which meant they weren't in this run to do anything but finish it. "Hi." Claire jumped off the sidewalk to push into their group.

She tried to remember even one of their names, and found her mind blank. Claire made eye contact with one of the more heavyset girls. "You're, ah . . . I forgot your name."

"Melissa."

"Right, Melissa. We pass each other in, ah . . ."

"C building."

"Right."

"What are you doing?" Again, the questions came, the answers were the same.

The conversations were brief, but gave Claire what she was looking for. Before she sped up to the next group, she parted with "You know the guys behind you are just there to check out your asses, right?"

They all looked, laughed, and waved her off.

And so it went. As she inched her way to the leaders of the pack, she tried to make contact with all of them, especially the stragglers. The ones who ran alone, though there didn't seem to be many of them. Once they left the neighborhood surrounding the school, and onto some of the busier streets, the stoplights gave her a decent chance to catch up. They were on their last mile and she was certainly feeling it. It wasn't unlikely for her and Jax to go for long runs on the weekends, or hit an obstacle course for the fun of it, but she hadn't done any of those things since the Auburn-Bremerton operation had begun.

She and Jax had made a pact that they weren't going to be those women who lose their fitness level after they left Richter. And that course rivaled any boot camp Claire was familiar with. This five-mile run was telling her she and Jax needed to take it up a notch.

The last mile of the run she was up with the top varsity girls, who ran with purpose. Although they were still chatty.

"Good God, you guys do this every day?" Claire asked, pushing into the mix.

Her presence was met with surprise and a little less awe than from the younger classmates.

"This is a short run."

"Yeah, sometimes we do ten miles."

"That's ugly," Claire said.

"You must have pissed off Bennett." The girl talking was in her World Affairs class. Brianna. And from what Claire had witnessed, she'd be the one to beat for the two mile on the Auburn team.

"Good guess," Claire said.

There were three of them, and they all laughed.

"Do you run cross-country, too?" Claire asked them as a group.

They nodded.

"So you've been voluntarily running this shit for four years?" Claire's head started to tick. Marie had dropped out of school three years ago. One of them may have known her.

"It's an illness," Brianna said, laughing.

"You guys are crazy."

They chatted a bit.

"Have you always been on varsity, Brianna?"

She shook her head. "No, Bennett doesn't put lowerclassmen on varsity if they can't place with the older kids. Once I found my pace and strategy, I got better."

"What's that?"

"Stay at the top and skate until the last lap."

Claire looked ahead. Only varsity boys were in front.

"They don't count, huh?"

"Not at meets."

Claire saw the school in the distance, picked up her pace. "What about out here?"

"This isn't a race."

"I'll never understand distance runners."

Claire moved faster and found the other girls right on her heels.

The four of them ran up behind the guys, who weren't running to win, and pulled alongside.

"Hey," Claire acknowledged them.

"What are you doing out here?"

"Dying," Claire said between breaths. "Where is the damn finish line?"

"We come up the back side and stop midfield."

Claire knew this was going to hurt, but she did it anyway.

"Well, shit." She estimated they were a little more than a quarter mile to their destination, and she needed to make sure she ran with these guys again. "See you there."

It took some serious concentration and effort to keep her legs moving. But she did.

And right behind her, so did the rest of the varsity teams.

Her chest was on fire, her legs burned, but she put her body into the race, and when she turned the corner and saw the field, she stopped thinking altogether.

The rest of the track team that was wrapping up their day stopped and watched. There were nine of them from the distance run stretched out and hauling ass. As a rule, the distance runners didn't spend their endurance conditioning runs racing for fun. But there was laughter and jostling for first place. To make it better, some of the sprinters on the field started yelling her name, while others called out to their friends.

Two of the guys overshot her, as well as Brianna when they reached the fifty-yard line. By the time they reached the end of the grass, they were sucking in air like guppies out of water.

Claire walked in a circle, patting backs and giving high fives.

"You might want to save a little for the invitational," Bennett said, coming up behind them.

Claire braced both hands on her knees. "Your fault," she accused him. The sight of Cooper jogging over made her smile brighter. "You said to keep pace and come in pushing the leaders." Claire extended her arms. "Mission accomplished."

"You're giving me gray hair, Porter."

She laughed. "Looks like someone beat me to it."

He was shaking his head, but he was smiling. "All right, walk that off and get in a long stretch. I don't need any of you cramping up and getting hurt this early in the season."

Claire saluted him.

Cooper had a hand over his eyes, a smile on his face.

She knew he wanted to say something. Instead, he turned on his heel and walked away.

CHAPTER TWENTY-THREE

Cooper rolled into the shop early on Friday.

He knew Kyle was already there because of the monitoring system he'd put in place shortly after taking on the job.

In the shop, Kyle's Jeep was up on a lift, one of the wheels was off, and he was using a hammer with some serious aggression on the control arm. The usual pink box was missing, and the music hadn't been turned on. From the way Kyle was swinging the hammer, it was obvious something was wrong.

"What did the car do to deserve a beating?" Cooper asked, making his presence known.

Kyle rammed the hammer down two more times before tossing it on the floor with a loud bang. "Piece of shit. I don't know what I was thinking buying this."

Two of his seniors took that moment to walk in the shop. "What's up with you?" one of them asked.

Cooper reached for his wallet, pulled out a twenty-dollar bill. "Why don't you guys go grab some donuts?"

They took the hint and left, leaving Kyle and Cooper alone.

He gave Kyle a minute to calm down.

"You wanna tell me what this was all about?"

Kyle ran both hands through his hair. Took his time answering. "It's Elsie."

Cooper sighed. "Nothing will drive a man more crazy than a woman." When Kyle didn't elaborate, Cooper asked, "She break up with you?"

A shake of the head. "No. But I'm starting to think I need to break up with her."

"You guys seem tight."

Kyle grabbed a shop towel. "We were. Then she started hanging out with some new friends and she's changed."

"Changed how?"

Kyle sighed. "Suddenly her life sucks. She's complaining about her parents, acting like she's miserable. She wants to go out and party . . ." He glanced at Cooper as if he'd just told him something incriminating.

"I get it," Cooper said. "I was seventeen once, too."

"It's too much. When I go with her, she runs off with other people. I don't know . . . when I talk to her about it, she tells me I'm smothering her."

Cooper opened his mouth to respond, only to be cut off.

"She's tanking algebra, for the second year. I'm in physics, I could totally help her, but she'd rather see her tutor, who's probably trying to get in her pants."

Cooper was about to blow off the whole conversation as typical teenage drama.

"Her tutor?"

"Someone from Bremerton. Or used to go there. I don't know." Kyle turned to the tire on the ground, kicked it, and yelled, "Fuck."

Tony walked in through the shop door. "That doesn't sound good."

Cooper looked over. "Girl problems."

"Screw women. Cost too much."

That pulled a smile out of Kyle.

Cooper did a double take, saw Tony's profile, and paused.

"I think Elsie is cheating on me," Kyle told his friend.

"With who?"

When Kyle didn't answer, Cooper did. "Her tutor."

"The douche from Bremerton?"

"Yeah."

"That blows," Tony said.

The seniors came back with the donuts. One brought the change over to Cooper and dropped it in his hand. "Thanks."

When someone turned on the music, Cooper knew sharing time was over.

~

With trips to headquarters on hold, Claire and Sasha joined the team online. Their once-a-week meeting had now turned into an every-other-day update.

The faces of the team lit up on one monitor; the other was a story-board similar to the one in their main office with names and pictures.

Sasha and Claire sat at the living room table of their temporary home. They had headsets on and notes in front of them.

As the team slowly blipped online, their images popped up on-screen.

Claire waved at the camera when Jax appeared. "Hey, Yoda. You doing okay?"

"Yes. You know the asshole hasn't even called, hasn't even tried to change my mind."

"Proof he isn't the right guy."

Neil's image flickered before he disabled his camera.

Manuel joined in from headquarters along with Lars.

Finally, Cooper's face appeared. "Hi," he said to the group.

It was nice to look at him and not hold back her smile.

"Is Sasha here?" Jax asked.

"I am."

Claire tilted her laptop to bring Sasha into the frame.

Neil's voice boomed in her ear. "I want to keep this brief and organized. No extra chatter."

Claire held her hand over her mic, turned to Sasha. "Is he pissed?" Her words were a tiny whisper.

Sasha's lips were tight, her eyes reflected a lack of concern.

"Good. First up. The device by your front door is a camera. Limited range that activates with motion," Neil told them.

"Audio?" Claire asked.

"Not enough to pick up inside conversations. We're leaving it." Neil kept talking. "Is everyone looking at the map?"

Claire directed her attention to what was on the situation board.

After a series of affirmatives, he moved on. "We need to narrow this field of vision. Let's start with eliminations."

Jax started. "We can remove Cummings."

"Completely?"

"Make him a strikethrough for now. I see no evidence to spend any time or manpower on him. He may have a wandering eye, but there is no trace of anything else."

Someone on Neil's end updated the map as they spoke.

"Where are we with Russell?"

"I tagged his car. His movements are to school and back home with the occasional stop at a strip mall. There are two restaurants, a convenience store, nail salon, real estate office, and a mail location," Manuel informed them. He gave the address of the mall, and someone updated the situation board.

"Lars, let's find out if there are any city cameras we can tap into."

"Got it."

"More on Russell? Jax?" Neil kept things moving.

"There was a note on my car windshield today. I'm assuming it's from him." She held up the note that had been placed in a plastic bag.

"He says he needs a passport photo for my gift. And he put his space number where his car is parked in the senior lot."

"Good. Anyone else on your list we can eliminate, Jax?"

"No. Ally is still fluid. She knows a lot of people from both sides of town."

"Cooper, you're up," Neil directed.

Claire watched him as he spoke, his concentration on his task very focused.

"Couple of developments today and a possible new lead." A picture of the party Claire and Jax had attended popped up on the screen. "Everyone got that?"

A chorus of yeses was heard.

"His name is Tony Mazzeo. Twice a week, at Kyle's request, I open the shop early. Let the gearheads use the place. This guy is alumni. How old would you guess him to be?" he asked the group.

"Twenty-five."

"Twenty-three to twenty-eight" was Claire's guess.

"Nineteen," Cooper confirmed.

Claire looked closer. There was no way.

Even Sasha shook her head.

"He was a transfer in the last half of the year. More typical senior, only spent half a day on campus, a lot of time in auto. He is a friend to Kyle. A direct connection between Auburn and Bremerton since he was seen at this party."

"Every Auburn kid at that party has a connection," Claire argued.

"Do any of the other Auburn kids look this age? This doesn't smell right," Cooper added.

Tony's name and image moved to the top of the board.

"Anything else?" Neil asked.

"Elsie."

The girl's name had Claire listening closer.

"She may have a new boyfriend at Bremerton. She and Kyle have been fighting, and outside of the teenage drama part, a few things came up. She has a new group of friends, isn't acting herself, and this algebra tutor is being blamed by Kyle for the crack in their relationship."

The hair on Claire's neck started to stand up.

"The tutor and the new boyfriend are one and the same?" Manuel asked.

"I don't know if we can call him the new boyfriend, but yes."

Claire spoke up. "Can we pause here for a second? Jax, the night Ally and Elsie came over, did you tell Ally you needed help with algebra or—"

"No. The other way around. Ally said she was failing, I suggested the study date. The other day she said something about seeing a math tutor as well."

"Are we talking teachers or student tutors?" Neil asked.

Jax shook her head. "No idea. But that should be easy enough to uncover. Girls' night at Claire's house."

"Okay, Claire, you're up," Neil said.

"I can't eliminate anyone. My recon with Marie and the yearbooks didn't shed light on anything. Outside of the class photo and the cross-country photo, there was no mention of Marie Nickerson. Cooper arranged for me to run with that group today. It gave me time to look at the most vulnerable kids that match Marie Nickerson's personality. And it gave me connections to the girls that were on the team when Marie was at the school. I need to put in more legwork. That's about all I have right now," Claire concluded and sat back from the computer.

"Any change in Eastman's actions today?" Neil asked.

"No. I asked him if he had any new equations he needed help with so I could sleep in the rest of the week. He called me a smart-ass and I agreed. You'd never know he was in the yard planting a camera."

She heard Jax laughing and watched Cooper smile.

"Okay, Sasha . . ."

"Leonardo Eastman is the name on the lease agreement at the apartment. He appears to live alone, however, this two-bedroom apartment has a young boy's room with the appropriate toys. Either Eastman is an exceptional housekeeper for his son, or the boy hasn't visited in some time. The rest of the place is a mess."

"Hoarder status?"

Sasha moved her head into the frame of the camera. "Look up from your screen," Sasha told Cooper.

He did.

"That kind of a mess. We'll watch through the weekend and find an opportunity to get inside for a more thorough search next week."

"Do we have a landline tap?" Neil asked.

"No landline. But there is an alarm system. Nothing fancy."

"Okay."

"The prints on the glass from the party belong to a Brian Contreras, twenty-six years old. He's used several surnames, but Contreras appears to be the one he was born with. Has a rap sheet going back to when he was sixteen. Spent some time in juvenile hall, mainly drugs and gang affiliation. Only he's been off the police radar for close to four years."

"Leopards don't change their spots," Cooper said.

"What about Gorge?" Neil asked.

"The images we have from the party weren't good enough for a positive ID."

"And the content in the glasses?"

"Whiskey. Nothing else," Sasha reported.

"If there isn't any more new news . . ." Neil paused. "All right. At the invitational, I want as many players in this circle in the stands. I want to see movement. Who is interacting with who. Jax, try and make Russell pick up the photo in person. We'll have Lars and Isaac on the sidelines. Sasha, time to have a face-to-face with Eastman. Claire's concerned aunt only has time during the meet. Did the party after get canceled?" Neil asked.

"It was moved to tomorrow," Jax said. "That's the word from Ally."

"Any idea where or when?"

"That news drops on Instagram thirty minutes before it begins," Jax elaborated.

"You're starting to sound like Emma," Neil pointed out.

"By-product of going back to high school."

"You have to use their language to fit in," Claire reminded Neil.

"Okay. We'll have Jax show up when Sasha leaves for work. Make a point about going to a party where Eastman's bug can pick it up . . . see if Eastman makes any moves. As soon as the information is delivered, we'll mobilize. Any players we have on the board are our first priority. Any questions?"

The line was silent.

Claire found herself looking at Cooper's image on the screen. Wondered if he was smiling at her.

"Call in with any changes."

With Neil's final instructions, everyone disconnected the call.

CHAPTER TWENTY-FOUR

As soon as the online meeting was over, Cooper called Claire privately. It took three rings for her to pick up.

"Hi. Hold on." It sounded as if Claire had put her phone on a table and was talking to Sasha. Cooper listened to her voice, not understanding a word.

It took nearly a minute before Claire got back on the phone. "Sorry. My aunt and I need to go shopping and buy food we actually want to eat."

"Do you write all your shopping lists in Russian?"

She laughed. "No. But since Sasha's Russian is better than mine, I'm trying to use this alone time to my advantage."

"It sounds good to me," he said, a hum in his voice.

"Me speaking a different language does something for you?"

"I think I told you that."

"This is weird."

Cooper felt his smile slipping. "We're back to that?"

"No. I know headquarters is listening in."

He switched his phone to the other ear. "They only hear your voice."

"So only you can talk dirty?"

Suddenly Cooper's mind shot right there and that was all it took to have him shifting his hips in his seat and adjusting his jeans. "Are we going to talk dirty?"

"Not with Isaac listening."

With that image, the heat he'd started feeling had ice cubes raining down. "Probably a good call."

"Yeah."

"My mind didn't wander off of you all day."

"We're in the same boat."

He knew she wasn't going to be as verbal as she'd been in the past. Not with their colleagues listening. "I always knew kissing you was going to be spectacular, but my imagination didn't come close to the reality." He heard her breathing into the phone. Some of that warmth started to return to his bloodstream.

"It made me want to do it again . . . soon."

"Things are starting to turn in the case. I'm more than motivated to find a resolution."

"You're not even the one running five miles a day."

"Running off the frustration created by not being able to even look at you the way I want to might be a good idea."

"Well, okay, Coach. Maybe on Monday, instead of watching, you put on your running shoes and join us."

"Maybe I'll do that." *Not gonna happen.*

"Dare ya."

He moaned. "That's not fair." She knew he didn't duck and weave a dare.

"You think about that. I told Sasha I wouldn't be long. I'd like to get a decent night's sleep. Help make up for the tossing and turning I've been doing."

He liked to think he was the cause. *"Spreche mit dir morgen."*

"Talk to you tomorrow," she repeated in English. *"Gute Nacht."*

Cooper disconnected the call and stared at his phone. Three years out of the six he spent overseas learning a new language was paying off.

~

"Bring a backpack and skip the makeup. I told my aunt you broke up with your boyfriend and we were going to spend the weekend dissing guys and making plans for our summer." Claire stood outside the decoy condo in full view and earshot of Eastman's surveillance.

Jax was on the other end of the line. "I'll be there in twenty minutes."

"We'll have a good time." Claire lowered her voice. "Any word on where the party is yet?" They were both watching Instagram for the Bat Signal. Between Ally's feed and Sean's, they should have something within the hour.

"No."

"Soon as my aunt leaves, we'll get ready to bounce." Claire ignored the camera in the shrubs and walked back in the front door.

Sasha was decked out in her flight attendant uniform and had a suitcase at her feet.

Once Claire was out of range of Eastman hearing her, she addressed the team through her com link. "Anything on Eastman?"

Isaac reported back. "He stopped eating his microwave dinner and looks like he's preparing to leave his house."

Claire and Sasha looked to each other and smiled.

By the time Jax showed up at the front door, Eastman was parked up the street and huddled in his car.

"AJ is in position to follow Eastman. Sasha, you're clear to vacate." Neil spoke through their earpieces.

Jax had already moved to the single bathroom to change clothes and get party ready.

Claire stayed out of sight when Sasha left the condo, her eye on Instagram.

Outside, the sky had darkened, and the smell of rain sat ripe in the air.

Eastman didn't move.

All they waited on was the party details.

"Anything yet?" Neil asked twenty minutes later.

"Nothing," Claire reported.

Jax was texting Ally.

Claire was starting to think the party was a bust.

A ping on her phone had her looking at a direct message from Sean.

"Got it." Claire rattled off the address, and Jax looked it up on a map.

"Doesn't look residential."

"It's not," Neil told them. "We're en route."

"Right behind you."

Wearing skintight black leggings, a tiny halter, and a matching leather jacket, Claire slid on her ankle boots and grabbed the car keys.

Jax wore ripped black jeans and a sparkly gold sweater off the shoulder. The choker on her neck had a camera.

Claire would depend on her cell phone.

Together they pulled out of the driveway and headed toward the party.

"Eastman is three cars behind," AJ said from the back of the line.

Claire kept an eye on her rearview mirror while Jax gave directions.

Her cell phone rang right before they were getting on the freeway.

Elsie's name popped up on the screen.

"Hey, girl."

"Did you get the information about the party?"

"Yeah, Jax and I are headed there now."

"Can you swing by and pick me up?" Elsie asked.

"I thought Kyle was taking you."

"He's being a dick. Doesn't want to go."

Without any objection from the team, Claire consented.

"Okay. I'll be at your place in ten minutes." Claire moved into the left lane to make a U-turn.

"Park across the street and text me."

She hung up the phone and told the team the address she was headed toward.

"AJ, hold up on the side street during the pickup. We don't want Eastman seeing you."

"You got it."

With an eye on the rearview mirror, Claire noticed Eastman hang back when she turned into the quiet residential neighborhood.

When she parked, Eastman pulled into a driveway and killed his lights.

"Do you ever get the feeling we're playing cat and mouse?" Claire asked Jax.

"As long as we're the cats."

They laughed, texted Elsie, and waited.

Within a minute, Elsie bounced out of her house, a backpack in her hands.

She tossed the pack in the back seat and jumped inside. "Thank you so much."

She closed the door and Claire pulled away from the curb.

Jax swiveled around in her seat. "Did you have to sneak out?"

Elsie shook her head. "Told my parents we were gonna head to the mall, then have a sleepover. Hope that's okay."

"My aunt's gone, so you can stay over."

While they talked, Elsie was pulling her bulky sweater over her head. Under was a tight tank top, appropriate for a teenage party.

"What's up with you and Kyle?"

Elsie groaned. "He's acting strange. Totally bailed tonight. Which . . . whatever. He's a drag at these things. I'll have more fun without him." The girl kept in motion, different shoes came out of her backpack, and more makeup was put on her face.

Claire turned on the freeway. In her ear she heard Neil telling them the position of Eastman and AJ. The team was already at the venue. "Looks more like a rave than a house party. Lights and loud music. Signs indicate there's some kind of Hollywood movie shoot going on," Cooper reported.

"Do we know who's throwing the party?" Jax asked.

"Jim told me it was Brandon and Russell." Elsie applied a fire shade of red to her lips.

"Who is Jim?"

"My tutor. He goes to Bremerton. You might know him," Elsie told Jax. "Jim Cromer."

Jax shook her head. "Doesn't sound familiar."

"Total geek. I think he thinks if he can impress me with party information I'll hang out with him."

"How does the geek get all the good party info?" Claire asked. More for the team than for the girl in the back seat.

"He knows Russell. I think Russell tutors, too."

Claire and Jax exchanged glances. Seemed like some of the lines in their investigation were starting to cross.

"Jimmy Cromer. Senior at Bremerton. Honors student. Runs for Bremerton's track team. Distance. Never wins." Sasha's voice sounded in Claire's ear.

"Everyone knows someone," Claire said.

"I heard this party was going to be huge."

"She's not wrong," Cooper said.

Jax gave the last of the directions, and before long they found the movie-set markers posted on corner fences that wound around an industrial park.

"Holy shit." Elsie pushed up between the bucket seats of Claire's car as the venue came into view. Two blocks away and they could hear the music.

Cars were parked everywhere as kids flooded the party.

"Wow."

Claire parked the car, noticed when Eastman drove past with AJ on his tail.

The sky had started to drizzle misty drops, which had the girls walking faster toward the entrance of the party.

At the door, Claire took notice of two new male faces. They could pass for high school seniors, but her guess was early twenties.

The guys looked them up and down as they walked past.

Inside was a haze. Lights flashed from a small stage where a DJ was blasting music. People were dancing and carrying on.

The building itself was a corner shell of what looked like an industrial center, although the inside didn't look like it was being used for anything other than the party.

"This cost some serious money."

Elsie's eyes were open wide. "I had no idea."

"Does anyone look familiar?" Jax asked as they mashed through people.

"Not really," Elsie answered.

"Let's stick together," Jax suggested. Her eyes leveled with Claire and back to Elsie.

"Good idea. You guys drink if you like, I'm driving."

Elsie looked surprised. "You're not going to drink anything?"

"Not worth it."

They weaved in and out of the crowd and found a cooler filled with drinks. Jax and Elsie both grabbed a hard seltzer and they started to circulate.

"Need a mic check," Neil told them.

"I can barely hear myself think," Jax said over the music.

"Let's move toward the back, see if we find anyone we know," Claire replied.

They walked away from the music and searched the room for players.

~

Cooper's attention was tuned in to Claire's voice.

Unlike the house party, this one seemed to attract kids from every school in the district. At least three times the number of kids from before. And like Claire, he felt he was looking at an entirely new group of people.

Sasha had changed into black spandex, her hair pulled back in a sleek ponytail.

Neil sat at the monitors.

Manuel and Isaac were outside the van and scoping out the building.

"AJ, what's the status?" Neil asked.

"Eastman is sitting in his car, looks like a glow of a computer reflecting up at him."

"Back of the warehouse is a utility van," Isaac reported and then gave the license plate number.

Sasha reached for the door in the back of the van.

"What are you doing?" Cooper asked.

"The people throwing the party will have parked close to the entrance or exit. Let's run some plates and get some names."

Neil offered a nod, and Sasha slipped out the back.

Lars moved from his perch and sat beside Neil.

They took notice of Sasha's feed. Her camera focused at the level of the vehicle's license plates as she skirted around in the dark.

"Ally just sent a text, said she's on her way in." Jax's voice came in clear.

"Hey, guys." Cooper heard a male voice.

"Hi, Sean."

Jax's camera came into view.

Sean Fisher stood staring at Claire. Not that Cooper could blame him. Claire was seriously hot.

The unmistakable sound of Ally's high-pitched voice was heard in Claire's and Jax's microphones.

"Time to circulate," Neil probed. *"I want to see the faces of the people in charge."*

Neil watched the monitors, took screenshots.

As the images that Sasha took splashed through, Cooper and Lars typed them into the system and started generating names.

~

"This looks like something you'd do," Ally told Sean shortly after Neil told Claire and Jax to get moving.

"What do you mean?"

"Your parents have connections to movie sets. Seems like your kind of gig."

Claire watched as Sean shook his head. "This isn't a set. This is a great way to stop people driving by from asking questions. I doubt the cops will show and break this party up."

"Ingenious, if you ask me," Claire found herself saying.

"Elsie?"

Claire turned to find Tony Mazzeo pushing through their circle.

"Hi, Tony."

"Where's Kyle?"

"He didn't want to come."

Claire saw Jax turn toward Tony, her choker aimed his way.

"That's too bad," Tony said. His gaze moved a little too slowly over Elsie's frame. "He's missing out."

Jax must have sensed the same ick feeling that ran through Claire because Jax moved in closer.

"Who's this?" Tony asked.

"I'm Jax," she said, her shy smile in place.

Claire wanted to laugh. Jax had a way of putting on the innocent look but could strike faster than a pissed-off rattlesnake if someone got too close.

"You ladies look amazing."

Claire noticed Sean turn away with a shake of his head.

At the same time, someone walked behind Claire, and she felt fingertips glide over her ass.

As snakes strike, she twisted toward the person behind the fingers, a beefy hand in her grasp.

Her eyes met her startled accoster.

He was big, as in he hit the gym kind of big. Early twenties.

"I'm sorry, you must have mistaken my ass for someone else's," she said as she twisted his wrist until he had no choice but to move back to stop the pain.

Sean stepped toward him. "What do you think you're doing?"

"Let him go, Claire," she heard Neil in her ear.

She released the guy's hand.

"Sorry."

Claire stepped back. "I'm sure you are."

The guy disappeared into the crowd.

Ally was laughing. "Did he just grab your ass?"

Claire shrugged.

Tony's eyes met hers. "Have we met?"

She shook her head.

"This is Claire," Elsie said. "Tony is a friend of Kyle's."

Tony looked beyond her. "Lots of ass grabbing going on in here. I wouldn't take it personally."

"That's totally not cool, Tony," Sean spoke up.

"Looks like your girlfriend here can take care of herself," Tony said.

Claire didn't correct him, waited for what he was going to say next.

Tony looked left and right. "You guys have fun." He started walking away, stopped at Claire's side. "Try not to hurt anyone."

He walked away.

Sean blew out a breath. "I hate that guy."

"Who is he?" Jax asked.

"He graduated from Auburn last year," Elsie explained.

"You're kidding? What was he, on his fifth senior year and someone finally gave him a free pass?" Ally spoke up.

Claire and Jax looked at each other.

"Guy's a douche."

"I can't disagree, but why do you think that?" Claire asked.

Sean shrugged. "I used to score some pot from my dad's stash. Sold him some last year, then he kept asking if I could get other stuff. Pushy. And Ally's right, the guy doesn't act like us. Rubs me wrong."

Ally moved closer to Sean. "Cool how you stuck up for Claire."

Sean put an arm over Ally's shoulder and the other around Claire's. "I'm the only guy here, I gotta watch out for you girls."

Hours later, after Elsie and Ally had one too many, and Claire and Jax couldn't find Russell or Brandon . . . or any of the players from the first party, it was time to go.

Sean had buddied up with a couple of his friends and waved them off.

Claire drove Ally home, aware that Eastman had stayed the course and was still following behind.

She dropped Ally off at the street, and waited for her to sneak back in.

Once she texted from the inside, Claire pulled away.

At the condo, Claire gave her bed to Elsie, who was half-asleep in the car. As soon as her head hit the pillow, the girl was out.

Claire went through the motions of finding a waste bin in case Elsie woke up sick. She put a bottle of water by the bedside with two painkillers next to it.

She and Jax moved into the living room, closing the door behind them.

"Okay, guys. Talk to us."

"Eastman waited for the garage door to close and left. Appears he's headed home," Cooper reported.

"Any sign of the party throwers?" Jax asked.

"None."

"That's odd, isn't it?"

"We have a lot of plates to run. Need to put them next to the school rosters. We have to assume most of the cars are in parent names."

"Get some sleep," she heard Neil tell them. *"We'll have more tomorrow."*

Claire put two thumbs up in the air and stared at the camera hidden on a shelf.

She and Jax both pulled their earpieces out.

"This party felt completely different from the other one," Jax said.

Claire looked down the hall. "A lot of drunk girls."

"And only a few drunk guys."

"Lots of grinding on the dance floor, sex in the dark corners. Unsupervised high school party?" Claire asked in a whisper.

"Half high school, half twentysomethings."

Claire agreed with a yawn. "Take Sasha's bed. I'll take the couch."

"It's a big bed, I won't cuddle," Jax teased.

"One of us should be out here in case Elsie thinks she should sneak out."

Jax nodded and unfolded from the sofa. "'Night, Loki."

After taking turns in the bathroom, Claire curled up with a pillow and a blanket.

Cooper had sent a text.

Sean has a crush on you.

She laid her head down. I like older men, she texted back.

Get some sleep. You look exhausted.

She stared at the camera. Are you still watching me?

Does that make me a voyeur?

Only if I were naked.

The three dots scowled on the screen for several seconds.

If I ever have the pleasure of seeing you naked, I want to be at your side, not miles away.

Claire felt heat in her cheeks and a smile on her lips. She started to type when he sent another quick text.

I love that smile.

She waved a finger at the camera.

Night relief walked in. I'm headed home so don't make kissy lips at the camera.

Claire giggled quietly. Good night.

CHAPTER TWENTY-FIVE

Monday rolled around, and both Jax and Claire skipped school and spent the time at headquarters combing through pictures and names. The party had bumped up Tony's name on their board and dragged Sean's closer to the bottom.

The location of the weekend blowout was owned by an out-of-state corporation, who, when called, stated they had no idea that their empty building had been used for a party.

The DJ owned the utility van that had been parked behind the building, and from what the team had surmised, his presence at the party was nothing more than paid entertainment. And since they didn't find any recent checks added to the DJ's bank account, they assumed he'd been paid in cash.

Claire found herself staring at Marie's mug shot and her class schedule before she disappeared. The investigation of her family indicated they'd moved from the apartment shortly after the girl went missing.

"There's always a possibility that the party was exactly what it looked like. A rave set up by rich kids to celebrate life," Jax pointed out when they'd come to a lot of dead ends.

"Yet the rich kids didn't show up. Or if they were there, they were hidden in the shadows. That doesn't ring true," Claire said.

"I'm going to meet this Jim Cromer tomorrow. Hang out in the stands during track practice."

"He's the only lead we really got."

"Better than nothing," Jax said.

They were the only two in the situation room at headquarters. They left notes for the rest of the team and on the direction they were going as they rolled into the next week.

The next time the entire team would be rallied was Saturday. If Jax was needed off campus, she could bail. Claire, on the other hand, wouldn't be able to run at the invitational if she missed any more school.

～

On Tuesday, Claire walked into her "lunch date" with Bennett. The same one she'd had every school day since he moved her into his class. He would sit at his desk, eating. She sat at hers doing the homework she didn't bother with the night before.

She pulled a book from the shelf, plopped it on her desk, and wandered over to the pictures of previous track and cross-country teams that were tacked on the walls.

"How did you feel after your workout with the distance team?" was how Coach Bennett greeted her.

"Not bad, actually. You should try it sometime." She found the picture that had Marie Nickerson in it.

"Are you always a smart-ass?"

She looked over her shoulder and smiled. "I save it for you and Mr. Eastman."

He full-on laughed. "So you're giving Mrs. Wallace a breather."

She groaned. "That woman should move to Stratford-upon-Avon and call it done." She searched out Brianna and then looked for the previous year to see if she recognized her. The image of what Marie looked like in her mug shot kept flashing in her mind. The woman looked thirty now and not nineteen.

"Are you going to open that book?"

"Hmm, yeah, sure," she said, distracted. "Hey, Coach. Do you remember all of the kids in these pictures?"

"Most," he said.

"Okay, who is this?" she asked, pointing to a random kid in a random year.

He moved from behind his desk and put on his glasses. "Dan Corsaletti. Pole vault."

"Oh, yeah? What about this little dude?"

"Patrick Durby." The coach moved to a group shot three years later. "Here he is, senior year."

Claire looked twice. "Damn. He found a membership at Gold's Gym."

"It's crazy how much you guys change in the four years you're here."

"What about her?" Claire pointed to Marie.

He peered closer. "Uhm . . ."

"Aha!"

"No, now wait, it's coming. Marie Nickerson? She wasn't on the team long. A year or two, I think."

Claire shrugged, watched him from the corner of her eye. "You could totally be lying to me."

"Like the way you lie to me?" he asked.

It took everything in Claire to keep from changing her expression. "What do you mean?"

"You told me you weren't a distance runner."

Oh, thank God. "Oh, that?"

"Is there something else you're lying about?"

She rolled her eyes. "I'm the smart-ass, never can tell."

He tapped her book as he walked back to his desk.

She moved to sit down. "Do you tutor all the track kids that need it?"

He laughed. "This isn't tutoring. This is babysitting."

"So if someone needed a tutor, who would you send them to?"

He put his glasses back on and pulled a stack of papers in front of him. "I don't think you need a tutor. You need discipline."

"Okay, fine . . . but who tutors?"

He wrote something on the paper in red ink, flipped to the next one. "Dunnan is in charge of the tutors. I'm too busy with track."

"What does it take to be a tutor?"

He looked up and dropped his hand on the papers, completely annoyed. "You have to pass the class and show the ability to problem solve."

"Does it pay? Like real money?"

"Yeah. Not a ton, but it's a good way to work and go to school."

Claire slapped her hands together and gave them a firm rub. "Okay, then. Let's do this."

"Let's do what?"

"Pass the class. Give me your final."

He narrowed his eyes, took his glasses off slowly. "What are you talking about?"

"Listen. My aunt said that if I pass all my classes and stay out of trouble, she'd let me backpack through Europe for six months after I graduate. I need to make some cash so I have more than ten euros a day to spend."

"You're serious?"

She folded her hands and blinked several times as if a halo suddenly appeared over her head.

"Listen, Claire, even if you did pass my final, which I doubt can happen since we haven't covered the material yet, I can't just let you out of the class."

"I'm not asking to leave the class. But I can skip all this labor." She pointed to the book. "And take that off your hands." She glanced at the stack of papers he was grading. "I'll be your TA and maybe you can leave campus for lunch once in a while and eat more than a soggy sandwich with processed cheese. That stuff will kill ya, you know."

"You sound like my wife."

She cringed.

He nodded a few times, rolled his chair closer to his computer. "All right, Miss Smart-ass." Glasses went back over his eyes, and within a few seconds he was printing out a test.

He walked over to her desk, papers in hand.

She reached for them. He held them back. "You need an A."

"B."

"B+. And show your work."

He put her in a solo desk in the front of the room. She had an hour and a half to complete the test.

Bennett set a timer and sat back down.

Claire went to work.

When the class bell rang, the room filled up, but she stayed focused on the test. The idea to infiltrate the tutor pool had come to her after she and Sasha had returned from the grocery store. The badass attitude got her into the party crowd, but the kickass student gave her access to whatever was happening in that world. So instead of catching up on that sleep she told Cooper she needed, she spent most of the night refreshing her brain on the more complicated math problems she'd see in a test.

Coach Bennett's voice and instructions to the room full of kids became a hypnotic background noise.

Three minutes before the bell, Claire double-checked her work and waited.

As the kids ran off to their next hour of torture, Claire took her test to Bennett.

"Here."

"You still have time."

She shook her head, grabbed her backpack. "I'm good. Those last two bonus questions had me. I took a stab at 'em."

Bennett flipped to the last page. "I'll give it a look, tell you how you did after Saturday's invitational."

"You can't tell me tomorrow?"

Bennett stared at her. "Has anyone ever told you that you lack patience?"

"That's torture."

"Try meditation. It works."

$\sim$

Friday morning was met with donuts and Kyle.

Tony didn't show.

Cooper spent extra time in the teacher's lounge, talked with some of the staff.

The only employee that drew his attention was Leo Eastman.

Cooper arrived to practice in track pants and running shoes.

He saw Claire walk on the field, noticed the new attention she received from the distance runners on the team. She gravitated toward the sprinters, and smiled when she saw him.

She sat on the field, put one leg out in front of her, and started stretching. She looked him up and down. "What's this, Coach? You plan on running today?"

"Since practice is minimal, and only meant to keep you limber and ready for tomorrow, I thought I'd run off some of the cobwebs."

He received a sufficient amount of teasing from the smaller group, but hit the track with them anyway.

He purposely stayed out of Claire's orbit until the second lap.

"How are you feeling about tomorrow's meet?"

"I think I'm ready."

"Should be a good start to the season," one of the varsity guys said from the other side of Claire.

"It's my track-meet cherry about to get popped."

Cooper was pretty sure the kid on her left wasn't expecting that.

Claire glanced over, grinned. "Sorry, guess I'm a little nervous."

He found his inner coach. "Just run fast and don't get hurt."

"Run fast. Don't get hurt. Maybe you should have said that before today," Claire teased and started to run faster. "It's only four laps, right?"

Ah, damn.

He had no choice but to keep up, even though he wouldn't mind staying right where he was. Behind her watching her butt as she rounded the corner.

She set the pace, and everyone stayed with her.

With one lap left she went a little faster, but nothing crazy. Watching her was like watching a racehorse stuck on a lead rope.

At the end of their mile run, Claire gave him a once-over. "I guess you still have it in you . . . for an old guy."

"She got ya there, Coach."

One of the guys put an arm over his shoulders. "Gonna happen to all of us."

Claire was ear-to-ear smiles.

His heart twisted the way it always did when her eyes sparkled with that smile.

They both looked away at the same time.

Laughter slowly faded as they met up with the rest of the team. Coach Bennett gave them the details for the invitational. The entire team was expected to show up even if they weren't competing. That included the JV team. They talked everything from uniforms to what they needed to eat for dinner. "And don't even think of going to a party. I will smell it and your performance will suffer."

There were a few snickers.

"That party was canceled, Coach. We're good," Claire smarted off.

Cooper laughed, placed a hand over his mouth to try and keep it together.

Even Bennett chuckled. "All right. That's all for today. Report to your coaches when you get here. You have to sign in a half an hour before your event. Late arrivals are scratched."

Cooper watched the team as they exited the field. His eyes found Claire and lingered only for a few seconds. He huddled with the coaches, talked out a few details. ". . . and, Coach Mitchel, the kids seem to really respond to you. Your call on Claire Porter was spot-on. She has some real potential. Good coaching keeps 'em on track. I hope you'll consider coming back again next year. The team could use you."

Guilt bit him in the back of that praise. "I'll consider it," he told the man.

He thanked everyone for their time and they broke up.

Bennett walked over and shook Cooper's hand. "I hope you do."

"I will."

Bennett grabbed his duffel bag, tossed it over his shoulder. "You'll never guess what the track smart-ass did this week."

"You mean Claire."

"Yeah."

"You didn't pull her off the roster for tomorrow, so I'm guessing it wasn't that bad."

"She challenged me to take the final in my class so she can get out of the homework."

"What? Did you give it to her?"

"I did. She tossed it at me, said the bonus questions were hard."

Cooper could picture the exact look she'd use saying those words. "And?"

"I looked at the bonus questions first. Damn if she didn't get them right."

"That's a good thing."

Bennett shook his head. "They were calculus equations. If my students attempt them, I give them credit. I don't expect anyone to get them right."

"And the rest of the test?" Cooper asked.

"I graded it Tuesday night. Nearly perfect, but I'm not telling her until after tomorrow."

Claire had mentioned a couple of times during the week that she was anxious to get moving on the tutor angle.

"Making sure she runs tomorrow?" Cooper asked.

"There's a lot of energy in these stands. Gives the kids that extra kick and excitement they don't get during practice. I want her hooked on the sport. I get the feeling she didn't really want to be here when she first started. Now that seems to have changed."

"I guess we don't need to worry about her having an academic probation keeping her off the field," Cooper said.

"Tomorrow's a madhouse. If you see her parents, let 'em know I'd like to talk to them at some point. Wait, she lives with her aunt."

"I think so."

"Either way. I'd like to talk Claire into going to college. Track coaches will want her. She might have to miss a season until she earns a foreign language credit—"

Cooper covered his sudden laugh, turned it into a cough. "Bug," he said, swallowing. "If I see her, I'll let her know you'll be getting in touch."

They shook hands. "It's a long, hot day tomorrow. Bring a hat."

CHAPTER
TWENTY-SIX

Jax stood at the fence line of the track while the crowd started to fill the stands. Over twenty schools were competing and could be told apart by the different colors on the uniforms. For the first time in a week, Jax saw Claire in person and not in a Zoom meeting.

She waved her over and gave her a hug. "Geez, could those shorts be any shorter?" Jax teased.

"Sasha approved them."

They both laughed. "I bet she did. Have you seen Elsie?"

"No. But I haven't seen anyone yet."

"Who's coming?"

"Elsie said she'd meet me down here. Ally said she'd be here at nine."

"And Russell?"

"Not completely sure." She'd left a note on the car saying that school security was watching like a hawk and she didn't want to get anyone in trouble.

"I can come up and sit with you between races. But no student cell phones out here." Claire looked left and right. "The coaches have phones."

Jax was careful not to say anything about the case. People were everywhere. "I don't think I expected this big of a crowd."

"Me either."

The announcer's voice boomed over the PA system, welcoming the runners and their families.

Claire looked down the field. "My coach is hot, huh?"

Jax laughed. "A bit old for you."

"Maybe." Claire turned back. "Nice necklace."

Jax played with the camera around her neck. "Thanks. My earrings didn't match with this outfit." She tilted her head to show Claire she didn't have a mic.

"They're too dressy for this." She started to bounce. "Okay, I see them calling us over."

"Do awesome." Jax put her fist out, bumped Claire's.

Jax stayed where she was and looked around. Her cell phone rang. "One is behind you, halfway up on the left. Two is photographing on the other side of the field," Neil said over the line. "Three is in the office."

She ducked her head. "I told you I was going to a track meet, Dad." Lars was holding a camera and standing several yards away. Isaac sat in the stands.

"It's hard to hear you when the announcer is talking. Leave your hat on. Take it off only if there's trouble."

Jax adjusted the rim of her ball cap.

"Four is holding back and will initiate contact."

"Fine, but I don't know how long this is going to take."

"We're clear."

"Fine," Jax said to an empty line.

She was about to text Elsie to see where she was when the girl ran up to her. "Hey, hey."

"I was worried you were going to bail," Jax told her, giving her a hug.

"No way. We have to see our girl race."

They made their way up the stands, smack in the middle, and took a seat.

~

The stands kept filling up.

Cooper was shocked.

Claire stood beside him staring with the same amazement in her eyes. "I would expect this for a football game."

"It's only because it's an invitational," Chelsea told them. "Next week's meet will only have two sets of parental support. And many of them leave the second their kid is done with their event."

Cooper turned back to his sprinters. "All right, guys, if you haven't warmed up, get on it." They took the hint and started to move to the center of the field.

~

The first time the starting gun went off, Claire flinched and stopped herself from taking a protective stance.

The crowd in the stands was cheering and yelling out school and student names. The energy on the field went up a thousand percent.

Every corner was filled with activity.

For Claire, there was nothing to do but wait for her heats. One for the eight-hundred-meter relay and one for the one-hundred-meter sprint. Both were spread out far enough to where she had plenty of downtime. She had an hour before her first race, and since Cooper was highly involved with the sprinters, he was between the start and the finish line coaching.

She marked the positions of her primary team even though she couldn't communicate with them at all on the field.

Jax was in the stands with Elsie at her side. No sign of Ally.

Claire made eye contact with Sasha and was waiting for her signal to leave the field to join her.

When the signal came, she took a swig from her water bottle and dropped it on top of her backpack. She walked past her teammates who were lining up to run. "C'mon, Miller. You got this."

She hopped over the three-foot chain-link fence and walked over to her "aunt."

"I see you dressed down for this," Claire teased.

Sasha smiled and, in a very American accent, said, "This is as casual as I get."

She wore dress pants that billowed in the wind. The kind of high waist fit that only the long-legged, lean woman could pull off. Her white blouse was just as stylish. Her sleek black hair was pulled back in a ponytail, her large-rimmed sunglasses a signature to her outdoor look.

If there was something about Sasha that impressed her from the beginning, it was how effortless she made every outfit look.

Behind Sasha, Eastman was looking their way.

Claire waited until he was close enough to hear. "I'm surprised you made it."

"I told you I would and here I am."

Claire turned her look to Eastman, then glared at Sasha.

"Hello, Miss Porter," Eastman said, smiling.

"Out for a stroll and stumbled back to school on a Saturday, Mr. Eastman?" Claire asked.

"School event," he said, opening his arms to the field. "And I am a schoolteacher. I always want to support my students."

"Are you telling me there is no coincidence that you make time to come," Claire said as she pointed at Sasha. "And you show up to a track meet?"

Sasha removed her sunglasses. "Don't be ridiculous and stop being rude. I called Mr. Eastman since those parent-teacher nights never seem to match with my schedule."

"I told you I was doing fine."

"Which is exactly what you said at your last school. And now we're here." Sasha turned and extended a hand. "I'm Sasha, Claire's aunt and guardian."

"Well, tell her how I'm doing," Claire challenged Eastman.

Eastman stared directly in her eyes. "Other than the obvious chip on her shoulder, Claire has made some significant improvements."

"See!"

Sasha kept a straight face. "Fabulous. Now don't you have to go run or something?"

Claire rolled her eyes and worked her way back onto the field.

The starting gun shot again, and the crowd cheered.

~

"Ally's not coming," Jax told Elsie after reading her text.

"What? Why?"

"She said she got busted last night after getting back from a party."

"What party?" Elsie asked.

Jax shook her head, started to text her that very question.

The announcer went through a series of calls, running down the stats of the athletes on the field. When Claire's name was mentioned, Jax put her phone down to watch.

"Eeeek, here she comes."

Jax looked around the stands to see who had cameras pointed at the runners. Not that it mattered; there were many athletes and no idea who was watching who. Jax went ahead and turned her camera to video mode to show Claire later.

CHAPTER
TWENTY-SEVEN

There were five heats for the one-hundred-meter sprints. Even if she came in first for this one, there was no way of knowing if another heat's winner was faster. Not until they were all over. The starting gun went off for the group in front of hers. She jumped up and down a few times, swinging her arms.

Cooper stood at the finish line.

Sasha watched from the fence, Mr. Eastman at her side.

Her teammates were staggered along the inside field.

The girls she ran the relay with were at the start. "Hey, Claire," one of them called out.

She looked over.

"Run fast and don't get hurt!" the three of them all yelled at the same time.

"Runners line up," the ref told them.

Claire positioned her blocks in the fourth lane to her settings, dug her spikes in the ground, and crouched to her starting stance.

She stared down the lane, her focus on the finish line.

The noise in the stands faded, and her heartbeat sped up with anticipation.

The gun fired and she ran.

Names were shouted, hers in the mix.

She didn't look left, didn't look right. Everything was blocked out but the goal.

The race was over in seconds and Claire was across the line, not letting up until she ran out of room.

Catching her breath, she shook the hands of the runners in her heat and walked onto the grass, nearly getting tackled by her girls.

"Oh my God."

"You smoked 'em."

She hadn't noticed who crossed the line first because she simply didn't look.

Cooper jogged up to her, shaking his head with a huge smile.

"How did I do?"

He pointed to the digital score. She saw her name, and her time, right in the first spot.

She acted like an excited athlete and hugged her coach. It was the first contact she'd had with him in a week and she wanted to linger.

"Now that's how you win a race, Porter." Coach Bennett came up beside them, and she gave the older man a hug, too.

"That's number-one smart-ass to you."

Bennett didn't stay long. "I wanna see that again in the relay," he told her before walking off to another event.

"Rest up, walk it off, and don't eat anything heavy," Cooper told Claire and the others before walking away.

She looked over to where Sasha was standing and waved.

Sasha gave her a thumbs-up, and then pointed to her watch.

Claire nodded.

"Who is that?" Chelsea asked.

"My aunt."

"You don't look anything alike."

"Adoptions work like that."

She noticed the other girls looking at each other.

"Is she leaving?" Leah asked.

"She's a flight attendant and has to fly out tonight."

As Sasha walked out of the stadium, Claire watched Eastman follow her.

"That's super cool. Do you get to fly anywhere you want?" Claire wasn't sure who asked the question.

"Only if she's in the mood."

Behind Eastman, Isaac slipped out of the stands and followed him.

At her backpack, she plopped on the ground and changed out of her spikes and into her running shoes. With Eastman out of the stands, it was time for Claire to check in with Jax.

Before she ran off, she cheered on the rest of the girls running the one hundred before making her excuses. "I'm going to say hi to some friends."

Jax and Elsie met Claire at the bottom of the stands.

"You were wicked fast," Elsie exclaimed.

"I think you came in second overall," Jax told her.

"Are you guys having fun?"

"I'm gonna be honest," Elsie said. "It's a lot more exciting than I thought it would be."

"Where's Ally?" Claire asked.

"She was grounded." Jax shrugged.

"That bites."

"Do you want to see what they have at the snack bar?" Elsie suggested.

"Sure."

They weaved through the crowd, and Elsie started telling Claire about her boy problems.

". . . I was telling Jax that he stopped wanting to do what I want to do. I kinda wanna break up with him, but then what happens with prom?"

"He totally bailed on last week's party," Claire said.

"He was pissed that I went without him. What does he expect? That I just stay home when he doesn't want to go out? He's the one that's going to be in a dorm in August, probably join a frat or something. I bet he goes to a ton of parties and won't ask me to go."

They turned toward the concession stand and took their place in line. "I left my money in my backpack," Claire told Jax.

"I got ya. You can pay me back later."

"Jax?"

They all turned to her name being called.

Claire recognized him right away. "It's Brian, right?"

"Yeah."

"What are you doing here?" Jax asked.

Brian looked around, checked out the kids standing in line behind them. "I had to pick something up. Milo told me you'd be here, asked if I'd help out."

Jax acted surprised. "Oh, yeah." She reached into a side pocket of her purse and pulled out an envelope.

Brian handed her a card. "Milo told me to give you his number, make it easier."

"This is really cool. Thanks." Jax put the paper in her back pocket. "I thought I'd see you guys last weekend."

"We took off early. We like things smaller," he told them.

"It was a lot of fun," Elsie told him.

Brian smiled at Elsie, a flirty lift in his eyes. "You were there?"

"Yeah, it was great."

"Maybe next time I'll stick around longer."

Claire kinda wanted to puke.

He started backing away.

"Thank Milo again for me," Jax said.

"I will. He said he's really looking forward to seeing you."

Jax put on the appropriate excited female smile one manages when she's just heard the cute boy wants her number. "Tell him I said hi," Jax called out to Brian as he walked away.

The line inched up and someone bumped Claire from behind as they were trying to get past.

She glanced around and saw Lars following Brian.

~

Cooper watched with anticipation as Claire's next race set up to run.

He knew she wanted nothing to do with screwing up the other girls' chances at medals and titles. And no matter if she blew it on purpose, or helped them win, they couldn't claim the prize once this case was over. She'd told him earlier that she'd rather watch them smile now and deal with the fallout later. Maybe they'd understand.

Cooper liked to think they would.

The gun went off and the race began. Everything looked textbook, until the second baton was passed. Fifty meters in and Leah managed to miss a step and went down.

Cooper started toward her, but the girl jumped back up and started to run, only now she was limping, in obvious pain.

Cooper heard the announcer over the PA mention an issue on the field. But Leah kept going until she crossed the line. Claire hesitated, but the team yelled at her to go, which was how they trained.

Claire took off to finish the race.

The team swarmed Leah in seconds.

"Let me in." Cooper shoved through, crouched down to her level. "Where does it hurt?"

"My ankle." Leah had tears in her eyes.

Cooper reached down, gave it a gentle poke.

She jumped.

"Do you think you can stand?"

She nodded yes, and he and one of the students helped her to her feet.

Claire came running up behind him, hand on his shoulder. "Is she okay?"

Leah tried to put weight on her ankle and buckled.

Cooper bent down, lifted the girl into his arms, and walked her off the field. He heard the crowd and the concern of the announcer.

"What happened to *run fast and don't get hurt*?" Claire tried to tease her.

Leah laughed through her tears.

"Do you think it's broken, Coach?"

"I left my X-ray vision and my Superman cape at home. But my guess is it's a sprain."

Leah laughed a little more.

Cooper found Claire's eyes and caught her smile.

They settled in the first aid tent where Leah's parents rushed to her side.

Bennett showed up and told her not to worry, she'd be running again before the season was over. Even Cooper knew that was a long shot.

He stayed with her while they iced and bandaged her ankle. Claire and her relay team did a good job of distracting her. Once they'd done all they could, Leah's dad took over, picked her up, and left to find an urgent care.

Claire walked with Cooper back onto the field. "That sucks," Claire muttered.

"Sure does. She's good and this is her senior year."

"You're a softy," she told him.

"Coach Mitchel?"

He turned to see the coach from Bremerton walking toward him.

They shook hands. "Sorry to see your runner go down."

"I think she's all right."

"You seem to have a knack for this coaching thing." The other man smiled and patted him on the back.

"It's certainly growing on me."

"And this one." The coach looked at Claire. "You're pretty fast, young lady."

"Claire, this is the coach from Bremerton. Coach Dale . . . Sorry, I forgot your last name."

Dale waved him off. "No worries. Coach Dale works."

"Hi," Claire said.

"Keep running like that and I'll see you at state." He said goodbye and walked back to his team.

Cooper's phone buzzed with a text from Neil. How is the kid?

He turned the message for Claire to read.

"You guys are *all* softies."

"Okay, let's finish this up. Go out there and get those distance runners motivated."

Claire turned to leave, and it took everything in him not to slap her butt as she went.

~

Claire and Jax left the school together and sat in on a conference call while they drove to their Tarzana home.

"Just the bullet points, team. It's been a long day for all of us. There's a full report in your inboxes." Neil took a breath and continued. "Eastman kept the conversation with Sasha Claire-centric. Nothing incriminating. The entire conversation is on audio file for you to go over. When Sasha left the school, Eastman followed her like he'd been trained to do so. She drove home, changed, and left for her long haul with a layover. Eastman then followed her to the airport until she turned into the extended stay parking lot. He waited for over an hour before he left. As you will hear in the audio file, Sasha set up that Claire was spending the long weekend with a friend until she came home."

Claire turned to Jax. "Yes!" she said in a forceful whisper. She couldn't wait to sleep in her own bed.

"Isaac followed Brian to the strip mall where he disappeared inside a mailbox location and stayed for two hours. He left with Gorge and continued to the Sanders home, where they're still located."

"Any other activity at that house we should know about?"

"Nothing that isn't expected. We've planted a front driveway surveillance camera for now and will increase if needed."

Claire rolled her head back in her seat, thankful Jax was driving.

"Any new details on your end that we may have missed?" Neil asked.

"You saw what I did all day," Cooper said from his car.

"Claire?"

"I played high school athlete. Nothing new on the field."

"Jax, your audio wasn't ideal. We will change the setup in the future. Anything to report?"

"Elsie wants to break up with her boyfriend, but is afraid she won't have a prom date." Jax turned to Claire and giggled. "I asked her about algebra and her tutor, but she didn't offer a name. I'm not sure if that was by design or indifference. Ally was grounded for a party she went to the night before. When I started asking about the party, her grandmother got on her phone and said Ally's phone privileges were revoked until further notice. I'll get more information when we're back in school."

"Okay . . ."

Claire waited for the words *Have a nice weekend.*

"Jax, enjoy your weekend."

"Oh, no." All Claire wanted right now was a stiff drink, a bathtub, and a good night's sleep.

"Claire, Cooper, there is a five a.m. charter flight at LAX with your names on it."

Suddenly sleep didn't sound so needed. "The Bahamas?" Claire asked.

Neil was silent when he was annoyed.

Claire filled that silence with images of a beach and sand . . . and Cooper finding second base.

"Seattle. Marie Nickerson showed back up."

The Bahamas dream would have to wait. Claire sat forward. "Is she in jail?"

"She's in a hospital. In protective custody. They have her under the name Hope Boyer to throw off anyone looking for her. Claire, I need you to interview her as a PI, so bring your identification. Cooper, I need you to keep Claire safe. You both know the players we've identified. If any of them are seen, your identities need to change, so bring backup ID and any disguise you need to go with them. All other travel details will be on the plane."

"Hey, Boss?" Cooper started.

"Yeah."

"This protective custody, is this Warren's doing?"

"Yes. He's working with the commander in the precinct Marie was found. A detective in homicide will meet you at the hospital."

"Did she kill someone?" Claire asked.

"No, but someone nearly killed her after taking two other *young* lives. The commander is giving us and Warren a shot before he takes this to the feds."

"Has anyone interviewed her yet?"

"She's not talking. I'm hoping you can change that, Claire."

"Copy that."

"Be safe. No unnecessary risks." Neil disconnected the call.

CHAPTER
TWENTY-EIGHT

Cooper pulled into Claire's driveway long before the sun even thought of coming up.

Dim lights were on inside the house, and Claire's silhouette filtered through the closed drapes. Much as he didn't like the thought of working, or the danger level of that work, he couldn't be happier to be at her side.

He cut the engine and walked through the misty morning to her front door and knocked.

"Almost ready," she said in a low voice after letting him in. Claire walked back toward the kitchen.

He followed her into the quiet house, mindful that Jax was probably as dead tired as they were.

Claire buzzed around the kitchen, pulled down two travel mugs, and proceeded to fill them with coffee. "I'm going to need a gallon of this today," she pointed out.

Cooper simply watched her with unabashed joy.

She wore tan linen pants with a cream silk blouse. She had heels on her feet, but not the sky-high ones she wore when going to a club. Her hair was down, but styled more like Claire the PI and not Claire the high school senior. And her perfume . . . He'd forgotten the scent but remembered it now. She hadn't worn it in his presence since before the assignment started. It wasn't floral, or some essential-oil type thing. It smelled like the dark woods on a moonlit night with just a hint of jasmine musk.

"Boy, I'm tired." She turned around and stopped with his stare.

Cooper stepped forward, took both mugs from her hands, and set them on the counter before pulling her into his arms. He pressed his lips to hers and savored the softness of them. So much strength in every inch of her body, but here, like this, she wilted and let him hold her.

He enjoyed her kiss for as long as he could without turning a morning greeting into more.

When he pulled away, her eyes fluttered open, and that frantic woman who was busy working her way out of the house was replaced with dreamy eyes and a giant sigh. "Good morning," she whispered.

"I wish we were going to the Bahamas."

"Me too."

He handed her back one of the filled mugs and took the other for himself.

Claire set the house alarm and locked the door behind them.

After she was safely tucked into the passenger seat, Cooper pulled out of the driveway and headed toward the airport.

She sipped her coffee and slowly started to wake up. "Did you get any sleep?" she asked him.

"Yeah, but not enough."

"What are the chances of Neil giving us a charter with a bedroom?"

Cooper laughed. "Slim to none."

She reached over and placed her hand on his arm as if she'd done so a thousand times. He wondered if she knew just what that did to him. She started to laugh softly.

"What?"

"I remember the first time Neil put me on a private plane. We were headed back from London. I remember the plane being huge. Bedroom in the back, big reclining seats in the main cabin with a giant TV, and a sofa equipped with seatbelts. It was impressive. Sasha and AJ were this bundle of sexual frustration. When they went in the bedroom, I put my headphones on in case they were loud." She laughed at the memory. "They didn't do anything. Or if they did . . . AJ was much too quick for Sasha to have stayed with the man."

Cooper didn't really want to think of any of his friends going at it, but Sasha accepting a quickie sounded out of character. "Neil was on that flight?"

"Yeah. He let me drink on the plane, but as soon as we touched down in Texas, nope."

"I remember him being such a hard-ass with you. Watching you needle him and making him crack, everyone noticed that. No one dared say a word, but man, that was great to witness." Cooper drove onto the nearly empty freeway, thankful the flight was on a Sunday morning and not a weekday.

"Does it feel strange to you that he's putting so much into this case?"

"How so?" Cooper asked.

"Most of the time it's surveillance and protection. Part bodyguard, part house spy. Celebrity events, high-profile protection. A lot of which is quite boring, actually. But this is new. Exciting." She rubbed his arm with the tips of her fingers. "Exhausting, but exciting."

"It probably does feel personal to Neil. Emma looks like our JV girls. With all the girl parts pushing out and the boys taking notice. You know that's gotta dig at the big man. A guy like him hears that someone in town is snatching up these kids and making them sex slaves. That would drive a normal man to kill, and we both know Neil isn't completely normal. I mean, I trust him with my life, and I also know he'd take someone out who threatened his family." Cooper turned his hand into hers and interlaced their fingers. "We're his family."

Claire squeezed his hand. "Is it strange that I jumped in with this family and never looked back?"

"Do you ever think about trying to find your real family?" he asked. He knew she'd been left at an orphanage door. Didn't even have the parental respect of a real adoption.

She shook her head, then paused. "Maybe in the beginning. Right after I graduated from college. But it's not a driving need in me. That might change someday, who knows. You know what Neil told me once?"

Cooper shook his head. "What?"

"Say the word and I'll find the facts. But when you do, be ready to hear them."

"I wonder if he already knows." Cooper wouldn't put it past the big guy.

"I've thought that more than once. But I'm not there. Sasha told me her search for her biological parents stopped her from living her life, and when she found them, it nearly killed her." Claire stared blankly out the windshield. "I don't want something to consume me like that."

He lifted her hand to his lips, kissed the back of it. "You have people who care about you who will never let something take over your life."

They used the valet lot associated with private charters and whisked through security. Their names and identification were their tickets.

Cooper couldn't help but see that Claire belonged in this lifestyle. She handed off her luggage to an attendant at the bottom of the steps to the private jet like she'd done many times. Truth was, Cooper had as well. Neil didn't travel domestic when they were on a case. And when he was with his family on the many trips back and forth to London, where his wife was from, a family plane was used. Come to think of it, Cooper couldn't remember the man ever using a domestic plane.

Neil liked control.

And Cooper liked Neil's style.

The jet could seat five people with full reclining chairs, a small galley, and of course a bathroom. The captain greeted them and introduced them to the copilot. He plotted out the flight plan and told them what to expect, weather wise, during their flight. After that he disappeared into the cockpit, leaving one attendant. A ridiculous service, as Cooper saw it, considering the flight was only three hours and they could pour their own coffee.

The attendant stowed their luggage and offered that preflight beverage, which they both declined.

Cooper double-checked the closet, where he found the "appropriate devices" one might need to protect a loved one.

Claire set a bag with her computer and notebooks in the seat she planned on using and disappeared into the bathroom.

Once they had everything in order, the attendant closed the cabin door. And in the time most people took to get through normal security, they were taxiing to the runway.

Their seats faced each other, keeping Cooper from touching her, but at least he could watch her.

"Are we going to work, or try and catch some sleep?" he asked.

"I need to formulate my questions. I didn't give it much thought last night before I fell into bed."

Once the flight was in the air, the attendant busied herself with preparing their breakfast. Cooper leaned over the table and lowered his voice. "I thought maybe she was a chaperone, but I don't mind someone else cooking breakfast."

"We're on a private plane, and you're impressed with the fruit cup and microwave omelet."

He tapped his chest. "I'm a simple guy."

While they watched the sunrise, sipping coffee and eating fresh fruit, and not the cup variety that Claire suggested, Cooper marveled at how she switched gears. Yesterday she was pretending to be a smart-ass kid giving adults a run for their money, and today she was the quintessential professional that looked like she could take on a courtroom without a law degree. And she could do it in five languages.

Claire vacillated between her options out loud, asking for his opinion on occasion. She'd write down notes on paper, and put others on her computer.

She picked at her food and drank that gallon of coffee she threatened.

And Cooper soaked up every minute he was with her.

It was raining in Seattle. Their rental car was waiting curbside, again a treat from Neil. "Hotel first, or hospital?"

She glanced at her watch. "Hospital. We don't know when our opportunity will be to talk to her. If we need to come back later, we will."

Cooper followed the navigation to the hospital. When they got close, Claire reached in the back seat and removed one of the handguns from the suitcase Neil had arranged. She did a weapons check, chambered a round, and tucked it in her purse.

Cooper made a noise and she looked over. "Still works for you?" she asked.

"That's so hot."

"Put it away, Cooper. We don't have time for that right now."

That comment had him doing a double take. "So much better than the other way you used to say that."

They bantered with a smile and a simple touch, all saying their relationship had changed.

They pulled into the parking lot. Cooper repeated Claire's actions and put his weapon in a shoulder holster. Technically, she was the only one that was supposed to be carrying a gun.

But *technically*, Cooper didn't give a shit. Someone tried to kill the woman they were about to go see, and he wasn't about to believe that someone wouldn't come back to finish the job. They locked everything else in the trunk and exited the car.

"Let's do this."

Claire's fist came out, and he bumped it with his.

~

Claire walked by Cooper's side as they entered the hospital. They stopped at the information desk and asked where Hope Boyer's room was located.

As expected, they were asked to wait in the lobby for an escort.

Two uniformed police officers exited the elevators and approached the information desk.

Claire and Cooper walked up to them. "I'm Claire Kelly and this is my associate, Cooper Lockman." It had been so long since she used her real name, it felt foreign on her tongue.

Claire identified herself with the private investigator badge that sat next to her primary identification. Her ID was checked quickly and given back.

They scrutinized Cooper's a little closer. "Bodyguard and private security?" the officer holding Cooper's identification asked.

"My retired military credentials are on the next page."

After checking, the police officer gave it back. "Thank you for your service, Mr. Lockman."

Claire and Cooper followed the officers and entered the elevator.

"Are either of you interviewing the witness?"

"No, ma'am. Detective Phelps is on the floor waiting for your arrival."

Neil must have known they wouldn't waste time getting to the hospital.

Cooper kept completely quiet, his body tense, eyes sharp.

The elevator stopped on their floor. Claire heard the click of her shoes as the scents that permeated medical buildings filled her nose. The first section of the floor was bustling with hospital staff, nurses, and doctors. Many stopped to watch them as they passed by. They took the first corner and angled down another long hall before stopping in front of a single door with a phone on the outside.

Along with a few nerves, some of Claire's spidey sense began to tingle. She wasn't sure if it was anticipation at what might be the break in the case they needed, or worry that something was going to go wrong.

One of the officers spoke into the phone, and someone buzzed them in.

The door emptied them into an ICU. One of the officers stayed behind, a single chair his only comfort.

The unit was significantly quieter than the one they'd passed through. Less staff and even fewer civilians.

All the rooms were completely visible from the central nurses' station. The only patient privacy was a curtain that could be pulled around a bed. Very few were pulled. Claire averted her eyes to avoid looking at the other patients in the unit, most of whom were either on a ventilator or hooked up to so many tubes and machines it was hard to tell if they were a man or a woman.

They arrived at Marie's room, the curtain pulled so they couldn't immediately see her.

A middle-aged woman in street clothes hovered outside the door. She smiled as they approached.

"Detective Phelps?" Claire asked.

"You must be Miss Kelly."

The two of them exchanged identification. Cooper showed his and stood back.

Detective Phelps shuffled them a few feet from the open door to Marie's room. "I'm glad you could come so quickly. She fades as the day goes on."

"How is she?"

"Good as can be expected, I suppose."

"We weren't given a lot of details," Cooper told her.

A nurse walked into Marie's room with a bag of IV fluids.

"My commander's orders were to tell you what I know."

"Have you identified the other two victims?"

"Not yet."

"Has she told you who they were?" Cooper asked.

Phelps looked at Cooper. "She hasn't told us anything. The staff came up with the name Hope. Boyer was a random computer name."

"Excuse me, Detective?" The nurse that had walked into the room interrupted them.

They all turned.

"We're going to have to do a dressing change soon. If anyone needs to talk to her, now would be the time."

"Thanks, Millie."

One of the housekeepers took that moment to walk past them pushing a cleaning cart out of the ICU.

Claire used the distraction to take a deep breath.

Phelps turned her attention to Cooper. "I guarantee you she won't talk if you go in there. She doesn't trust men."

Claire placed a hand on Cooper's arm. "I'm okay." She turned to walk into the room, paused. "What is the extent of her injuries?"

"They didn't tell you?"

"We have a lot of questions and not a lot of information."

Phelps looked between them. "After brutal abuse, they tried to burn her alive."

Claire felt bile rise in the back of her throat. Hearing those details wasn't something she was looking forward to.

Her expression must have shown her unease, since Cooper placed a hand on her shoulder.

Claire reached in her purse and turned on a recording device before squaring her shoulders and walking into the room.

CHAPTER
TWENTY-NINE

The mug shot of Marie Nickerson looked nothing like the teenager who morphed into what looked like a breathing airbed.

Her eyes were closed. Bandages covered her neck and chest, her hair had either been burned or shaved to the scalp. Bruises in all stages of healing were a dark rainbow of colors. What wasn't bruised was swollen. She lay on the bed like something out of a cartoon meme, of a person in a body cast with all four limbs stretched away from her body. Knees supported by pillows in a slightly bent position, arms extended and elevated. Her hands were both completely bandaged.

And there was something about the scent in the air Claire knew she'd remember for her entire life.

Marie's eyes fluttered open, a moment of question swam in what looked like a sea of pure despair.

"Hello, Hope."

The girl closed her eyes.

"My name is Claire." She moved a little closer. "Do you mind if I sit down?"

She didn't answer.

Claire pulled a chair closer to the side of the bed that housed fewer medical devices. She sat and secured her purse in the chair beside her.

The sound of the bed humming and the devices on her legs squeezing them filled the silence.

"It looks like they're taking really good care of you."

Marie turned her head away, slightly.

Get her talking, Claire's inner monologue chimed. Anything to start the flow of words. Any words.

"Do you want me to call you Hope? I was told the nurses gave that to you. Everyone seems to care about your recovery."

Still nothing.

"There's a lot of protection, too. Everyone's making sure you're safe."

Marie swallowed and looked at Claire without turning her head. "You a cop?" Her voice was tired and hoarse like a ninety-year-old woman who'd smoked all her life.

"No. I'm not a cop."

"You're a shrink." And that didn't interest her by the way she closed her eyes again as if ending the conversation.

"God no. I'd be a terrible shrink. I'm a private investigator."

Marie looked now, turned her head. "You don't look old enough."

Claire chuckled. "I'm older on the inside."

Her words brought the first sign of any emotion, and Claire ran with it. "I was forced to do well in school. And not in the typical way most think of." She sighed. "Do you know why Beethoven was so great at such a young age? His father all but chained him to a piano, and he was forced to do nothing but play from the moment he could sit up and put his fingers on the keys. His first concert performance was when he was like six." Claire shook her head, spoke slowly. "People get good at things they're forced to do."

Marie was looking at her now.

"I bet he felt old before he was ten," Claire let her voice fade.

A few seconds passed.

"You can call me Hope."

Claire squeezed the fist in her lap to keep from showing too much excitement.

"I bet you're feeling pretty old, Hope."

"You sure you're not a shrink?"

Claire smiled. "Would a shrink tell you that you kinda look like crap right now?"

Hope laughed and came up coughing.

"Oh, I'm sorry." Claire reached for the water that sat on the bedside table. "Do you want some water?"

Hope nodded, and Claire brought the straw to her dry lips for her to take a sip.

"Thank you."

"I probably shouldn't have said that."

Hope closed her eyes. "It's okay. Everyone comes in here and looks at me like I'm going to break."

"I think you're stronger than that."

She went silent again.

"You have to be. Pretending like you're something you're not for so long."

"I'm leftover trash."

Claire swallowed, kept her teeth clenched. "They tell you that? The cowards that did this to you?"

She didn't say yes, didn't say no.

"You know what I see? I see a young woman who was handpicked out of a crowd of children and manipulated into this life. You're older now, so you know kids can do stupid things sometimes. But when someone is older and they're telling you the stupid things you're doing are right, you start to believe them. Maybe you keep doing those things, and maybe they start to feel stupid again. Maybe they hurt more. Or maybe you're just older. But somewhere in the back of your head you know this isn't the life you want."

Claire opened her oversized purse and pulled out several pictures she'd printed out before coming. "This is what I see." She leaned forward and made sure Marie saw them. The first was a shot of the youngest cross-country runners bringing up the rear of the pack.

Marie's eyes focused, and recognition seeped in.

She dropped the page to show another. This one a scene from the quad, with young girls that hadn't found their confidence yet but were surrounded by older students. "And I see this. Don't these girls look young to you?"

A tiny nod was Claire's answer.

"Someone targeted you. Maybe they saw a shy girl, or an unpopular girl . . . someone who liked to sneak a little liquor and experiment. Maybe you just wanted to lose your virginity because your best friend did and she told you it was great. Or maybe someone already took that from you and you didn't think anything after was worth savoring."

Marie flinched, and Claire knew she hit the right combination. She tucked that knowledge away to deal with later.

"And what I and the people I work with think is that the guy who pulled you away from all this, that guy isn't working alone. We think he has a lot of help and we're getting closer to finding them. And I want to find them and stop any of these kids from experiencing what you've been through."

Marie stared at the pictures, wetness behind her eyes.

"We want to know everyone involved. I know you have names in your head. I know you're scared they'll find you if you say them out loud. But they all think you're dead so they aren't looking for you. They're moving on to the next kid."

Claire showed the image of Marie's cross-country team from when she was there.

"I don't know any other way of life," Marie said.

"A lot of nineteen-year-olds don't know what to do with their lives, but they have the rest of it to figure it out. Protecting these people just gives them the opportunity to make sure you *are* dead the next time."

And with that, Claire sat back and stayed silent.

When it seemed Marie wasn't going to say anything else, Claire gathered the pictures and tucked them back in her purse. "If you change your mind and want to talk, I can come back."

Claire stood and tried to smile.

Marie closed her eyes.

Damn it.

"The guy who put me here wasn't the same as the one I left California with."

Claire sat back down.

Marie looked her in the eye, then directed her attention out the window. "His name was Brian. He went by Big Brian."

The curtain surrounding the bed moved slightly, and Phelps quietly walked in and sat down.

Cooper stood out of sight of Marie, poised at the door.

Marie glanced at Phelps and continued. "I met Big Brian at a party. Fancy house party with kids from all over the place."

"Do you remember where the party was?" Claire asked.

She shook her head. "Big house, long driveway. Really nice house with a huge backyard. I remember a firepit with a bunch of kids passing around a bong."

Claire made a note to get a picture of Milo's house for Marie to identify.

"Brian had a nice car. I thought he was a senior, maybe nineteen. Later I realized he was already in his early twenties. Not that it mattered. He was older, liked me. Listened." Marie shook her head, closed her eyes. "In the beginning we'd meet at hotels, make use of the back seat of his car. He never hurt me." Marie made eye contact briefly. "Not directly anyway. My father . . . there was a night my father had been drinking, told me I couldn't leave the house. I didn't like being at home alone with my dad." Marie's stare grew cold.

"Your father hurt you," Claire said.

Marie nodded.

"Sexually." Claire didn't phrase it as a question.

A slight nod was all Marie offered.

"With Big Brian it was my choice. He made me feel safe. When he suggested I run away, I packed a bag and didn't look back. Only it didn't last."

"What happened?" Claire asked.

"Big Brian hooked me up with a fake ID. Took me to the Venetian in Vegas."

Claire sat forward.

"He took me shopping. I remember thinking . . . 'Where did he come up with the money?' But I didn't bother asking. I felt like a princess. He bought me a fancy dress, like something you'd wear to prom. Left me in a spa for half the day. Hair, makeup . . . you name it. I thought he was my savior. At sixteen, I thought Big Brian and I were going to be together forever." Marie closed her eyes. "I'm so stupid."

Claire set her hand on the side of the bed. "You were being manipulated."

"Brian took me to a party. Nothing like a high school thing, this was in a penthouse overlooking Vegas." She went on to describe some of the other girls at the party, then returned to the man who took her there.

"Big Brian said he had a lot of rich friends he wanted me to meet. Encouraged me to be nice. The guys were older. They wore suits. I tried to act the age on my ID. Big Brian pulled me aside, told me one of the men at the party offered ten thousand dollars if I'd sleep with him. We laughed a couple times. Talked about how crazy that sounded. Big Brian hands me another glass of champagne and then starts talking about what we could do with ten thousand dollars. We could get a nice apartment and a real start on life. *It's this one time.*" Marie paused. *"It's this one time."*

Claire beat down her own emotions as Marie revealed everything.

"The guy was old. I was drunk enough to not really care. He had a thick accent."

"Do you know what kind of accent?"

"No. Didn't matter. The party lasted for three days. At least that's what I concluded once I woke up. Blips of men and bedrooms and Big Brian telling me I was doing the right thing. And I was high. I know now someone had given me something. I don't remember how I got from one hotel to another, just that there were different places and a different group of men. When I came down, Mykonos was there."

"Who is Mykonos?"

Marie looked at Claire. "The man who owned me."

Claire listened while Marie spelled out what that meant. Mykonos made it clear that he owned Marie. That she needed to do anything and everything he told her and she could live a comfortable life, or he'd send her to a dirty country where she'd be whored out for pennies.

Twice Marie tried to get out.

Twice Mykonos sent her out for a lesson.

Marie explained how she'd lived with a handful of his girls that were rotated through like chattel. They'd come in young, some as young as fourteen. Some would filter in and be gone within a week, mainly the young ones.

By the time she turned nineteen, she almost never saw Mykonos. He would come in, sometimes he'd use her and reward her with a weekend away from Vegas. The rewards were always a hotel where a convention was going on. Marie had made it clear that she never searched out the men. They were always there, and arrangements were made. Whoever Mykonos had hired to stand beside her pointed at the men, and she was told to do whatever they wanted. No one ever handed her money directly.

When Claire asked how Marie got away, her voice was so monotone it sounded as if she were a robot. As if all emotion had been drained like the last drop of blood.

"Two months ago, Mykonos sent me to San Francisco. I looked in the mirror and didn't recognize myself. I wanted out. I made it as far as a bus station. Mykonos told me I wasn't worth the money to fly me out of the country for another lesson. I was relieved at first. But then he told me if I wanted to be on the streets in America, he'd make sure I knew what that looked like. I was drugged in the back of a van. My eyes were open but I couldn't move. From the van, I was put in the trunk of a car. I knew I was in Seattle. When Mykonos's man handed me over to Ice, I knew things were not going to be the same."

Marie described how Ice took over. The fancy hotel parties where she was the party favor were gone, and the dark corner of an occasional motel was where she turned tricks. Ice, or one of his guys, was always there. The men were dirty and mean. But Ice was meaner.

When she was busted and processed, she never even considered telling her story. Who would believe her? She wanted to go back to Vegas, where at least she had clean clothes and some freedoms. She knew it wouldn't be as good as it had been, but it was better than Ice.

Only that didn't happen. She knew she was never going back to Mykonos when Ice removed half of the pinky on her left hand. Mykonos didn't like his merchandise permanently damaged.

Ice still pimped her out. The men didn't care about a mutilated hand. It gave them permission to hurt her more.

Claire listened to the whole story with her stomach in her throat.

The day Marie had been taken to the warehouse, two other girls showed up. One was Russian, and spoke very little English. The other was American, and from what Marie figured out, both of them were like her. And they were scared. Like they knew what was coming. She tried to talk to them, but they wouldn't say a thing.

Marie overheard a fight between Ice and his guys. She heard them talk about finishing the job. Make a little more money and get rid of them. It was then she understood the fear.

The three of them were showered and put in clean clothes. Marie thought that she could talk her way out of whatever was planned.

Only speaking wasn't allowed.

And when Ice lined up the other members of his gang, he made his last dollar on her. If she cried out while they raped her, one of the other girls would get cut.

She lost track of time, stopped feeling the pain.

Marie stopped talking at that point. And when Claire asked if Ice lit the flame that killed the other girls and nearly killed her, all she did was nod.

~

"I didn't think she was going to talk," Detective Phelps said, bent over a fresh cup of coffee in an isolated conference room a few steps away from the ICU.

Cooper sat beside Claire, saw the fire in her eyes as they reviewed the testimony Marie had provided.

For the first time in their assignment, they had names.

"I thought I lost her. Thank God I brought the photographs," Claire said.

"This is much bigger than it first appeared," Phelps told them.

"Do you have any idea who *Ice* is?"

"Obviously a street name. We'll start our search with the known gangs out of White Center where she was found and work our way out. We'll get a sketch artist in as soon as we can. The downfall of these guys is their love for street credit. Their name is everything to them. We'll find him."

Cooper had already texted the name and the location of the abandoned industrial building to the team. Along with a request to the precinct commander that had given Claire and Cooper access to the witness to give them more time before releasing the case to the feds.

"Mykonos sounds like a big fish," Phelps suggested.

Cooper leaned back in his chair. "The party in Vegas, the first one Big Brian took her to. She describes a lot of girls, most of them young, some with accents, foreign and domestic. And all of them painted up like six-year-old pageant divas. Whoever arranged that party and cashed out those girls is the bigger fish."

"We need Las Vegas vice on this," Phelps said.

Cooper exchanged looks with Claire, both of them had the same concern.

"We need time. Big Brian sounds like someone we're already following. But he's not smart enough to have put all of this together. We need to know who fed her to Big Brian," Cooper said.

"It sounds like she did that all on her own."

Claire shook her head. "That's how our unknown fish stays underground. From the first meeting to Vegas is less than a month. Poof, she vanishes. How does this case look if Big Brian pleads that his biggest sin was not knowing she was sixteen? That she had a fake ID to prove it? They go to a party in Vegas and she runs off with some rich guy? Just taking Mykonos into custody without finding the players that handed her to him in the first place only gives those players a chance to disappear."

Phelps nodded her agreement. "And since I'm sitting here with a private investigator and a bodyguard at the request of my commander, and not a detective from your local sheriff's department, I'm going to assume there's a dirty officer involved."

"If there is, we'll find them. But if Mykonos is taken in, and whoever Big Brian works with is tipped off, everything crumbles."

Phelps rolled her shoulders. "I'll report everything to my commander."

They all stood.

Claire tucked in the file of information Phelps had for them into her purse.

After they shook hands, Claire asked, "Is she going to be safe here?"

"Anyone trying to get to her has a lot of people to get through first."

"If she wants to talk to me again . . . ," Claire said.

"We'll call you."

Cooper and Claire walked out of the hospital side by side. Once they passed the main doors, he felt her hand slip into his.

CHAPTER THIRTY

They checked into an upscale hotel that had views of Puget Sound.

Neil had booked two rooms with an adjoining door. Claire suggested just taking one, but Cooper said something about *rubbing it in* and the affection he had for his perfect smile.

It was almost five, and the sun was still a good hour away from setting. They both decided a hot shower and a real meal would be the best way to ease the tension of the day. And since they had two showers to use . . . they did.

Even though Claire's thoughts were on the case, it didn't escape her that she and Cooper were about to have their first real date. She was thankful she'd thought about that when she packed.

Cooper had used the concierge at the hotel to book a nice restaurant. Claire put on her best outfit.

She slipped the black dress over her head and flattened the fabric along her waist. A look in the mirror made her smile back.

She knew, without a doubt, that Cooper would call the dress a Sasha Special before the evening ended. Her guess would be less than an hour.

It was sexy and short, but not tacky. And the shoes she wore were eye catching and high without being sleazy.

Claire swept her hair up in a messy bun and put on a pair of glittery earrings. The earrings had been a gift from Gwen when she graduated from college. She was fairly certain the diamonds were real, but she'd never ask. Neil refused to take credit for them, but she gave it to him anyway.

Sitting at a vanity table, she finished her makeup with a rose tint on her lips.

Looking at her reflection in the mirror, Cooper walked up behind her and traced the spot on her neck that reached her shoulders. She closed her eyes and leaned into his hand.

"We should go before I try and change your mind about the importance of food," he told her.

The rain had let up before they left the hospital. The sky held a scattering of bright white clouds that stood poised on a variegated blue sky.

They took a hotel car to the restaurant, where their table offered views of the Sound and displayed streaks of purple and gold from the sunset.

"Did you talk to Neil when I was in the shower?" she asked once they were seated.

"I did, briefly. The team is burning the midnight oil to find faces to go with the names. By the time we're back, we should have more answers than questions and a direction to go."

"I hope so. The thought of the people who did this getting away makes me physically ill."

The waiter came over and asked if they wanted to see the wine list.

"Do you want wine?" Cooper asked. "We can, but I know nothing about wine."

Wine with a romantic setting always sounded like the perfect combination, but after their day that wasn't what she wanted. "Vodka martini, two olives," Claire told the waiter.

Cooper handed the menu back. "Make that two."

"Thank you."

The waiter walked away.

"Today was brutal," Cooper said, reaching over and placing his hand over hers on the table.

"Today made it personal. Putting a face and story to the victim. I don't know how anyone does this every day." And she didn't. The crime scene photographs, images of Marie from the hospital before she'd been taken into the burn unit, and what about the two that didn't make it out? What were their stories? "Let's talk about something pleasant. Concentrating too hard is throwing up roadblocks in my head."

Cooper traced her fingers with his. "Should we talk about how we're in Seattle and there isn't a chance that anyone from school could walk by and see this?"

That definitely helped her mind free space. "It's almost like we're having an affair."

"Maybe when the case is over we can have a role-play weekend once a month." He tilted his eyebrows in an expectant way.

Cooper was thinking long term, and yet they'd only shared a couple of stolen kisses.

She lowered her voice, leaned forward. "You have to get to second base before we can talk about next month."

He laughed. "Unless you're wearing that Sasha Special just to tease me, I'm guessing I can unveil your need to cover all the bases."

Claire took a quick look at her watch. "Forty minutes," she said.

"What?"

"You called this a Sasha Special. I knew you would. It took less than an hour for you to do it."

"You're stunning in anything, but dresses like that make me very *hungry*."

The drinks came and they ordered their dinner.

"Do you know how many times I've sat and imagined this night with you? Sitting in a nice place, sipping something, and holding your hand. And more importantly, you not trying to break mine for doing it?"

She took hold of his thumb and twisted it just a little.

"It might take me a little more time to catch up to all you imagined," she said.

He kissed her fingertips, looked out the window in a nonchalant way, and said, "I think, if you're not too tired when we're done here, we can go back to the hotel and run the bases a time or two. Replace the dreams with reality and make it our history." His eyes returned to her with a soft smile.

No man had ever asked permission to sleep with her. It always just happened. But apparently Cooper felt the need. She lifted her glass. "To life today that becomes our history tomorrow."

They both sipped, then put their glasses down. "Now, if we're done talking in metaphors . . . the answer is yes, I'll share your bed tonight."

It was easy to tell that Cooper tried hard not to smile like a child with a new toy.

He squeezed her hand and leaned forward to speak in a whisper. "Is it too early to ask for the check?"

She bit her lip and watched as his eyes lingered. "You're going to need the steak for the energy it's going to take. Until then, put it away."

Dinner was part nutrition, part flirtation, and part frustration.

She slipped her shoe off at one point and found the inside of his calf under the table. When he started eating faster, she slowed down and felt the energy build.

On the way back to the hotel, Cooper's hands played with the edge of her skirt, out of the view of the driver.

They talked about baseball and stealing bases while Claire gave Cooper the opportunity to touch anywhere he pleased. He kept it decent, but that didn't stop her body from turning up the heat.

The talking stopped when they exited the car.

Hand in hand, Cooper led her to the elevators.

She was breathing hard just knowing Cooper was finding it difficult to talk, and he hadn't even touched her yet. Well, touched, but not *touched*.

The elevator door opened and a couple walked out.

Cooper pressed the button to their floor and the close door button at the same time.

Claire watched, hoped that no one stuck their hand between the doors to stop them from being alone.

The door closed and Cooper twisted her around. He pinned the hand he'd been holding to the wall and pressed his frame against hers. His mouth crashed down in complete possession. Hot open-mouth kisses were made even more scorching because of the public place they were in.

The bell in the elevator pinged as if signaling the end of round one.

Cooper backed away as the doors started to open.

His hand stayed on the small of her back on the short walk down the hall.

The electronic keycard was out of his wallet and they pushed into the room breathless.

Cooper reached for her, one hand on her neck, the other on her waist. Everything about their meeting of lips was pure passion. Claire closed her eyes and let him lead her wherever he wanted to go.

Her fingers spanned the width of his back, digging in the pure muscle she felt.

He released her lips long enough to catch a breath, tilted her head to the other side, and returned with more fervor.

When she felt his hand follow the curve of her spine and then squeeze the globe of her bottom, she broke their kiss. "You're stealing bases."

He smiled before lowering his lips to her shoulder and taking a small bite. "I'll cover all the bases." Slowly he kissed along her collarbone and then the swell of her breast that was visible in the dress she wore. Both his hands swept up and settled on the edges.

Her nipples tightened in anticipation of his full coverage of second base.

While he reminded her what it felt like to be touched, Claire pulled his shirt from the waistline of his pants and enjoyed the feel of bare skin.

It was hard to believe she was there in his arms as he drew sensations out of her so powerful they left her lightheaded.

Cooper slowed down, his thumbs flickering over her nipples through her dress.

She loved the slow tease of his touch, followed by a kiss and a tiny pinch. "You've been practicing second base," she told him.

He pushed the edge of her dress aside. "My pillow tells me I need therapy."

He made her laugh and repeated the tease, kiss, and pinch.

"Your pillow talks to you?"

He abandoned one for the other, repeated the actions. "Every night."

Her body responded, nerve endings firing in all directions. "What else does your . . . oh, God yes. Do that again."

"Demanding minx. I should have guessed that about you." He pinched a little harder.

Her hands dropped from his back, down his ass, and flirted with his hip. They were still standing in the center of the room.

She reached for his belt, and Cooper found the zipper on the back of her dress.

A wiggle of her hips and the dress slid to the floor.

Cooper's hands froze on her shoulders, and he stepped slightly away.

"What?" Claire asked, looking into his eyes.

"You. You're so beautiful."

She wore a lace bra and matching thong. Body image was never something Claire struggled with. She'd been given smallish breasts that worked well with her frame. Her slender hips gave way to a toned butt she exercised daily. If there was a lesson of Sasha's that Claire would remember forever, it was the one where she explained that if Claire loved her body, accepted every curve, sex would be so much better.

Watching Cooper study her shape drove that point home.

Claire stepped out of the dress, pressed both palms to Cooper's chest, and backed him toward the bed. His knees caught and she pushed him down.

"I think I'm in trouble."

Instead of messing with the buttons of his dress shirt, she tugged it off over his head. "You started this," she told him, reaching for his belt. "We could go back to *just friends* if you've changed your mind."

Their eyes locked.

"Bite your tongue," he said.

She shook her head, stopped playing with his belt, and reached lower, captured the length of him through his pants. "I'd rather bite yours."

Their lips met and Claire stretched out on top of him, legs straddling his hips. She pushed into the friction their bodies created. Sparks of what was to come made everything inside of her tighten with need.

Cooper caught fire, and suddenly his hands were everywhere. The clip in her hair was out, tossed to the floor. Her bra followed. And they kissed like starved animals going after food.

He rolled her over and stood on the edge of the bed long enough to remove the rest of his clothes. When he returned, his hand traveled from her knees to her feet, took each shoe off slowly. He licked his lips, tugged her closer, and slowly played with the length of her legs. "Third base looks phenomenal."

She opened for him, ran a hand over her own stomach, and slid a finger inside her panties. "You should have a taste, see if it works."

He pushed the lace aside and did just that. He started on the outside and slowly moved in. All Claire could do was lie back and enjoy every ounce of attention Cooper was giving her.

Sparks and flutters. "To the right," she instructed. "Yes, right there . . . oh."

He was so incredibly good at what he was doing, just the right amount of pressure, his movements changed when she felt her body getting close. Her foot reached his back, a hand on his head, and then there was no feeling except the build and sudden gush of release. She called his name, and her body went limp while she caught her breath.

"Note to self," Cooper said as he inched her panties down her legs. "Claire loves a thorough inspection of third base."

She chuckled and opened her eyes.

He shuffled through their clothing and found his wallet. A condom came out, the wallet tossed back where he found it.

Claire reached to help him put it on, made sure she inspected the length and girth of the man. "This is a thick bat you have here."

The condom on, she played a little more. Turned Cooper's chuckles into moans and when he'd had enough he reached for her, scooted her hips higher on the bed, and climbed on top of her. He kissed her, the taste of her own essence on his lips.

She felt the tip of him reaching, until Cooper finally slid home.

Full. The man completely filled her.

"So good," he whispered in her ear.

And it was.

He took his time, said sweet things, and worked her up again. And when their cadence marched in sync with each other, and the need became too much to even kiss, Claire rode out the last wave and crashed right beside Cooper on the shore.

The only sound in the room was the two of them breathing, and maybe the beat of their hearts.

"Good God, Claire, you've ruined me." He stayed on top of her, in her, but kept some of his weight on his elbow.

"I hope that's a good thing."

Later, when she was tucked into his arms, her head resting on his shoulder, she had to confess. "Cooper?"

"Yes?" His reply was sleepy.

"I don't even like baseball."

His laughter bubbled and his arms held her closer.

"Neither do I."

CHAPTER THIRTY-ONE

Their time together was too damn short.

Cooper woke before her and just watched her sleep. He knew he was in deep. Knew before he returned to the States that with Claire, he flirted with falling too hard only to be left with a shattered heart in the end.

But after the few stolen hours that they used to their full extent, Cooper let himself hope.

He'd never made love to a friend. Yes, he became friends with his lovers, and when things ended for whatever reason, he still considered them friends. Of course, that never lasted. Cooper knew he risked losing a friend when they became lovers.

All those thoughts and more tossed around in his head as the private charter climbed to a cruising altitude.

Claire had opened her laptop the minute they'd settled in their seats.

Without looking up from her computer, she said, "You do know you're staring."

"I have to soak you in now."

She had long eyelashes. How had he not noticed them before?

"What are you thinking about?" Claire asked, still typing.

"Your eyelashes."

That made her look. "My what?"

He loved her smile. "When you sleep it's like they're resting on the pillows of your cheeks."

She gave up on work and put it away.

After several moments of silence, Claire turned her head and looked out the window.

"Does anything about *us* . . . scare you?" she asked.

"I was more afraid there would never be an *us*."

"Now that there is?"

He shook his head. "What scares you?"

"Losing our friendship."

"That's never going to happen." He said his words fast, as if doing so would guarantee the outcome.

Claire's smile waffled. "Lewis will never be Jax's friend. Sex changes things."

Cooper leaned forward and took her hand in his. "You're going to have to trust me on this one. Besides, it sounded like Jax's relationship with Lewis was only about the sex. That isn't *us*."

She met him in the middle of the table, pressed her lips to his. "We're pretty amazing at the sex thing."

"I haven't even started to show you what it's like for a man to worship your body."

"I think you made a pretty good start."

It was his turn to ask for a kiss.

"Should we make some rules?" she asked.

"What do you mean?"

"Well, if you wanted to see someone else—"

"That's not going to happen."

She gave him a look that said she didn't believe him. "In case you wanted to."

Maybe she didn't understand the six years of absence was enough to tell him what he wanted. Then it dawned on him. What if she wanted to keep their relationship open? The thought was enough to drive him mad.

"I stopped seeing two women at the same time when I left the military. Maybe it's too soon for us to be talking about exclusivity . . ."

"It is?"

"Isn't it?"

She shrugged. "Maybe for people who aren't friends first?"

He found his smile again. "Okay. Just you and just me."

Claire squeezed his hands and smiled. "Can I wear your letterman jacket?"

He laughed. "I never had one."

"If at some point, even if you think it's not going to happen, you meet someone you want to explore something with, we talk first," Claire said. "Same for me."

"I think that goes without saying, but if you want to write up the rules, by all means."

"I don't have to write them down."

He laughed at that. "Yes, you do. And you'll do it in five languages."

~

They drove directly to headquarters.

The team was there and looked like they had been the entire weekend.

Jax jumped up from her computer when she saw them, walked over to Claire, and pulled her in for a hug. "We all listened to the interview. God, that must have been awful."

"Satisfying, but not fun." Claire looked at Cooper, giving him credit for her not breaking down.

Jax stopped hugging her and narrowed her eyes. "You look very relaxed."

"It wasn't *all* work."

"How you doing, Yearling?" Lars asked.

Claire realized everyone was looking at her . . . well, all but Sasha, who rolled her eyes before focusing on the computer she was in front of.

Neil looked her in the eye. "Great job getting her to talk."

"Having the track team photographs was key."

"Smart," Sasha said.

"Is she going to be safe?" Claire asked Neil directly.

"I have eyes on her. If something looks out of place, I'll assemble a team."

"What do you mean, 'eyes'? Is there a team in Seattle you aren't telling us about?" Claire asked, half joking.

"Not a team." Neil stared down at her, eyes unwavering.

In that moment Claire's mind flashed to the ICU. The staff moving around the unit . . . the housekeeper that had pushed a cart through the door. "Oh my God . . . Olivia."

Neil's lips pushed together.

"You're kidding me," Sasha said, turning to stare at Neil.

"In the ICU." Claire looked at Cooper. "When we were talking to Phelps, she was disguised as a housekeeper." Claire could see her clearly now. Olivia was ex-Richter. Only she didn't escape the clutches of evil that the school harbored.

"I don't remember," Cooper admitted.

Claire returned her stare to Neil. "It was her, wasn't it? She's the one keeping an eye on Marie?"

Quiet filled the room.

Olivia was an assassin. Or had been, before Neil and the team tore apart the fabric that cloaked Richter.

Neil's silence confirmed her suspicion.

Who better to watch out for an assassin than someone who'd been in that role in the past?

"Marie will be safe" was all Neil added.

Cooper rubbed Claire's back before walking to the front of the room. "So where are we at?" He stared at the situation board, hands on hips.

It took a few seconds before the shock that Olivia was not only alive but working for Neil wore off.

Jax answered Cooper's question. "Marie positively identified Big Brian Contreras."

"That's a huge check on the board," Claire said. "What about Mykonos?"

"Mykonos Sobol," Sasha reported and handed Claire a picture. "Extended family with money and power. They are the kind of family that goes to jail for tax evasion instead of prostitution and murder."

"Russian mafia," Cooper said, deadpan.

"Affirmative."

Lars picked up from there. "Vegas vice has been wanting to bust him for years, but no one talks. Two times he was booked, both times the witnesses recanted and later disappeared. Marie's testimony is exactly what Vegas needs."

Every time Claire heard Marie's name, she worried more for her safety, felt better knowing the person protecting her.

"Any direct link between Mykonos and Milo?"

Isaac spoke up. "I'm working on that now. So far, nothing."

Claire's mind flashed with the pictures of the bodies in the police report. "Do we have the autopsy reports yet on the two deceased?"

"I'm told we'll have them tomorrow," Neil told her.

Cooper pointed to a new photograph on the board. "I'm guessing this is Ice."

"Detective Phelps already got back to us on him," Lars informed them. "Marie gave a positive ID. Similar to Brian, he was headed toward his third strike when he and his guys cleaned up their act. The running theory is when Marie was sent there to *learn her lesson*, Ice needed to make sure she did. When she got busted, she wasn't going back to Vegas directly to Mykonos, so Ice was told to kill her. But instead of doing that right away, he makes more money off of her, then lines up all of his guys and makes them participate in all the brutality before the girls are set on fire."

"Which makes all of them accomplices to murder," Jax concluded.

Claire started nodding as the pieces fell into place. She moved to a clean board and picked up a marker. "Local gangs only organize with leadership. I've met Brian, he's not sharp. But he doesn't talk like a thug and he doesn't have an abundance of ink or piercings."

"He's not a bad-looking guy," Jax pointed out.

"Let's look at the money," Neil said, taking the pen she wasn't using out of her hand. "Marie is taken to Vegas and sold." Neil wrote Brian's name on the board, put a dollar sign next to it. "Mykonos has her for three years, makes an untold amount of money. By her descriptions, many of these events were high end. These men are expecting more than anything they can find on the street. Chances are they don't even pay for the girls individually, more like a bonus for spending more than a hundred grand a day in a casino."

"That's how it sounded to me when Marie was talking," Claire told him.

He wrote several dollar signs around Mykonos's name. "He sends her to Ice. Ice gets paid." More dollar signs next to his name.

Claire took the pen from Neil. "Three years ago, girls started to be selected, which is why Detective Warren sent in undercover cops. Now that we know what happens to those girls after they disappear, we know there's serious money for the one who sells them." She drew a big dollar sign. "It's given to Brian, and the school connections, and the dirty cop, if there is one. So it has to be big money. And if I'm spending a lot of money, I want to get what I want. A busty blonde with blue eyes, or a fifteen-year-old that looks like their sister . . . or whatever perverse thing drives them."

Claire studied the board, capped the pen, and put it down. "We need to find the want ads?"

"No, what we need to do is flush out these leads at the school," Neil said. "And we have less than a week to do it. Now that we know this is over the state line, the commander in Seattle can only hold off on getting the feds involved a short time. He's giving us that courtesy. Let's not waste the time. I don't want any person in this shit show getting away. We can't depend on Brian pointing fingers or not ending up dead so he isn't able."

They all had their assignments for the next day.

Cooper needed to put a tracker on Tony's car. Hopefully the guy cooperated and showed up for the shop day.

Claire needed to obtain the roster of tutors and find the connection to Bremerton, work Eastman and see if she could get anything else from him.

Jax needed face time with Russell. And get as much information about this party Ally went to.

And Manuel, who Claire was starting to think spoke only when spoken to, was on watch for any change in activity.

The rest of the team were doing all they could to infiltrate the mail store frequented by Brian and Gorge, and provide more visual and audio to the Milo residence.

Cooper pulled Claire into a quiet corner when it was time to leave.

"I would feel so much better if you and I could stay together when we're not at school." He kept a hand to the side of her neck as they talked. "Especially now that we know what we're dealing with."

"It's the seventh-inning stretch."

That took away his worried expression.

"I'm pretty good at taking care of myself. And Sasha . . . we all know she's capable."

"Call me when you get home."

She tilted her lips to his and savored how they felt.

And when they couldn't justify standing in the corner making out any longer, she broke away and said goodbye.

Back in her flight attendant uniform, Sasha drove them home.

They made three miles of complete silence.

And without prompts, Claire said, "It was incredible."

Sasha's eyes smiled though her lips didn't. "The look on your face when you walked in the door told me the sex was good."

A couple more miles passed by.

"This Mykonos and his family . . . this changes the case," Sasha said.

"I know. I saw Marie."

"Be careful."

Claire felt the warmth of those two simple words. "I will."

CHAPTER THIRTY-TWO

Instead of waiting for Russell to approach her, Jax waited for him to park his car in the senior parking lot.

Manuel was watching from around the corner.

Russell pulled in and, like most of the students, sat in the parking lot and talked with his friends until the bell rang.

When it did, Jax approached him. "Hi, uhm . . . you're Russell, right?"

He was all his profile said he was. Tall, at least six two, and thick. "Do I know you?"

Jax shook her head. "I was at your house party a couple of weeks ago. I met your uncle."

Russell looked away from her face and down to her chest. "The blonde," he muttered.

"I'm sorry?"

"Right." He started walking again. "We don't do that delivery thing here."

She tried to act disappointed. "Oh."

His eyes looked her up and down, before quickly looking away. "If you have Milo's number, you should call him anyway."

"I can do that." The whole conversation felt strange. Like he didn't want to be there.

Claire's words from the briefing the day before about Mykonos ordering a busty blonde sounded in her head.

~

"Are we beating up the cars today, or working on them?" Cooper walked into the shop, happy to see Tony's car up on one of the lifts.

"Loverboy made up with the girlfriend," Tony said, looking over at Kyle.

"Elsie seems like a nice girl." *And she needs a date for prom.*

Kyle and Tony were working on the rear brakes.

"I took her out on Sunday and we had a long talk."

Cooper walked over, tried to appear interested in what they were doing. "So no more tutor from Bremerton?"

"Nope." Kyle handed Tony a tool. "I told her I could help. But her mom doesn't believe we can actually study when we're together."

"Elsie's pretty hot," Tony said.

Kyle kept working. "I know."

"How is she going to pass algebra?" Tony pulled the question right out of Cooper's head.

"Claire."

"Do I know Claire?" Tony asked.

"She's the new girl. She was with us at that party . . ." Kyle stopped talking, looked at Cooper. "Shit."

"What?" Tony stopped what he was doing, looked between Kyle and Cooper.

"Claire's on the track team."

That seemed to spark Tony's interest.

Cooper turned his head. "I heard nothing. Unless it's before a track meet. No parties before the meets."

Kyle smiled. "Thanks, Mr. Mitchel. I finally feel like I got my girl-friend back, I don't want her to think I'm dissing her friends."

"I'm glad it's working out," Cooper said. He looked at the job they were doing, looked at the time. "This looks like it's going to take more time than we have this morning."

"We were hoping you didn't mind if we left it here until Friday to finish," Tony said.

"That's not a problem." The more Cooper looked at Tony, the less he saw a newly graduated high school student and the more he noticed a grown man with wisdom in his years. Like suggesting he leave his car there instead of asking. A kid would have asked. But with the car stuck in the garage, there wouldn't be any tracking of Tony's movements that way. "Do you have another car?"

Tony narrowed his eyes. "A buddy is letting me borrow one of his."

A buddy with two cars? Nineteen-year-olds don't have friends who lend them cars. Cooper grabbed a donut. "Be sure to lower the lift before you take off," he instructed.

~

Claire walked into homeroom with one of her earbuds in her ear, and stopped at Eastman's desk. "Since my aunt didn't yell at me when she got home, I'm guessing you gave a good report."

"I told her the truth. Said you were improving and were a little less of a pain in the ass."

"I need to try harder, then."

Sean walked behind Claire on the way to his seat. "Hey, Claire." She twisted, said hi.

"My aunt is hot, don't you think?"

Eastman did a double take.

"Don't pretend you didn't notice. You know, you're single, she's single, could work."

"Are you suggesting I hit on your aunt?"

Claire smirked. "Dude, my aunt would never go out with you in a million years. She has excitement standards, and you're a schoolteacher."

"Have a seat, Porter."

Twenty minutes went by fast. She hoped her needling would have resulted in something. Instead, Eastman jumped on a couple of the students in the class, and talked about the limited time to graduation.

Claire left the room frustrated. Every hour at school was one closer to her last. Without new information, or confirming information, the players at the school level stood a chance at getting away.

Her mind was stuck on the image of the charred remains as she walked the halls to her next class.

"Hey, Claire." Sean walked up behind her.

"Hey." There was no intel to gather in Wallace's class . . .

"I heard you took second place at that track thing this weekend."

"Yeah . . ."

"That's cool."

They kept walking.

"Hmm . . . Sean, do you know of any parties that happened last Friday?"

He shrugged. "There's always something going on, but nothing big."

Hopefully Jax could draw something out of Ally.

Sean stopped her. "Claire, uhm . . ."

He was fidgeting. And he'd done something different with his hair, or maybe it was just washed. How different could a guy change his hair unless he shaved it off?

And the memory of Marie's shaved head surfaced.

Claire closed her eyes, shook it away. "What?"

"I know it's kinda lame, but we only do this high school thing once . . ."

"Yeah."

"I want to know if you wanted to go to prom."

Claire stood shocked.

"With me." Sean smiled.

She did *not* see this coming. *Fuck!*

"Oh . . . I wasn't planning on going to prom."

His face fell in disappointment. "I get it. Like I said, it's lame."

"I'm sorry."

Sean swallowed hard. "We're cool." He turned and walked away.

Son of a bitch!

~

During Cooper's lunch, when the shop was empty, he took a picture of the VIN on Tony's car, sent it to the team, and made a call.

Neil answered, "What do you have?"

"I just sent a VIN on Tony's car. And since it isn't leaving the school until Friday, hopefully we can get something useful from the car itself." With the phone to his ear, Cooper opened the passenger door, rifled through the glove compartment.

"License plate number?"

He rattled off the number on the plates, then found the registration papers, took a picture of it, and sent it in.

"Got 'em. Keep looking."

"I will." Cooper disconnected the call as frustration started to build.

~

Claire graded papers instead of getting a lecture during algebra and was told to come back at lunch so Coach Bennett could review her grading before sending her into Dunnan's tutor pool.

Making sure she wasn't late, Claire made it to Bennett's classroom before the lunch bell rang.

"You're early." Coach Bennett had already pulled out his soggy sandwich.

"I'm an overachiever, what can I say." Claire dumped her backpack, found her eyes scanning the pictures on the wall.

Marie's face was never far from Claire's thoughts. Her throat started to constrict. Damn it . . . she did not need to tear up.

"I looked over the work," Bennett said.

"And?" She kept her back to him and tried to get it together.

"I think you need to go to college."

"I heard."

"You're bright, Claire. I've been doing this for twenty years, and it takes me longer to grade these papers."

She swallowed the lump that rose in her throat after looking at Marie's smiling face on the cross-country team picture, and turned around. "I should go to college so I can be the head of the math department at a high school?"

"I know this isn't glamorous, but it's what I chose."

"What, besides the heartburn from that lunch, is the perk behind going to high school for the rest of your life?"

Bennett smiled.

"My schedule's easy. Most of the kids aren't as much of a challenge as you. As you can see by this room, track is my passion. And don't think I haven't seen that in your eyes, young lady, because I have."

She snorted.

"The district sends me twice a year to different symposiums. It's like a free vacation."

"Your idea of a good time is questionable, Coach." And yet something *clicked* in the back of her head.

"Well, I don't teach for the pay, so I'll take my kicks when I can. Especially if someone else is footing the bill."

"So you go to a convention where you party with all the other math nerds?" *Click, click, click . . .*

"Fine, don't become a teacher. But go to college and become something."

She had to give the guy kudos for his effort. "Maybe tutoring will change my mind."

Bennett sighed. "We have a little problem with that."

Not what she wanted to hear. "Oh?"

"Dunnan doesn't want to work with you."

"What?"

"He has to take the time and supervise you tutoring someone before he puts you in rotation. And he's not convinced you're worth the time."

Claire felt that lead slipping away. "You're the head of the math department, convince him."

"I'm not his boss."

"C'mon, Coach. What do I have to do?"

She turned back to the wall of pictures, placed a hand on Marie's.

Marie's tears trickled down her beaten face.

Claire felt all the pent-up frustration about to boil over.

She could go to Mr. Green, make the administration take over, but if anyone was watching, they'd know something didn't add up.

She needed more time.

The team needed more time.

"We might be able to set you up with an outside system so you can make the money for your trip."

An outside system took time.

Claire felt a single tear drip down her cheek. She slammed the side of her fist on the wall and turned around.

She had to get out of there before the floodgates opened.

The coach called after her when she grabbed her backpack and left his room.

CHAPTER THIRTY-THREE

Coach Bennett filled Cooper in on what had happened with Claire.

Without talking to her, he knew exactly why emotion had overtaken her. He, too, felt like the hourglass was turned upside down and someone was shaking it.

"I wouldn't be surprised if she skipped track today," Bennett told him.

"She'll be here." *Even if she hated it.*

"If she shows, pull her aside, talk to her. I would, but I don't think she'll listen to me."

"Isn't there any way to get her into the tutor job?" Cooper asked.

"I'll see what I can do. Maybe get one of the kids that can't afford to pay for a tutor to come in so I can sign off on her skills."

Cooper looked at his watch. "C'mon, Claire."

The team was halfway through their warm-up before she walked down to the field.

Instead of joining in, she sat under a tree with her back resting against the chain-link fence on the far end of the field. Her eyes followed the runners.

Cooper knew where her thoughts were.

Bennett walked up to him. "Part of the job is listening to teenage girls cry, and teenage boys rant."

Cooper made it to her side and sat on the grass beside her.

She'd been crying.

"You okay?"

She closed her eyes. "I don't cry."

"Did Richter burn that out of you?" he asked. Their end of the field was empty. Being overheard wasn't a concern.

"I'm so frustrated, Cooper." She picked at the grass by her side.

"We all are. But this is when we need to keep it together."

"I know that."

He picked at the grass, gently touched the side of her hand that sat between them. "You didn't process her. I expected tears when we left, maybe on the plane . . ." He kept his voice low.

"I have no business doing it now."

He couldn't argue that.

"Do you know how hard it is to sit here and not pull you into my arms?"

She avoided looking at him, and nodded. "I'd just cry harder."

"That would make me hold you tighter, then I might accidentally kiss you. Then everyone would talk."

She looked up at him, nudged his arm with her shoulder, and smiled.

He could die a happy man if she just kept smiling at him like that. "Dunnan doesn't want to work with you because you're a pain in the ass."

"I have repented and changed my evil ways," she said, a lift in her voice.

"What do we really need from him?"

She picked the grass more. "Get into the pool. Find which troubled students go to which tutors and are any of them a player? We're running out of time."

His pinky reached for hers. "Every time I thought that today, I found myself staring at the clock. My mind would go blank. Nothing productive happened."

"Glad I'm not alone."

Cooper stared downfield, saw Bennett working with the sprinters. The man was just as big a teddy bear as Neil. He really wanted to help Claire. "Sometimes we get so stuck in the weeds . . ."

"What?" Claire asked.

"Wouldn't the head of the math department have access to the tutor need and tutor pool on his own computer? At least for the students at *his* school?"

Claire stopped picking the grass.

"Aren't you our resident hacker?" Cooper turned his head, his eyes collided with hers. "Sometimes to steal the car, all you have to do is ask for the keys."

Those tears were gone. "I want to kiss you so hard right now," she said, smiling.

Cooper settled with helping her off the grass and a hug.

They walked over to Bennett together.

"Hey, Coach?"

Bennett turned around. "You all right?"

Claire looked at the ground and talked slow even though Cooper saw her fingers twitching. "I'm better. I just need to go . . . I need a few minutes."

"Of course."

"I forgot something in the desk where I was grading papers. Mind if I go get it?"

Bennett shook his head, pulled the keys from his pocket, and sin- gled out the right one. "Lock up when you leave."

"Thanks."

Cooper watched her run off.

"Is Claire okay, Coach?" The relay team had moved in when Claire left.

"She's fine."

"What's wrong?" Chelsea asked.

Cooper didn't respond.

Leah, who was sporting crutches, said, "I heard Sean Fisher asked her to prom and she turned him down."

Cooper bit his lip until actual pain to keep from laughing.

~

Claire and Jax sat in their Tarzana house with a situation board of their own.

Aunt Sasha had left the decoy house and Claire hadn't returned.

The rest of the team was at headquarters or out in the field.

"The mail location in the strip mall is owned by an Aram Aghassian. He owns three of these types of stores. Two in LA, one in Orange County. They rent out mailboxes, send post through all the major carriers, have a notary service, passport photos, and sell all the things you need to send Nana a package on her birthday." Isaac was the one reporting.

Claire and Jax had him on speaker.

Jax was typing in names on her computer and putting faces to them. Between the two of them, they had identified several pairs in less than an hour. Finally, Claire felt like they were getting somewhere.

"Any link to Milo?"

"Only through Brian and Gorge. However, after photographing several of their patrons, it's safe to say this location has an unusual number of customers that have spent time in jail. The security cameras are visible in the usual locations, front door, back door, and register. Typical alarm system, but we can't locate a monitoring service." Isaac stopped talking.

Claire stared at a picture of one of the juniors at her school. "That should give Detective Warren more than enough to obtain a search warrant."

"We'll have our own knowledge of what they're hiding before we waste anyone's time," Neil said.

"I wish I could be on that detail," Claire said, more to Jax than the team. Running around in the dark wearing spandex and breaking into places sounded like a lot more fun than a giant jigsaw puzzle of high school kids.

"Not this time, Yearling." Just hearing Cooper's voice made her smile.

Jax shoved her aside with a grin. *You have it bad.* She mouthed the words but they were easy to read.

"Does that mean you're going and playing Spider-Man?"

"Without the tights."

Claire laughed.

"Milo Gusev does have links to the Sobol family, though he is not blood. Gusev has a lot of nephews. They come to America for a semester abroad. Last year he housed Ivan Zahbin during his junior year. The year before that was a niece. He has been on 'guardian of a minor' papers at Bremerton for the third year in a row."

Jax had stopped typing and looked at Claire. "That would make sense of how Russell reacted today. I finally intercepted him in the parking lot. He didn't have a single interest in my fake ID. Suggested I call Milo, which I did. But he didn't answer."

"Does Russell know what's going on?" Cooper asked.

"He knows about the fake IDs, but beyond that? Who knows? He can't be completely oblivious," Jax reported.

"But he's seventeen. A minor, and Milo is harboring that age group." Lars had a point.

"What about Tony's car?" Claire asked, having heard more about that when she'd talked to Cooper on her way home from school.

"Registered to Tony Mazzeo. The car was bought a little over a year ago. Right at the time Tony was a senior at Auburn High. The registered address is an apartment complex. Since the name on the mailbox is Chen, he has either since moved, or he was never there. Which would line up with him being an undercover cop," Cooper told them.

"So we have two undercover cops. One working the teacher level, Eastman, and one working the student level, Tony. Boy, doesn't that sound familiar." Claire summarized the situation as she saw it. "I wish we could flush one of them out."

"We're not flushing anything until the feds are there and everyone is in custody. One leak before we're ready to roll and someone in the chain gets a tip . . ." Neil didn't have to finish his sentence. They all understood the consequences.

"Jax and I will get this road map figured out, send pictures before the night is over. Tomorrow we'll need surveillance at Jax's decoy apartment. We've invited Elsie and Ally over for an algebra lesson. Make a last attempt to find any connection we're not seeing."

"We're out, then. And, ladies, all audio and video is live until this is over."

Claire looked around the room, knew exactly where all the microphones were. "That's fine."

"Be safe," Jax said.

"Let us know when you're clear." Claire couldn't help but worry. And when they disconnected the call, Cooper had already sent a text. Spider-Man never gets caught with his mask down.

~

There were parts of Cooper's job he didn't get to exercise nearly enough. As he put on black utility pants, protective armor, and a field jacket before he started tucking everything he thought he'd need for the job, he felt his excitement grow. Neil and Sasha geared up in the same way. Neil was taking a position on the outside, and he and Sasha were going in.

The three of them got in the van along with Lars, and Isaac took the wheel.

Back at headquarters, Manuel and Rick were on the monitors.

Nothing in the strip mall was open twenty-four hours, which made their job a little less complicated. Not that they'd be walking in the front door.

Their plan had been mapped out and time stamped. Get in, find out what they're hiding in the place, plant a bug of their own, and get out. And more importantly . . . leave no trace.

Cooper popped a stick of gum in his mouth, found the repetition of chewing something calmed his nerves.

It was almost one in the morning. The storefront had been empty since nine. The adjacent business had been closed since eleven. They had done a thorough head count in all locations, coming and going, since Cooper and Claire returned from Seattle. The lights were off and nobody was home.

As they got closer, they secured their headgear.

The chewing gum started to lose its flavor, so Cooper tapped his fingers on his knees.

"Must you?" Sasha asked.

Cooper gave her his best smile.

"You know, you're still a really hot older sister." He'd told her that once before, and lived to tell the tale.

Neil stayed silent.

"Don't make me remove your balls now that Claire has become so fond of them."

Cooper lifted his eyebrows, chewed his gum a little louder.

"Three minutes," Isaac said from the front seat.

The three of them put the face coverings over their features.

Cooper pulled the wrapper out of his pocket, shoved the gum inside. "Save this for later," he said, putting it in front of Lars, who sat at the computer board.

"Neil." Isaac slowed the van to a stop and Neil jumped out.

"For a big guy, he sure is silent," Cooper mused aloud.

Isaac did a drive-by. "Be ready."

Cooper's hand was on the back door.

"Three, two, one."

Their feet were barely on the ground and the van was off.

"Radio check." Lars's voice sounded in his ear.

"This is one, in position," which meant that Neil had already climbed onto an adjacent building with a weapon at the ready should he need it.

"Two," Sasha said next. "One minute to position." She was halfway up a drain spout.

"Three." Cooper waited at the back door.

"Headquarters. Everything is clear." It was always good to hear Rick's voice.

"Four," Lars said from the van. "Waiting on your cue."

Cooper looked at his watch, finger poised.

"Go," he heard Sasha say.

Cooper pressed the stopwatch when the power on the entire block went out.

He put on his night-vision goggles and waited.

Sasha was small enough to get into the access point on the roof. All Cooper had to do was wait for her to unlock the deadbolt on the back door.

It took her ninety seconds.

Inside, Sasha disabled the battery backup on the alarm system while Cooper scanned the main business area. He moved to the back of the building, where if there was anything to find, chances were it would be there.

There were two doors past a small storage room.

Boxes of mail filled the crowded space. Locks that took only seconds to pick. Sasha moved into that room while Cooper breached the other.

The room was about ten by eight. There was a table shoved to one side, some kind of printer on top. "Are you getting that?" Cooper asked the team.

"Crystal clear."

Sasha tapped him on the back.

Someone on the team made a sound.

Cooper turned around and looked at the wall filled with pegboard.

He moved closer to find dozens of pictures. Some passport-photo size and quality, some were random shots. Each picture had an envelope next to it with more copies of the photographs inside.

Sasha pointed to the left and made a sweeping motion down.

"We see it," Lars said.

And now, so did Cooper. The groupings of pictures were categorized. Blondes, Caucasian. Their age, height, and weight written on the corner of the picture. Next category, brunettes. Next category, Asian, Hispanic, African American, and so on, all girls and all under the age of nineteen. On the far right was a limited number of boys.

"Switching off infrared," Sasha said before she removed the goggles from her eyes.

Cooper did the same, and Sasha switched on a flashlight.

It was then that it all came together.

Sasha was on autopilot, scanning the wall with a camera so the base had it instantly.

Cooper recorded the rest of the room, down to the trash can.

In there, pictures had been removed from the wall and discarded. He picked up a few and looked through them. He found a picture of Ally. He dug further and found Elsie.

Sasha touched his arm and pointed.

Jax was on the board.

At the end of each column was a date sometime in the future.

"Two minutes."

Cooper and Sasha exchanged glances.

They'd gotten what they came for.

CHAPTER THIRTY-FOUR

Claire heard noise from the kitchen and assumed Jax had woken up before her and was making coffee.

When she descended the stairs, she found Cooper rummaging through the cupboards. "This is a nice surprise."

He turned, looked her up and down. She had worn a T-shirt to bed. On it was an image of a bear with the caption "Screw Mornings!" The shirt barely covered her butt. "Yes it is."

She walked up to him, knowing she looked worn out, but not giving a damn. "Good morning."

Cooper's lips reached for hers, and his hands took firm hold of her ass.

She laughed through their greeting. "What are you doing here?"

He rested his forehead on hers. "We need to go over some things."

"Coffee first." She turned out of his arms. "I should tell Jax to put something on before she comes down."

"Good call."

She turned to leave the room. "I feel your eyes on my ass."

"Affirmative."

Ten minutes later, they were sitting at the kitchen island and not the table since it was still littered with the work from the previous day.

Claire and Jax sat in stunned silence at the photographs obtained the night before.

"It's just like you said. They place an order and people like Brian go out to fill it."

Jax took her cup of coffee over to the dining table, held one of the photographs from the storefront wall.

Claire looked at Cooper, both had concern in their eyes. Jax had gone white when she saw her picture next to the call for a curvy white blonde, seventeen to nineteen years old.

"No one can say we don't know what we're doing," Jax told them. "We identified Elsie and Ally and obviously I managed to hit the club."

Cooper rubbed Claire's shoulder when she stood to go to her friend's side. There were still tutors they didn't know and didn't have pictures of. "I'm guessing Neil's got someone working on identifying all these kids."

"There's a lot of coffee being consumed at headquarters," Cooper confirmed.

"With Elsie and Ally's pictures in the trash, we have to assume they didn't fill some kind of box," Jax summarized.

"We'll find out tonight what those were."

"I'll see if I can get some information out of Ally today at school."

Cooper made a noise from the kitchen. "That's a negative."

Claire and Jax both turned to him at the same time.

"It's too dangerous. We have until the end of the school day tomorrow and Neil is calling it in. Since your picture is on that board . . ."

Jax opened her mouth, then closed it.

"You're more useful at headquarters putting this map together. Tonight at your girls' party, we'll have the team close by. You two get the girls talking."

"And if we don't flush out Eastman or Tony, and one of them is dirty?" Claire asked.

"At some point we have to hope the feds are good at their job. Whoever put them undercover did a Neil-precision job of it. We're not finding anything on either one of them. And without a positive ID, we can't check cash flow or travel records."

Claire turned to Jax, put an arm over her shoulders. "Use the Force, Yoda. Work Neil into that Bahamas trip."

That helped Jax smile.

"I'll get all this together," Cooper said. "You guys shower. I'll follow you on the way to school. And Lars should be here when we leave to drive you to headquarters."

Jax rolled her eyes. "I can drive—"

"That's a negative. Maybe on the next case where you're not a direct target."

Jax glared at him. "You know, Loki . . . your boyfriend is bossy."

Twenty minutes later, Jax was safely tucked in the passenger seat of Lars's car, and Cooper was following Claire.

Because Cooper had access to the shop parking lot, which was right off the student lot, he took advantage of that so he could keep an eye on her.

As she was walking by, Claire said hi to several students she'd managed to get to know.

He stopped himself from staring, but did catch her out of the corner of his eye as she looked over her shoulder one last time before disappearing on campus.

This would all be over soon. And if Neil didn't send them on vacation, Cooper would make it happen.

He unlocked and rolled open the shop doors. *I'm going to miss the place.* He looked at Tony's car as he walked by. He had a bug in place and hoped the feds could nail him if in fact he was one of the bad guys. Eastman was tracked as well. Not one of them wanted a loose end, but taking out the biggest players and keeping Marie safe had to be their primary goal.

The bell rang and his students started walking in the room. "Hey, Mr. Mitchel."

He heard that name so often, he was starting to adopt it.

"Hi, Coach."

"Morning, Gavin."

The bell rang and the stragglers ran in.

"Everyone, pull out a piece of paper, put your bags on the floor. Time for a pop quiz."

A collective moan went through the room.

He turned around and picked up a pen for his whiteboard.

Not one spitball.

He dropped the pen. "Never mind. Let's have a shop day."

Moans turned to cheers and they all filed out of the classroom and into the shop.

Sometimes it's good to be the boss.

~

Claire sat in homeroom, watching the backs of kids' heads. Her shortest class of the day had the last standing suspect in this end of the investigation.

She really hoped she wouldn't be staring down a courtroom testifying against him.

Every once in a while, Eastman would look up at her and she'd look away.

Sean ignored her altogether.

Claire found herself tapping her fingers when she was thinking. Just like Cooper.

"Have you taken to doing your homework before you get to school these days, Porter?"

"I'm fresh out of homework all week, Eastman," she told him. "Do you want me to do yours?"

There were a couple of snickers.

"I'll be sure and let your teachers know they're not challenging you enough."

Claire sat back, placed a hand over her heart. "Ahh, and I was starting to think you didn't care."

He actually started to laugh, and when he did, the kids in the class felt like it was okay to laugh with him.

"You've got balls," Dalia, who sat in front of her, said.

Claire shook her head. "I just know that in a few years, when I'm at some bar soaking up the scene, Eastman's going to be sitting there nursing a light beer. When he sees me, I'm going to make him buy me a drink, and he'll remember what a joy it was for me to be in his class."

Eastman met her gaze, respect shined in his eyes.

The bell rang and she grabbed her pack.

She wanted to catch Sean before he ran off.

Eastman stopped her. "Porter?"

"Yeah?"

He shook his head. "Never mind."

She took a step, turned. "We're good?"

He smiled.

Claire stuck out her fist. He bumped it with hers. "Don't forget that beer," she said as she ran out of the room.

She saw the top of Sean's head and followed it. "Sean?"

She moved closer.

"Sean?"

He turned back, expression blank.

"Wait up."

Once at his side, Claire slowed down. "Can I talk to you a second?"

He sighed.

She pulled him out of the line of students scrambling to their next period.

"Listen, I'm sorry."

"You said that yesterday. I get it. You're not interested." He did not want to be standing there.

"It wouldn't be fair. You're a good-looking guy. I'm sure plenty of girls here would love it if you ask them to prom."

Confusion sat around Sean's eyes. "You have a boyfriend or something?"

It's not the first time you've said this, Claire, it probably won't be your last. "I . . . Shit." She took a dramatic pause right out of a Shakespearian play. She leaned close, put a hand to his ear, and whispered. "I'm a lesbian."

Sean leaned back, a myriad of expressions passing over his face. Doubt, confusion, acceptance, and then that . . .

"Don't look at me like that's hot."

"Well, it kinda is."

"Sean!"

He went back to acceptance. "Well, at least it isn't me."

"Like I said. You're good-looking. It just doesn't do anything for me. But you know my friend Ally?"

"She a lesbian, too?"

"No." Claire spat the word at him. "She talks about you all the time. I bet she'd go to prom with you in a heartbeat."

"She goes to Bremerton now."

"And hates the kids there. She'd love a chance to come to Auburn's prom."

The walkways were clearing out. They were both going to be late.

"I'll think about it."

They started walking again.

"I know this is really juicy gossip. But can you keep it on the down low for a little while? There's someone I want to ask out and if this starts spreading it will probably scare her off."

Sean had that hot look in his eyes again.

Claire hit his arm. "I'm serious."

"Okay, okay."

The bell rang.

"Aw, damn," he cried.

Claire kept walking slow. "Just tell your teacher someone turned you down for prom, they'll cut you some slack." She put her fist out.

"I'm starting to think you do have balls."

~

They had pizza, chocolate, soda, and chips.

No liquor.

Apparently the old bat found a bigger lock for the liquor cabinet.

"I'm actually surprised she let me out," Ally said after the conversation about the lack of liquor.

Claire, Jax, Ally, and Elsie were spread out around the living room. They had the music on, food everywhere, and books pushed aside.

"What did you do that got you busted last weekend?" Claire asked.

"I went to a party."

"We knew that," Elsie teased.

"It was last minute. I shouldn't have gone."

Claire was halfway through a piece of pizza. "Did it suck?"

"Hundred percent. I was told there'd be a bunch of kids from Auburn. I get there and I only recognize a few people. Nobody I really know."

"Where was it?" Claire asked.

"Up in the foothills."

"I hate going to parties when I don't know someone," Elsie said.

"That's why you only go to parties with your friends. Always take a wingman, right, Claire?" Jax said.

"I never leave home without one."

"I thought I had one. Louisa is the one who suggested it. When I get there I can't find her. I think she ran off with her boyfriend. Totally ditched me."

"Do I know Louisa?" Jax asked.

"No. She goes to junior college in Glendale."

"That's kinda far away, isn't it?"

"She was supposed to be helping me with my algebra. She was harder to understand than my teacher. So when she said my favorite word, *party*, I'm like, let's go. I get there, and it just didn't feel right."

Claire thought of Ally's picture in the garbage can. Thought of Marie. "Don't do that again," Claire told her.

Ally didn't bother arguing. "I won't. I only drank half a beer and called an Uber. Halfway home I felt completely wasted."

"Oh my God, someone totally slipped something in your drink." Elsie said what they were all thinking.

Ally kept nodding. "Scared the crap out of me. That's the kind of thing that happens to other people. I didn't survive my mom to end up like her." The girl had tears in her eyes.

Jax reached over and put a hand over hers. "You're not your mom."

Ally took her napkin and wiped her eyes. "My mom was always high. She was so embarrassing. But all of us have been to a party, we have a little fun. Is it the same thing?"

"There are a lot of adults out there who drink that aren't alcoholics," Claire told her.

Elsie sat up. "I'd rather hang out with you guys, and if we score some beer, great. Otherwise we get carb drunk and talk about guys."

Ally leaned her head on Jax's shoulder.

"You were smart enough to get away, Ally. And the Uber is even better." Claire glanced over at the cable receiver where the camera was hidden. Although the team had probably already hacked into Ally's account and were tracing that address.

"You can call me anytime for a ride," Jax offered.

"That goes for all of us."

"Thanks, guys. I just feel really dumb." The girl was still tearful. Claire hoped she'd be that way for a while and never get caught like that again.

"Learn a lesson, but don't beat yourself up too much. It could have happened to any one of us."

Ally got herself together. "If I don't do some homework, my grandmother isn't going to let me come here."

Jax jumped to her feet and took the pizza box off the table, and Elsie and Ally pulled out their books.

"I got you covered. Algebra is easy for me," Claire said.

Ally moved to the couch, sat next to her. "Did Sean really ask you to prom and you said no?"

"Of course."

"Why? He's super cute," Ally asked.

"Because you dig him. Friends don't do that."

It looked like Ally was going to cry again.

"I also told him I liked girls, so don't tell him otherwise."

Claire saw Jax standing in the kitchen laughing.

"Why did you do that?" Elsie asked.

"Because once you're playing for the same team, guys open up. Then I told him you thought he was hot. If he doesn't ask you to prom, I might have to kick his ass."

Jax returned, sat on the floor.

"It's high school, people will talk." Elsie grabbed a handful of chips.

"The less you worry about what other people think, the sooner you'll live a happy life."

Elsie threw a chip at her. "You're such a dork."

CHAPTER THIRTY-FIVE

Cooper stretched out in Claire's bed and waited for her to get home. Maybe he was pushing the boundaries, but then again, they hadn't set those up yet.

He watched the monitor feed from the front door and knew when it opened it was Claire and Jax.

He'd parked on the street, so she wouldn't be surprised he was there.

The girls chatted as they ascended the stairs, their voices softened as Claire approached the closed door to her room. He heard them saying good night before she walked in.

"I thought you'd be asleep?"

He lifted up on an elbow. "Not a chance."

She kicked her shoes off en route to the bed, climbed up beside him, and rested her ear on his chest. "I'm so exhausted."

He kissed the top of her head and marveled at how easy she tucked into his arms. "It's almost over."

She released a long-suffering breath and pushed off the bed. "I need to brush my teeth before I drop."

He used the time she was in the bathroom to pull back the sheets and dim the lights.

She returned wearing a nightshirt, this one showing a bear stretching with sunshine in the background. The clock on the nightstand said eleven p.m.

"Cute," he told her.

She'd brushed out her hair and washed her face clean.

Claire returned to the tucked position at his side, her free arm wrapping around his waist.

"What's the word from Neil?" She knew their deadline was up. The girls' party was the last push to find more names and details. Which worked out, to a small extent.

"The commander in Seattle went to the feds. They're scrambling to make as many arrests tomorrow at the same time to avoid anyone getting away."

"What about Warren?"

"Everything is out of his hands at this point. If Tony or Eastman are his guys, they won't know anything until after it's all done. Neil has a meeting scheduled with Warren late tomorrow night."

"I bet he'll be pissed that this went way over his head."

Cooper shrugged. "I think he knew it was bigger, that's why he hired us. His hands were tied to his jurisdiction. Ours aren't."

Claire snuggled a little closer. "I wish we knew more about Tony's movements."

"Me too." They hadn't seen the man since he left his car in the shop.

"What does tomorrow look like on our end?" she asked.

"Business as usual. We go about the day like we have since this started. We can't step outside of normal or risk someone being tipped off. We want the feds to sweep in, take it all down at the same time."

"You think that's how it's going to go?"

"I think it's no longer in our hands to worry about. We've done all we can." That didn't stop him from worrying about her safety. "We stay hypervigilant."

"I know." Her voice was sleepy.

Cooper reached over and turned the light off, then snuggled close. She looked up, asked for a kiss.

Their lips met for what he thought was going to be brief, but Claire had other ideas.

Cooper's arms pulled her closer, his hand brushed over the curve of her hip. "Girl, where are your panties?"

He felt her squeeze his bare ass. "Making out with yours."

In the light of the moon shining through the window, Cooper traced the side of her face, memorizing the feel of it. "If you're too tired . . ."

Her exploring hands said she wasn't *that* tired. "Stop talking and kiss me."

"Yes, ma'am."

~

Cooper and Claire bustled around the kitchen first thing in the morning. They both synced their phones with headquarters and put the nearly invisible earpieces in place so they could obtain up-to-the-minute reports as the day progressed. She and Cooper were told to call in a verbal check every hour.

Claire's watch and cell phone had tracking enabled. At the last minute, she secured a third device disguised within the clasp in her hair.

Jax dressed in what they'd labeled DEFCON five clothing. It was a field outfit; much like what Cooper had worn two short nights before. If at any time the team needed to mobilize, all they needed to do was jump in the van.

Claire gave Jax a quick hug, whispered "Bahamas" in her ear, and watched her drive away with Lars.

Cooper set the alarm and locked the door. The garage door was already open, her car tucked next to Jax's.

She enjoyed a parting kiss. "I think we've done a really good thing," she said between kisses.

"Let's say that tonight when it's all over."

"See you at track."

Cooper pursed his lips. "I'm going to miss track."

"Me too."

He opened the car door for her, closed it after she was in.

Like the day before, he followed behind her, watched her as she parked in the school lot and walked onto the campus.

The audio feed in her ear switched on. *"Checking feeds. Report back."*

Claire reached for the cell phone that lived in her back pocket.

Headquarters picked up on the first ring. "Yeah?"

Claire was pretty sure Lars had answered the phone. "Did you know that the female praying mantis eats her lover after they mate? Sometimes while they're still going at it. Talk about dying for sex." The system was simple. When she made a call, she had to ask a question so the team knew there was no threat. Granted, she could have asked, *How are you?* But where was the fun in that?

"We're clear."

Claire looked at her phone. "Rude much?"

She bounced into homeroom and paused.

Eastman's chair was empty.

He almost never came in late.

She walked to her seat, set her backpack on the floor.

Some of the sparkle faded like fireworks dying in the night sky. *Don't be a wanker, Eastman.*

Time ticked.

The room filled.

She did not want to call this in.

"Hey, Claire?" Sean greeted her.

A quick fist bump. She kept her smile.

The bell rang . . .

Five seconds passed.

Fuck!

And then the bastard walked in the door like nothing was wrong.

Claire slumped in her seat.

"I was starting to wonder if you were going to show up."

Claire turned to Sean, who'd called the man out.

"Did you miss me?"

"You weren't gone long enough," Claire chimed in.

Eastman looked her in the eye. Something flickered.

"Mr. Eastman, did you know that the female praying mantis eats her lover, sometimes while they're in the middle of the nasty?" Claire asked.

"No way!" Several students turned in their seats, looked at her.

"Seriously, look it up. Found it on YouTube last night. It's sick."

Cell phones came out, and within seconds the class gathered around each other watching videos.

"That's epic," Sean said, laughing.

"Sometimes education happens on accident," Claire said, glancing at the video.

"How true that is." Eastman sighed, sat down in his seat, and let his homeroom scroll through YouTube videos on the strange mating habits of insects.

~

Cooper called in. "Did you get the spark plugs I needed?"

"We're clear." Lars hung up.

The shop was empty.

The two-stroke engines that were group projects were spread out on tables. He walked around, checked their progress. When he saw something wrong, he wrote a note. *Check your work.* When the work was perfect, he left a different note. *Help your neighbor find their problem.*

Cooper left his surveillance equipment alone. Knew they'd do a sweep before leaving campus altogether.

The bell rang and Cooper proceeded to his last day in school.

~

Because it was business as usual, Claire spent her lunch in Bennett's classroom, and she started it by putting an apple on his desk.

"What's this?" Bennett asked, picking it up.

"It's called fiber." She made a sweeping motion with her hand. "It's good for the plumbing."

He smiled. "Do I look constipated to you?"

"Honestly . . . sometimes."

He took a bite, looked at the apple. "Grab a chair," he told her.

She pulled one over and sat.

"I've put together a few common problems and answered them wrong. I know you can identify them, but I need you to talk me through them." He turned a paper toward her and continued to eat his apple.

She underlined the first part of the work that was wrong and turned it back. "How did you come up with this?"

Coach Bennett was already smiling.

They finished two problems even though he tossed some pretty lame reasons for his wrong answer to the questions.

Bennett pushed his pathetic lunch away and sat back. "If I gave you a college application, would you fill it out?"

"We're back to that."

"I never give up."

She laughed. "That way we can party at the geek convention in a few years?" *Click, click . . .*

"I'm past my party days."

Claire thought of the pictures of Ally and Elsie in the garbage. Both struggling in math, both sent to Bremerton to obtain tutors. Ally's tutor takes her to a party with spiked drinks. Elsie's quits after two sessions because she's impossible to teach. Which was bullshit since she'd left their study date confident she'd pass her test today.

"Do all the math teachers go to this convention?" Claire asked.

"District budgets don't give everyone a ticket. Mainly department heads."

Click . . . click . . .

"Do all department heads run the tutoring programs?" Claire got up from her chair, walked back to the wall of photographs as something close was clicking its way into focus in her head.

"Not all, but some. There's a lot of networking at the events. We share information our students can use. Like cost-effective tutoring, or even free. Why are you asking?"

Claire couldn't help but wonder if the random sampling of pictures on the want-ad wall would show math-challenged kids being funneled to Bremerton. "Who is the head of the math department at Bremerton?"

"That would be Dale Levine. I've known him for years."

"And does he run the tutoring program there?"

"Yeah, as a matter of fact. He took it back under his wing a few years ago. I thought he was crazy. Coaching track takes up all my spare time. But not for Coach Levine, apparently. He's a dedicated guy. Always asking if there's someone on my team struggling in math that he can pair up with the right person."

Claire's memory flashed. The man had smiled at her, told her he'd see her at state. "Jesus."

"Are you thinking of skipping Mr. Dunnan and going to Coach Levine directly?"

So many pieces *click, clickity, clicked* into place. Here she thought Dunnan might be the one directing at-risk kids to Milo and Brian, but instead it was the coach at Bremerton, with access to Milo through Russell. Or was there another connection between Levine and Milo? If they'd been watching Levine from the beginning, maybe they'd have all the answers. Claire kicked herself for not putting that together before today. "I should have done that all along."

"I can give him a call—"

"No!" She cleared her throat, spoke softer. The last thing she needed was Levine to get wind of anything. "That would totally undermine Mr. Dunnan, and you see him every day. Completely unprofessional."

Bennett nodded. "You have a point."

"Tell you what, I'll go over a strategy plan to approach Levine, Coach Levine," she corrected herself. "No outside help. I'll run it past you before I go over there. Maybe bring a bottle of his favorite whiskey?"

"That would be inappropriate."

This information needed to get out before the feds rolled. At least get the local authorities to pick the man up.

"Right. You have to promise me, no outside help. Not even a phone call."

Coach Bennett held back. "Fill out a college application."

Claire smiled. "I'll fill out three."

Bennett stretched his arms over his head and leaned back with a huge smile.

Claire grabbed her backpack and ran out the door, her phone to her ear.

"Yeah?" Lars answered.

"Did you know that an apple a day keeps the doctor away?"

"We're clear."

"Put Neil on speaker."

CHAPTER
THIRTY-SIX

Jax had never witnessed anyone control stone-cold rage the way Neil MacBain did.

When Claire had spelled out her discovery, the entire team turned to their boss. The link to some of the kids on that wall was right in his front yard. The set of his jaw and the tension in his shoulders said everything while he didn't speak a word. His daughter went to that school.

Jax didn't think that would last much longer.

It was then she realized why parents tucked their kids away in places like Richter. Although for many, that backfired. But if there is a magical school of safety, she'd bet her next paycheck Emma would be enrolled by fall.

Neil hung up with Claire and dialed another number.

"Detective Warren . . . Interrupt his meeting, tell him it's MacBain."

Neil put the call on speaker. Lifted a hand to indicate that no one was to speak other than him.

"Neil?"

"I need you to do something for me, no questions asked."

"As long as it's legal," Warren replied.

"I need you to take Coach Dale Levine at Bremerton into custody at exactly three this afternoon."

"You found something."

"Three o'clock. Not a minute before or after."

"What the fuck, Neil?"

"Do not use your men on this case. Take him in yourself if you have to. Keep it quiet."

"Shit's going down," Warren concluded.

"Three o'clock."

"Consider it done."

Neil disconnected the call, pointed a finger at Jax. "Call Ally and Elsie, find out what role Levine had."

He directed the next demand to Lars. "Everything on Levine. Bank accounts, cars, where he had lunch on Saturday."

"On it."

Neil was back on the phone. "Manuel. Find Emma, take her home. Call me when you get there."

~

The doors to the shop were rolled up, the sun beamed into the space. Cooper took his lunch with a few students that needed extra time.

He watched the time ticking away, knowing everyone was geared up and ready to claim victory on the arrests.

"How did I know I'd find you in here at lunch?"

Cooper turned to see Leo Eastman standing in the doorway, a smile on the man's face.

Cooper left the side of his students and offered Leo a handshake. "Dedication to the job, I guess. What brings you here?"

Leo's eyes drifted to Tony's car, then back again. "Couple buddies of mine are headed out this weekend, do some fishing. Wondered if you'd like to come along."

Cooper planned on spending the weekend in the Bahamas with Claire tucked into the hammock with him.

"I have plans this weekend. Besides, is it even fishing season?"

Leo shrugged. "Nothing illegal about sitting in a boat with beer."

Cooper laughed. "Fish jumping in the boat is just the icing."

"Next time, then."

"That would be great," Cooper said.

Leo turned, indicated Tony's car. "Is that your car?"

"No. Belongs to a kid that went here last year. He still comes in to use the shop."

Leo peered in through the windows. "I wouldn't let my car out of my sight when I was a kid. Did all the work myself."

Cooper couldn't help but wonder if there was a hidden message in there somewhere. "Tony is in here all the time. Helps a lot of kids."

Leo nodded, continued to look around the car.

"Funny, the first time I saw Tony I thought he was a teacher or something. Looks a lot older than nineteen," Cooper said, hoping for a reaction.

"A lot of these kids look like they could be in college. It's a curse, if you ask me. Their bodies grow up before their brains. Gets them in trouble sometimes." Leo stopped poking around, met Cooper's gaze. "It's important to keep an eye on the ones that are older than their years."

Like bugging the bushes outside of front doors? "Why is that?" Cooper asked.

"It means they have trouble at home, stuff they don't want anyone else to know, or they're at risk for older and smarter people taking advantage of them."

Cooper waited for Leo to look at him. "You sure you're a public school teacher?" he asked, point blank.

"I am today," he said.

Interesting choice of words.

Ten minutes later, once Leo had drifted away from the shop, Cooper called headquarters. "Are we still tracking Eastman?"

"According to our monitors, he's in his classroom. Why?" Neil asked.

Cooper explained the conversation and was told that should Eastman deviate from his normal routine, they would activate their team to follow him.

After Cooper disconnected the call, he once again glanced at the clock. It wouldn't be long now.

~

Claire changed clothes in the girls' locker room to get ready for track. Her eye stayed on her watch.

At 3:08 the first report came in, Lars's voice in her ear.

"Vegas vice has Mykonos Sobol in custody," Lars reported.

Claire jumped up and cheered. "That one's for you, Marie." She felt like crying.

"Two victim locations are being liberated."

"You okay, Claire?" one of the students asked.

"I'm on fire," she told her, stuffing the rest of her clothes in her backpack. "See you out there."

Claire held her cell phone, ready to make a call to headquarters.

She stepped out of the gym and rounded the corner past the senior parking lot to head to the field.

Someone honked a horn.

She looked up and saw Elsie in the passenger seat of Kyle's car. The girl was crying.

"Hey, are you okay?" Claire jogged over, and the driver leaned forward.

Tony stared back at her.

Claire's world froze.

That's when she saw the gun pointed at Elsie's chest. "Get in."

Her feet moved, and she reached for the car door.

~

"Ice is in custody," Lars reported.

Cooper was chewing gum and smiling like a crazy man.

"You running with us today, Coach?" one of the kids asked.

He'd put on track pants and was stretching with the rest of them. "Nice day to do it," he said.

"Strip mall is locked down! Brian and Gorge in custody."

God, he wanted to celebrate.

Claire needed to hurry up so they could smile like fools together.

He watched the path she normally took from the main gym, saw the team trickling down.

She was probably up there dancing in one of the bathroom stalls. He could see that image vividly.

Cooper narrowed his eyes, saw Eastman walking down to the field.

That put a bit of rain on his sunshine. *What are you doing here?*

Eastman waved him over.

Cooper jumped to his feet and ran across the gritty track.

They shook hands. "Twice in one day?" Cooper asked.

"I wanted to catch you before you left."

"Practice lasts a couple of hours."

Eastman shook his head. "That's not what I mean." He looked around.

"Mind elaborating?"

Lars's voice boomed in his ear. "Levine is deceased. I repeat, Levine is deceased. Single gunshot to the head in school classroom."

Cooper put his hand to his ear, turned a half circle. "What the fuck!"

"Cooper, Claire, report in now."

~

Tony tore out of the parking lot and away from the school.

"Claire?"

"Keep your hands where I can see them." Tony pushed the gun into Elsie's ribs.

"Calm down," Claire told him, her voice even.

Tony's eyes scanned his mirrors.

Claire pushed away the fear that was crashing in and focused.

Elsie whimpered and huddled next to the door as if doing so offered some protection.

The window on her right side went down. "Toss the backpack."

Claire scanned the area. They were in a residential neighborhood, and no one was on the street.

"Do it!" Tony yelled.

Her backpack went flying out the door.

He kept driving. "Cell phone."

She looked at her cell phone and hesitated a second too long.

Tony's hand that wasn't holding the gun came around and smashed against Elsie's face.

"Jesus!"

Claire couldn't toss the phone fast enough.

"Your watch."

Claire damn near ripped it off her own wrist.

Elsie's nose was bleeding, her body rocked with sobs.

"Hands where I can see them!"

Claire placed her hands on the seat behind Elsie. "Here they are. See." Her heart was racing, mind scrambling to find a way out.

"Let her go," Claire told him.

"You want me to let her go?"

He lifted the gun to Elsie's head.

Elsie screamed and Claire put her hand in front of Elsie's face. "Okay, stop. Please just calm down."

"Shut up," he yelled.

Claire tried to coax her friend. "It's okay. We'll get you out of here. C'mon. Shhh."

He looked over at her, didn't like how close she was. "Scoot back."

She started to move.

"Wait."

She froze.

"Get that shit out of your ear."

Some of her optimism was fading. She'd yet to hear that anyone knew they were missing.

Claire removed the device, knew what to do when he rolled down the window.

"Who the fuck do you work for?" Tony took the corner hard and started weaving through traffic.

Claire didn't answer.

"You're a fucking fed, aren't you?"

"No."

Elsie looked over, each breath sucked in a cry.

"You fucking are."

"No . . . I'm not." They needed to get out of this car.

Tony poked the gun at Elsie again.

"I'm a private investigator!" Claire yelled, wishing it was her in the passenger seat so she could disarm the bastard without getting Elsie killed.

Tony hit the gas, slammed his driving hand on the steering wheel. "Fuck me. Just fuck me!"

~

Cooper felt panic in his knees and it started to rise.

"Report in now!" Neil yelled.

"What's going on?" Eastman asked tensely.

Cooper patted his back pocket.

He left his keys, phone, and wallet back on the field.

He ran over to them, grabbed everything.

"Is everything okay, Coach?"

"Has anyone seen Claire?" he asked.

"I saw her in the locker room right after the bell rang."

That was twenty minutes ago.

He scanned the field, knew she wasn't there.

He ran across the lanes again, hopped the fence, and headed straight for the locker rooms.

Half the track team followed, along with Eastman.

A sinking feeling in the pit of his stomach started to spread.

He bolted in the locker room. "I'm coming in!" he yelled.

He ran through, looked down every aisle. No Claire.

"We're sending backup," Lars reported.

Cooper pushed past Eastman, back outside.

"Has anyone seen Claire?"

"I saw her jump in a car with Elsie and her boyfriend's friend."

Cooper marched up to the student talking. He was in one of his auto classes. "Which friend?"

"Tony, the guy that comes in the morning."

"Which way did they go?"

The kid pointed.

"Son of a bitch!" Cooper heard Eastman yell.

Cooper jumped in his face, bumped into him. "What the hell do you know?"

"Stand down."

Both hands reached for Eastman's shirt. "Start talking."

"Hey, hey!" Coach Bennett was pushing in. "What the hell is going on here?"

"You've been following Claire for weeks, planted a camera at her front door."

Eastman's nose flared.

Cooper pulled his fist back.

"Federal. I've been on Tony for a year. Waiting for him to fuck up."

"Who does Tony work for?"

"Local PD."

Cooper shoved him out of the way and screamed his frustration.

He pulled out his phone and ran to his car.

Neil answered.

"He has Claire. Tony has Claire." Saying it out loud made it real. "Elsie is with them."

Cooper popped the trunk of his car, pushed back the felt covering, and placed his hand on the biometric safe. It slid open and he grabbed his weapon.

The entire track team was standing there.

Cooper turned to Coach Bennett. "Get them out of here. Call the police."

Eastman was on his phone, jumping in Cooper's passenger seat. "Special Agent Leonardo Grant requesting backup." He rattled off his badge number.

Cooper tossed his phone in a drink cup, started the car. Neil's voice came through the speakers.

"Which way is she headed?"

"North."

He punched the gas.

CHAPTER THIRTY-SEVEN

Tony pulled the car into an abandoned warehouse.

Claire was told to get out of the car first.

He dragged Elsie across the seats, waved his gun in the direction he wanted Claire to walk, and kept Elsie close to his side.

Outside, the brightness streaming in from the sun was a complete contrast to the darkness unfolding in front of her.

Tony pushed Elsie away from him, causing her to trip and fall.

She scrambled away on her hands and knees like a hand-shy dog looking for shelter.

Claire stayed standing, presented a calm she didn't completely feel. "What do you want?"

He tossed a pair of handcuffs on the ground. They skittered to a stop at her feet. "Put those on her."

Claire reached down.

"No." He directed his gun at Elsie. "You, put them on her."

Tony obviously knew Claire was the biggest threat.

Elsie scurried over to the handcuffs and picked them up. She slowly got to her feet.

Claire brought both hands out in front of her.

Tony inched forward, yelling, "Do I look like I was fucking born yesterday? Behind your back."

Shit. Keep it cool, Claire. You've practiced hands-tied defense before.

"Claire," Elsie said.

Claire turned around and backed up slowly. "It's okay. Just do what he says."

Tony smiled as the cuffs clicked around her wrists. "Let me see," he said.

She shifted on her feet, lifted her arms behind her, and pulled at the cuffs. Much too tight to slip out of.

Claire stood in front of Elsie.

"You're so tough, aren't you?" Tony growled.

Claire kept quiet.

"Stand over there."

Claire walked several yards away from Elsie, hating the distance.

"Sit down," he yelled at Elsie. "Move a muscle and I'll pop you. You understand?"

Tony walked over to Claire, waved his gun around. "Face the wall."

Handcuffed with a hostage and a pissed-off cop with a gun.

She turned toward the wall.

"Spread your legs."

She steadied herself, feet at hip distance apart.

He moved in fast, kicked her legs wider, and shoved her head into the concrete wall. Her head buzzed with the impact.

She felt the gun on the base of her skull as his other hand ran up the inside of her shirt. "What else are you hiding?"

"Nothing."

She ignored his hand as he grabbed at her chest and ran the length of her bra.

Bile rose when he ran his fingers over her tight shorts. Groping her was a fear tactic. A successful one.

Claire did everything she could to hide any emotion. Showing fear would only encourage him.

"You like that, bitch?"

Tony squeezed the most private part of her body until it hurt.

She bit her tongue.

He wouldn't be searching her if he planned on just killing her, so she kept quiet and prayed to God the team had found the third tracking device disguised as a clip in her hair.

"Stop fucking the girl."

Claire turned her head to see the face behind the voice, was rewarded with a palm pressing her face into the hard surface until she felt her skin break and blood trickle down her cheek.

~

Cooper stood over Claire's discarded phone and watch. One in each hand.

She could be anywhere. The residential neighborhood emptied out close to a freeway and they were twenty minutes behind her if they were on the run.

He spun in a circle, looked at the houses. Or she could be feet away and he didn't know it.

"Tell me you have something," he said into the phone.

"Her receiver's offline."

Eastman . . . or Grant, as it stood, was talking to his people.

"Who is left? Who isn't in custody other than Tony?"

"Milo and Russell."

"How the hell did they mess that up?" Cooper asked.

Grant looked over with a shake of the head.

Cooper stared at the broken screen on her phone. "C'mon, Claire." Damn thing still worked, but he didn't know the password.

The watch pinged and so did the phone.

"Can you get into Claire's phone? I need a password."

"Try Loki," he heard Jax suggest.

He used the keypad, typed in the numbers associated with the letters.

It opened to a home screen.

"Perfect."

He found the app they used as a team and opened it.

Sure enough it was a slow signal feed from a noncomputerized tracker. "Are we tracking anyone on the H system?" he asked the team.

"No."

Clearly Claire had considered the possibility of being without her phone, watch, or car. Each blip on the screen was like her heartbeat. Every beat gave him hope. "God, I love this woman."

"What do you have?" he heard Neil ask.

Cooper forwarded the information to the team and put the car in drive.

~

Claire had been shoved on the floor next to Elsie.

The girl clutched onto her as if Claire were a life raft on the *Titanic.*

Milo knelt down, far enough away to avoid a shoe to the face. "I remember you. The paranoid one with the busty blonde friend."

Russell stood to one side, his gaze just as awestruck as Elsie's had been.

"Private investigator. I didn't see that. What does that make her?" Milo asked.

"A scared little girl," Claire told him. "Nothing more."

Elsie's hands were free, but the girl was too scared to use them.

Russell spoke up. And he did so in Russian. "We should go before anyone comes."

"We'll leave," Milo said, again in Russian. "After we clean up a few loose ends."

"What the hell are you saying?" Tony asked.

Milo took to his feet, walked back to Tony. "I thought I told you to keep all the cops out of my home."

"She's not a cop. Has never been to the station."

The two of them started shouting at each other, giving Claire an opportunity.

"Elsie?"

The girl was whimpering.

"See the pin in my hair?" Claire watched the men fighting. Felt Elsie's nod.

"Take it out and put it in my hand."

Too scared to move.

Russell looked at them, briefly, then back to his uncle.

Claire spoke slowly. "You can do it. Trust me."

Elsie's hand moved up Claire's back, stopping every time the voices grew louder.

Finally, Claire felt the pin leave her hair.

"You're the one who skipped the line and gave her friend a green light," Tony screamed, pointing the gun their way for a second before tapping his own chest with the thing. "I have a system that keeps all of us safe . . ."

Relief flooded Claire's body when she felt the pin in her fingers. She worked as fast as she could and still stay in control. She bent the end and found the keyhole to the cuffs.

". . . you and every damn family sidekick you bring in. How do we know he didn't narc us out?"

Milo turned to his supposed nephew. "Any of that true?" he asked in Russian.

"I don't know these people."

Milo looked at Claire right as she felt the lock go.

She made a noise to disguise the click.

"Good. Then you won't mind removing one." Milo removed a gun from the inside of his coat, cocked it, and handed it to Russell.

At first the kid didn't take it.

"Do it."

As Russell reached for the gun, Claire started talking. Her Russian was so rapid it took them both by surprise. "You don't have to do this, Russell. We don't have anything on you."

His eyes opened wide.

"What the hell . . ." Tony took a step forward.

Claire inched up the wall, hands still behind her back. "It was Tony we were following. He led us to your house and the storefront," she lied. All in Russian, which was pissing Tony off.

"What the fuck is she saying?"

"Don't do this, Russell. You don't want to go to jail. You have the rest of your—"

"Enough!" Milo yelled.

～

Cooper knew the team was three minutes behind him.

They heard voices in the warehouse. Men, arguing.

Where are they? He mouthed the question to Eastman, who was on the other side of the entrance.

The man pointed one finger, signaled left. Two fingers, signaled right.

The voices rose and finally, Cooper heard Claire's.

It took everything not to storm in.

"Taking position," Neil's voice informed him.

Eastman pointed to his watch, lifted five fingers twice. Ten minutes? Was he kidding?

Cooper shook his head. Pointed to the ground. Then held out a hand holding him off.

Voices in the warehouse grew louder.

"Russell, in my sights," Jax reported.

Cooper hoped she didn't have to squeeze that trigger.

"Tony's moving in and out," Sasha reported.

"I have Milo." Neil's voice was last in Cooper's ear.

"Tony's moving."

"Go!"

Cooper gave the signal and Eastman yelled the loudest. "Federal agent, put—"

~

Claire caught a glimpse of a shadow in the upper reaches of the warehouse.

The second she heard a voice, she moved, reached for Elsie to drag her away.

But Tony was too close and he was swift.

Claire was in a headlock with Tony's gun pushed into her temple.

She grasped at his arm and tried to lodge her chin into the space between his arm and her windpipe. Her sparring partners at Richter had always held on hard, but this was a different level.

Around her, everyone had shifted.

Russell had fallen to his knees, the gun he'd been holding on the ground in front of him.

Milo, the cocky son of a bitch, stood there without a care.

"Everyone, calm down." Cooper looked Claire in the eye, raw nerves close to the surface.

"Drop your guns!" The barrel of Tony's gun ground into her skull.

"Calm down." Eastman, who had burst into the warehouse with Cooper, stood with a gun pointed at Tony.

"Drop your guns now, fucking drop 'em. I'll fucking kill her." The more Tony yelled, the closer he sunk into the shadows.

Cooper lifted his hands, slowly placed his gun on the ground. "Okay. It's cool. We're good."

Eastman carefully made the same movements.

Claire knew he wouldn't have done that if there weren't other guns pointed at Tony.

"Kick them over here."

They both did. But Tony didn't reach for them.

"Come on, Tony. Let's talk about this," Cooper coaxed.

"What are you waiting for?" Tony yelled at Milo. "Pick up the gun."

Claire felt the tension surging through Tony's body by the way she was being held. He probably didn't realize that she was gasping for air.

"Pick it up."

She needed the barrel to leave her temple to escape with her head. Or she needed to know the team was watching her every signal.

Milo turned to Cooper and Eastman. "I want to see my lawyer."

Tony's body shifted, dragging her with him. "Fuck you!" He took a step closer to Milo. The gun was no longer pressed right up against her head, but it was still pointed directly at her.

Cooper's eyes glued to Claire's.

Too much more of this and she was going to lose consciousness. If she didn't make a move, she might not get a chance.

I love you, Cooper mouthed to her.

She felt the words in her soul.

"It's over, Tony," Eastman told him.

Claire looked up to the rafters, prayed someone saw her lips.

One hand let go of the grip he had on her neck and settled at her side.

One.

"Let her go."

Two.

"Fuck, fuck."

Three.

Claire went completely limp and shots were fired.

~

Cooper couldn't get to her fast enough.

When Tony went down, his fall took her with him. And for a brief moment, Cooper couldn't tell if the blood was hers or his.

"Claire? Talk to me." He was on his knees, hands on her shoulders. "Where are you hurt?"

"Everywhere." She looked up at him, coughed, and crawled into his arms.

"Oh, baby." Cooper clenched her tight, didn't think he would ever let go.

There were sounds of footsteps running toward them and sirens in the distance.

Jax ran to Elsie. "It's okay. We got you. It's over."

Cooper looked around, saw Russell lying on the ground, arms spread out. He was pretty sure the kid was crying.

Milo was on his knees, hands behind his head, Eastman standing over him with a gun out, a phone in his hand. "Two injured, one fatality," he was saying.

Neil walked past Milo on his way to Claire's side. As he did, he stopped at Milo, brought him to his feet with both hands. "No one hurts my family." And with one beefy punch, the man was back on his knees, holding his face.

"Three injured and one fatality," Eastman corrected himself.

~

Hours later, when the paperwork was filled out and the bandages had been placed, Claire stood beside Leo Grant in a private meeting room at the hospital shaking her head. "You have no idea how happy I am that you weren't the dirty cop."

Cooper hadn't left her side for hours. She was pretty sure he hadn't even gone to the bathroom. His arms were around her, on her, holding her, or simply never far away. And she was happy for it.

"I'm pretty pleased I didn't have to rearrange your boyfriend's face for the way he was looking at you."

The three of them laughed.

"What finally tipped you off?"

He folded his arms over his chest. "Remember yesterday, when you talked about the day you would be old enough to make me buy you a drink and reminisce?"

Was that just yesterday?

"You got me thinking. I seem to remember a couple of pretty girls at the end of a bar, one came over and the other slipped away."

"You saw us?"

"I didn't put it all together until yesterday."

Claire laughed, although smiling hurt. "That was pretty epic."

"Weren't you speaking German?"

"I've been speaking German since I was eight," she told him, in German. "Isn't that right, Cooper?"

He replied in a less practiced accent, but she'd certainly give him an A for effort. They had plenty of time for him to practice.

"I'll be damned."

"She speaks five languages," Cooper said proudly.

"What?"

"Six, actually. You have to count English. Classic overachiever," she said.

"And your aunt?" Grant asked.

Sasha had left the scene without ever showing her face.

"She's my aunt."

"Really?" The man had a little too much hope in his eyes.

"Put it away, Grant, she's happily married."

"That's a shame." He paused, looked around. "Your team is good. Your decoy home, the fights with the aunt."

"Your decoy home is a pigsty," Claire informed him.

"You've been inside?"

"Not me. My hot aunt."

Leo shook his head. "Good thing I never had company over."

They laughed at that.

"Tell us what you know about Tony," Cooper said.

Leo sat back, arms folded over his chest. He looked less like a teacher and more like a cop. "I was brought in at the end of last year, right before Tony's 'graduation.' I got to know him and the kids he spent time with at Auburn. I saw the reports he gave to Detective Warren. Things didn't match up. Tony gave bogus leads, had his team running in circles. He used his position to keep the cops from busting teenage parties."

Claire looked over at Cooper. "I remember Milo being surprised when his party was broken up."

"I watched Tony all summer. He'd spend every other weekend at a party, playing the role of Tony the teenager. My boss was going to pull me from the school until we realized that Tony was still showing up. He'd convinced Warren there was something brewing and gave him a reason to be there. I knew he was dirty. I just couldn't find the mud. After the first of the year, I told my boss we needed more people. I was never going to find the dirt as a teacher at the school."

"What happened then?"

Leo looked between the two of them. "You guys showed up."

"But Warren is the one that came to us. Not the feds."

"Warren needed to flush out his own cop with a new team. When he took that approach, my boss knew Warren wasn't on the take."

"You didn't know who we were?" Claire asked.

"Not directly. At first I thought you were just a pain in my ass. The kind of pain that ends up on the wrong side of the law if led the wrong way. I wasn't kidding when I said I wanted to help the kids. I pumped them for information when I could. Made sure they could tell me about their weekends without judgment. I planted that bug at your house when I started to wonder if you were really a high school senior."

"You planted the bug in a bush. Not much you're going to learn there."

"I would have gone farther if you'd done one single thing to be someone you weren't pretending to be. But you're good, Porter. Really damn good."

"It's Kelly. Claire Kelly."

"Of course." Leo looked at Cooper. "You were too much of a coincidence to me. I'm guessing Tony was watching you, waiting for a slip or some kind of a link."

Cooper nudged Claire's arm. "Kyle mentioned you early in the week, when Tony was there. Told him you were going to tutor Elsie. He went on to mention the party where you first encountered Milo."

"Someone had to tip him off about today's arrests," Cooper said.

"When did you find out?" Claire asked Leo.

"Last night. Only when I didn't see Tony's name on the arrest report, I knew he'd go off. That's why I was at the shop and on the field today. I figured he'd go after you," Leo told Cooper. "If he went after anyone."

"He knew what was going down. Must have tipped off Milo. Another bad cop at the station?" Cooper asked.

"Or Tony has extra ears of his own. Our internal investigation will figure it out. We always do."

Claire leaned her head on Cooper's shoulder, exhaustion finally catching up with her.

"I'm sure we'll be talking again soon," Leo said as he pushed away from the wall he'd been leaning on.

Claire smiled. "Damn right. You owe me a drink."

Leo smiled, looked at the bandage on her cheek and likely the bruises surrounding the cut. "I'm sorry this happened," he said.

"I'm glad it wasn't worse."

Cooper's arms slid around her shoulders as he pulled her in tight.

Cooper shook Leo's hand. When it was Claire's turn, she gave the man a hug instead.

After he left, Cooper dropped his forehead against hers gently.

"I thought I was going to lose you today." His voice was unsteady with emotion.

She knew the adrenaline had finally dumped and now reality was setting in.

"Gonna take more than one bad guy to take me out."

Cooper pulled back, placed his hands to each side of her face. His thumb traced lightly over the bandage. "I love you," he whispered.

Claire let a smile spread over her face. "That became pretty obvious a while back."

He smiled, nodded a couple of times. "I guess it did."

She waited for his eyes to find hers. "I love you, too."

"I was starting to think maybe that was the case. But it's nice to hear."

"Let's go home and sleep for a week."

EPILOGUE

"C'mon, Chelsea. Swing those arms! Don't let her get away!"

Claire stood on the sidelines on the inside of the field, stopwatch in her hand. She spoke to Cooper at the finish line through her fancy headset. "That looked like a personal record."

"It sure was," Cooper replied.

She waved at him downfield and put a check next to Chelsea's name.

"Coach Kelly?"

Claire turned to see the relay team girls standing there. "For crying out loud, it's Claire. You can still call me Claire."

Cooper and Claire had made a unanimous decision to finish out the year coaching the team. There was a strange mixture of confusion, feeling cheated, and anger when they'd explained who they were and what they did for a living. In the end, they were welcomed with open arms.

Elsie had spent the night in the hospital and a week away from school. Claire knew it was going to take a lot longer than a week for Elsie to heal. When everything was explained, Ally and Elsie both were shocked at how close they had been to becoming a statistic.

As it turned out, Kyle had let Tony borrow his car the day he'd kidnapped Elsie and Claire. Never once did Kyle understand what the outcome would be.

When Neil had put Warren on the task of apprehending Levine, word made it to Tony through one of his buddies on the force. Leo's investigation was still ongoing, but it didn't appear that this friend knew anything about what Tony was up to.

Neil's monitoring of the Bremerton campus clearly showed Tony walking into Coach Levine's classroom and exiting in a hurry shortly after. Computer files implicated Levine in taking a cut for three years. He filtered the students through his tutors. For three years Milo's supposed nephews and nieces linked tutors with students and so far, three of those students, including Marie Nickerson, had come up missing. It was hard to say how Levine got involved, and with Milo talking through lawyers, and Levine and Tony dead, they might never know all the details. The whole thing took some time to swallow, and honestly, Claire didn't think that would happen for quite a while.

Clearly Levine could have implicated Tony.

In the end, the outcome was the best Claire and the team could have hoped for.

Marie was in a protection program tucked so deep she'd probably never see her family again. But from what Claire had learned, that wasn't a hardship.

Neil said nothing about Olivia, or indicated if the woman was still watching over Marie. Claire secretly hoped she was.

And now Claire was staring down three of her runners who insisted on calling her by her last name.

"Okay, Coach Claire. What do you think of this dress for prom?"

Claire looked at Leah, then the dress. "What does the back look like?"

Leah swiped the screen on her phone to the right. Claire blew out a breath. "Can you see your butt in that?" It dipped that low.

"Not really."

"Who's your date again?"

Leah told her and Claire smiled. "Okay, that dress is fine."

"My date makes a difference?"

"Yeah, your date is too shy. He won't know what to do when you walk in wearing that."

They all laughed, and Cooper walked up behind Claire and rested his chin on her shoulder. "What are you guys looking at?"

"Prom dresses."

"Girls!" he said, chuckling.

"Oh, yeah . . . show him."

Leah turned her phone around and showed him the picture.

"No. Absolutely not," Cooper said, deadpan.

"What about Coach Kelly, can she wear that dress to prom?"

Claire looked up at him, waited for his answer.

"Yes. Absolutely."

More laughter.

The girls ran off and Claire relaxed in his arms. "Can you believe we're out here in this heat while Jax is in the Bahamas on some beach drinking a mai tai?"

"I don't care where we are, as long as you're with me."

"Awww. That totally sounds like a line."

"Even if it's true?"

"Yup."

She turned in his embrace, wrapped her arms around his waist. "I'm really glad you changed the rules."

He leaned down and gave her a brief kiss. "I love you."

"I love you, too." And she did, a little more and a little harder every day.

"How do you think Jax would feel if I moved in while she was gone?"

Claire looked at him like he was crazy. "I thought you already did." He'd stayed every night since the busts.

"Okay, then. That's settled."

"You might need to ask Neil."

Cooper pulled her in close. "I have other questions for Neil."

"Oh? What?"

"About changing more rules."

Her suspicious bone tingled.

"Don't I need to approve rule changes?"

"Sometimes you need a father's approval."

Never in a million years did she believe she'd be having this kind of conversation with Cooper Lockman.

"I'm a size six," she said putting her left hand out in front of her.

He kissed her a little too hard and a little too long.

The athletes close by started clapping.

Claire clicked her tongue and shook her head. "Public displays of affection in front of the kids, what will they think?"

He pressed his lips to her ear. "Wear that dress to prom and we'll really give them something to talk about."

AUTHOR'S NOTE

I feel the need to take a moment here to stress that Auburn High and Bremerton High as detailed in this book are completely fictional. I've placed them in Southern California in ambiguous cities I purposely didn't name. I did so to express that human trafficking can, and likely is, happening right where you live. In my research, I was shocked to learn of the prevalence of this tragic crime.

I want to thank all the teachers, coaches, and mentors that actively work to keep their students from falling victim. Thanks to the school administrators that do in fact have undercover operations in our high schools to flush out the criminals responsible.

I also need to take a moment to say that every track coach I've ever encountered has been nothing but incredible to their students, and to the best of my knowledge would never put their students at risk. But alas . . . I do write fiction, and someone has to be the bad guy. And sadly, in real life, the bad guy is often the one closest to the victims.

Slavery has never gone away, it simply went underground.

Education and awareness often lead to intervention. So please, educate yourselves and your children. The life you might be saving could be closer than you think.

Catherine

ACKNOWLEDGMENTS

It might sound strange, but I need to thank a few of my characters. Neil MacBain (*Fiancé by Friday*). When Neil first showed up on the page, I knew I had to write his story. Little did I know he would be a character that spans three of my series.

Sasha Budanov (*Say It Again*) was yet another of those characters that I couldn't let go. Which led me to Claire Kelly and the first book in this new series.

Thank you to Amazon Publishing and Montlake, Maria Gomez and the team, for allowing me creative freedom to continue writing these dynamic characters.

Thanks to my editor, Holly Ingraham, for helping me put this book into fighting shape.

To Jane Dystel, who is always the first one to read my work and champion every single book I write. Thank you.

Thank you, Jeanie Pugh, for just happening to be watching the sunset as I walked by with my plot all twisted in my head. Your suggestion to look up some of the case studies in San Diego on this subject helped me see the light. For all the kids I know you help in your position as a high school VP, thank you.

Now to the graduates I've dedicated this book to.

I wrote this story during the global pandemic of COVID-19. It wasn't until I was finishing my edits that I realized I had to dedicate this work to every graduate in the class of 2020. It's been such a crying shame to watch high school seniors miss all the things one looks for in their last year of school. No prom, no sports, no class party or events. And certainly no graduation.

I also want to acknowledge the college graduates, who may have missed out on fewer of those iconic events, but certainly didn't get the satisfaction of walking on a stage to receive a well-deserved degree.

Congratulations, graduates!

May your futures be filled with happiness, health, and success in all you do.

Catherine

ABOUT THE AUTHOR

Photo © 2015 Julianne Gentry

New York Times, *Wall Street Journal*, and *USA Today* bestselling author Catherine Bybee has written twenty-eight books that have collectively sold more than 5.5 million copies and have been translated into more than a dozen languages. Raised in Washington State, Bybee moved to Southern California in the hope of becoming a movie star. After growing bored with waiting tables, she returned to school and became a registered nurse, spending most of her career in urban emergency rooms. She now writes full time and has penned the Not Quite series, the Weekday Brides series, the Most Likely To series, and the First Wives series.